More
Dangerous
Than the Moon

More
Dangerous
Than the Moon

by RICHARD BUTLER

WALKER AND COMPANY
New York

First published in the United States of America
in 1968 by Walker and Company, a division of
the Walker Publishing Company, Inc.

Library of Congress Catalog Card Number:
68-16682.

Printed in the United States of America from
type set in Great Britain.

To
PAUL BRICKHILL

. . . qui miscuit utile dulci,
Lectorem delectando pariterque monendo.
HORACE

One

THE rain came with the west wind, tiptoeing stealthily across the heaving blackness of the Southern Ocean to scratch experimentally at the chartroom windows, leaving its breath on the glass in tiny droplets that blurred the five-second flash of the lighthouse twelve miles away to starboard into a spangled, iridescent glow. There was a pause while the squall gathered itself for the spring, its tail lashing the sea into whitecaps of foam. Then it launched itself out of the night with a hissing roar that drowned the rumble of the motor yacht's twin diesels. The light on Tasman Island was blotted out as abruptly as if the whole of Tasmania had foundered and left *Lorelei* slicing through the streaming blackness towards an island that was now as non-existent as Atlantis, and my world dwindled to the dimensions of the warm, dimly lit bridge—a rolling, ten-by-fifteen space capsule poised in the alien atmosphere of some lost, landless planet.

I switched on the clear-view screen, reduced speed and lit a cigarette, watching the late-summer rain drumming on the roof of the deck saloon like a curtain of thin steel rods that had come down between me and the stubby, sharply raked mast. Our twenty-five mile radar could have picked a better night to pack up on us. Without it I was now as blind as a bat, and we were already in the outer approaches to Hobart. But that, I reflected, was one of the minor occupational hazards that came with the job. We were on time for the rendezvous, and that was all that mattered. The weather itself was unimportant, because *Lorelei* had been built to stand up to far more than a rainsquall in the temperate waters of Tasmania. She was a sixty-foot resin-glass yacht of seventeen tons' displacement, moulded and

7

fitted out on the Clyde and powered by a pair of three-hundred-horsepower Cummings diesels with oil-operated $2\frac{1}{2}$–1 reverse reduction gears, a power unit that could take her through a hurricane. It had, in fact, already done so, her first owner—a Sydney automobile dealer—having been washed over the side and back again during a South China Sea typhoon. Before that dampening experience, one that had made him turn to model-car racing for his kicks, he'd taken her all over the Far East. This period of tropical service accounted for *Lorelei*'s one blemish—the sun-deck and control position above and aft of the deck saloon, an addition to her original superstructure that gave the helmsman the feeling that he was driving a floating hansom cab. It also gave the yacht a lumpy, top-heavy look that was entirely misleading, for she was as stable as any ship of her size. I often wondered whether the finance company I seemed to be supporting single-handed realised how lucky they were to own her. Her load of electronics alone must have cost a fortune.

And you can add to that, I thought gloomily, the repair bill for the radar that was now lying on a repair bench somewhere in Hobart. I peered out into the downpour, thinking again how comforting its revolving, watchful green trace would have been.

Without it there was no warning whatever of the other vessel's approach. Not until the searchlight beam caught me full in the face. The bar of bluish-white light flared out from dead ahead, a glittering silver cylinder, solid with driving rain, that seemed to push the yacht sideways with its impact as I spun the wheel hard a-starboard, blinded, and groped for the throttles. *Lorelei* heeled over sharply as the screws and rudder bit, her hull juddering with the thrust of six hundred horse-power trying to drive her in two directions at once as the port engine went full ahead and the starboard full astern. A muffled shouting came from below above the roar of the diesels and the drumming of the rain. There was the faint, faraway smash of falling crockery. The light still lit up the bridge like an atomic explosion, but it was swinging to port as *Lorelei* came about and the thousands of brilliant suns that swam in front of my eyes began to fade.

A hoarse voice said indignantly from down by my left foot,

'What the flaming hell's going on, Tallon? I got a kettleful of boiling water over me fist and the bloody teapot fell on me foot. What you done this time, yer no-hoper? Collided with a lighthouse?' Two-tooth Harry Lamb, one-time chief petty officer in Her Majesty's Royal Australian Navy, former inmate of Her Majesty's Prison, Wormwood Scrubs, and late of Pentridge Jail, Melbourne, hoisted his fifteen stone up the ladder from the deck saloon. He braced himself against the echosounder and wrinkled up his bearded face as he peered out into the glare. 'My word,' he said softly. 'What's this you've picked up, Tallon?'

'I'm not stopping to find out.' I slammed the starboard throttle full ahead. 'Whoever it is, let's see what he's got in the way of engines, shall we?' The rain eased off as suddenly as it had started and the deep booming note of twin diesels working up to full revs took the place of the roar of falling water. 'If it's a Customs boat he's going to need them.'

He trod out my cigarette which had fallen to the deck, and shouted above the bellow of the engines, 'Never seen a Customs boat with a light that big.' It still held us unwaveringly from out on the port beam and was being projected from a vessel that was not only keeping pace with us but, judging from the increasing intensity of the light, was closing us as well.

'I don't reckon we're getting anywhere with this,' bawled Two-tooth. He staggered as the motor yacht pitched. She was tearing through the water with her stern tucked down and her resin-glass hull flexing as if it was alive. 'They're coming in to use a loud-hailer. You'll have to heave to.' When I shook my head stubbornly he came and put his face close to my ear and said, 'Look. I've got an idea that's a Navy boat out there, Tallon. And if it is, we haven't got Buckley's chance of getting away.'

'The Navy?' I looked sideways at him. 'Are you crazy?' One of the factors that operated in our favour in the import business we ran was that in this part of the world there was no inquisitive radar network, no coastguards, none of those inconveniences that make life so difficult for importers in Europe. 'What the hell would the Navy be doing down here?' I shouted. 'They don't . . .' I stopped. Against the blackness

9

ahead there had appeared a string of reddish-orange dashes that floated eerily across our bows from port to starboard. And at the same time, above the clamour of the engines, we could hear the slow tok-tok-tok of a heavy automatic weapon, like a dry, mechanical laugh.

I reached forward with my right hand and slid the throttles back slowly and smoothly in their slots. As the roar of the engines and the whistle of violently displaced air died away Two-tooth said disbelievingly, 'They fired at us! Me own Navy! Gawd, you're not safe anywhere these days.'

I sat back in the padded helmsman's seat, numbed by the speed with which we'd come unstuck. 'How the hell did you know it was the Navy?'

'I didn't.' He moved out of the light and took his short black pipe out of the pocket of his leather jacket. For some reason he was avoiding my eye. 'But after I saw their searchlight I thought about what I heard a bloke say in a bar the other night —that the Yanks were sending the *Fort Knox* here on a courtesy visit. With the biggest aircraft carrier in the world on its way they'd be bound to lay on something special, I reckon.'

I nodded. This was curtains for both of us, and the fault was entirely mine, not his. I should have made it my business to find out about the nuclear carrier and the security precautions the Navy had organised. Instead, I'd run blindly into what looked like the middle of a SEATO exercise. The latest of a long line of mistakes, I thought bitterly. *Lorelei* began to roll in the swell as the way came off her and, in the sudden silence, the diesels purred like a pair of sleepy panthers, their exhausts muttering sonorously, while the night wind sighed in the aerials. 'You wouldn't happen to know,' I said heavily, 'of a good way of getting rid of sixteen packing cases in a hurry?'

'If there was time we could train up a couple of octopuses.' He was doing his best to sound tough and offhand, but he'd have done better if he hadn't been trying to light a pipe that had no tobacco in it whatever. The flame reflected in his steel-grey eyes as they met mine. Then he blew it out. 'I should have told you about that aircraft carrier,' he said quietly. 'I'm bloody sorry, Pat. What d'you reckon you'll collect this time?'

When he started calling me Pat, things were really rough.

I shrugged. Five, ten, twenty years, what difference did it make? Once you were inside, in the crushing monotony of congealed food and the stink of urine, time lost any meaning it might ever have had. An hour could be an eternity. Besides, the sentence didn't really begin until they threw you out. Then you were doing solitary. You were on your own, struggling single-handed to get back into the boat with all the other normal people, hanging on by your fingernails to a job—any job —until one day something happened to pry your grip loose. You might forget to throw in enough 'sirs' one evening when the head waiter was a bit more ulcerous than usual, or perhaps some fool would lose his gold watch after he'd used the lavatory you'd been put in charge of. And, naturally, if you'd done time for manslaughter because you'd hit your wife's boy friend who happened to have a bad heart—physically as well as morally—then it followed as the night the day that you were a lousy waiter, a thieving lavatory attendant and finally just—nothing. Then you were drifting again, easy meat for a shark like Zaghrali to drag you down to the depths again.

That was why, when my aunt died, I bought a cheap ticket to Australia out of the money she'd left me, and I put every cent of what was left into a down payment on *Lorelei* when I saw her in Sydney Harbour. She was going to keep me afloat—and Two-tooth as well, after we'd met up by sheer good luck in a pub off Pitt Street. We were going to run a big-game fishing outfit for the glossier side of the tourist trade up in Sunny Queensland. Striped marlin, black marlin, hammerhead shark —you name it, we'd get it for you, with a free photographic service thrown in.

But we hadn't got it. Not any of it. I must have been out of my mind to ever think we could. Because to run *Lorelei* I had to have money—big money. Money for diesel fuel in six-ton tankfuls, money for insurance, money for fishing chairs, Scotch whisky, rods, advertising, steel hooks, spring mattresses for client and friend, steak Diane and harbour fees. And to get the money I had to run *Lorelei*. That sort of vicious circle doesn't last very long—not with the repayments I had to find every month as well. So we'd come south to Tasmania, where you can get blue-fin tuna up to two hundred pounds in the summer, and where you can find shark if you go far enough out for it—mako, and even the fabled White Death. We'd hoped that our luck might change.

But the shark had got us instead. We'd drifted into what we were doing now, kidding ourselves all the time that working for Zaghrali was only temporary, that we'd be back in legit. business as soon as we had a bit put by. And now I was going to lose *Lorelei* and start the cycle all over again.

Two-tooth put his pipe away. 'We can start up again, Pat, after. The US, maybe. They've got a lot of coastline.'

'They've got a lot of prisons, too.' I went and stood beside him, peering out into the glare. A launch was put-putting towards us across the black water that glistened like treacle as it reflected the light.

There were five men in the boat. The seamen wore black waterproof reefer jackets with round caps and slacks tucked into calf-length seaboots, and there was an officer sitting bolt upright in the stern with a white roll-neck sweater under his uniform jacket. I tried to throw off the lassitude that hung round my neck like a dead albatross. A yacht owner who'd been fired on by his own Navy would be entitled to do a certain amount of foaming at the mouth. 'You'd better have a bloody good explanation for this when you come aboard,' I bawled truculently. 'I'll be sending a full report of this to Canberra the minute we dock.' It didn't seem to terrify them much.

They came alongside and the officer said something I didn't catch to one of his men who held the launch steady with a boathook while the other four swung up and over our rail, aft of the bridge. Two-tooth leaned forward and spat accurately into the sea, inches away from the bow of the launch. 'Scrape just one square inch of that rail, mate,' he said unpleasantly, 'and I'll give you three guesses what I'll do with that bloody boathook.'

The officer said something to me, but I wasn't listening to him. I was too busy staring down incredulously at the man in the boat below us. The lettering on his black-and-gold cap band showed up clearly in the harsh white light.

And it was in Russian.

Two

I FELT as if somebody had pulled the deck from underneath me. I stood gaping at the seaman, then at the officer, as I tried to adjust to the fact that, instead of being dragged off to chokey, we seemed to have landed the distinction of being the first POWs of World War Three. We seldom switched on our radio receiver on these outings, Two-tooth having read somewhere that the heterodyne oscillations could be used for detection purposes, and at the speed with which crises developed these days anything could have happened since we'd left Constitution Dock a few hours earlier. I was still trying to work out whether I ought to feel relieved or not when the officer said curtly, 'I ask you again: are you the owner of this vessel?'

I pulled myself together. 'I am. And you can start by giving me the name of yours. Because there's going to be . . .'

'I am of the Soviet trawler *Novgorod Seversk*.' His English was slow and heavily accented, but perfectly clear. 'My captain send me to make inquiries.' He came forward along the two-foot-wide deck, handing himself along the rail as the yacht rolled sharply.

My first impulse was to push him over the side. But that could lead to complications, and we'd already got enough of those. 'Apologies,' I said coldly, 'is the word you want. Come in here.' Two-tooth came up the single step into the chartroom after me, his beard failing to hide the pop-eyed stupefaction on his face that gave him the look of a sandbagged chimpanzee. As the Russian followed, I saw one of the seamen go past him, outlined against the flood of light, heading for'ard. 'Wait a minute,' I snapped. 'Where does he think he's going?'

The officer stood under the amber glow from the overhead

panel that was trying to compete with the glare of the searchlight. He was short and stocky with a flat, peasant's face that was dark with stubble round the jaw. His eyes bored into mine like a couple of X-ray tubes. 'To search the ship,' he said bleakly. He picked up the ship's log and opened it.

Like a spring being released, Two-tooth jumped forward, ripped it out of his hands and slammed it back on to the chart-table. 'Like hell he is!' He grabbed a fistful of the Russian's jacket in his huge left paw while his right swung back. 'And let's keep our grubby little hands off other people's private papers, shall we? Or we might find ourselves eligible for a posthumous Order of Lenin.' He bent down and stuck his beard into the Russian's face. 'It so happens,' he said in a voice like an electric drill going through sandstone, 'that we don't feel in the mood for being gone over tonight. Some other time, maybe. But right now,' he lifted the man up on to his toes, 'I'll give you ten seconds to get your bunch of bolshie brothel-bashers off this ship. After that, I'm going to . . .' His voice tailed off as he looked down at the big, blunt-nosed automatic that was grinding into his navel. A 7.62 Tokarev. I wondered if Two-tooth knew it hadn't got a safety-catch.

'Knock if off, Two-tooth,' I said quickly. I took a step forward and grabbed his arm. 'Let me handle this.'

Two-tooth let go of him and subsided slackly into the chair behind the chart-table. The Russian pulled his jacket down and stood breathing hard for a moment, staring at him. 'That was stupid, comrade,' he said, his voice dangerously controlled. 'If I had had to kill you, then I must kill this man also, and sink your ship. So be sensible, yes?'

'Sensible!' Two-tooth glowered at him. 'With comrades trying to blow us out of the water, crawling all over . . .'

'Silence!' The Russian had tensed, peering into the far corner of the bridge. He took a step forward. 'That woman. Is she dead?'

'In a way,' I said. I looked aft, at the dark-haired girl in the yellow sleeveless summer frock who was sitting motionless in the shadowy corner, her legs crossed and her hands folded demurely in her lap. She was slim and tanned and beautiful—and amazingly lifelike. She was a shop-window dummy Two-tooth had bought as a gimmick in Sydney, real hair and all. 'You see, she's never been alive. That's Lorelei, our mascot.' When he stared at me uncomprehendingly I said, 'A sort of big doll. She's supposed to bring us luck, but this seems to be one of her off nights.'

'*Kykna*—doll? For men?' He frowned at me. Then he cocked his head as shouts and the clang of metal came from below.

Two-tooth lurched to his feet, ignoring the muzzle of the Tokarev that swung and settled on his stomach. 'What are those bastards up to?' he snarled. 'If they as much as lay a finger on my engines . . .'

'They do not touch the engines.' The Russian was tensed up and jumpy, with the air of a man working with the odds against him. He snapped, 'They look around a little, that is all.' He was listening to the noises his men were making—the crash of doors opening and shutting, the lid of a packing case being prised off with the protesting shriek of nails wrenched out of wood, the thump of seaboots on carpeting.

'You won't get away with this,' I said quietly. 'Firing on, boarding, and forcibly searching an Australian vessel on the high seas is an act of piracy that not even your government will be able to talk its way out of. There'll be . . .'

'Firing?' he said angrily. 'We signal you with a lamp, but you take no notice. Then it is a flare that we fire—a Very light, *nyet*?'

'A signal lamp and a Very light?' I said incredulously. 'You think anybody's going to believe that? You know damn well it was that searchlight out there that nearly blinded me into colliding with you. Then you opened fire with one of those fifteen-millimetre Skodas you've got on board.'

'You are mistake.' He raised his voice belligerently. 'You lie. That is not what happen. What proof you got, eh?' He paused, looking from one to the other of us. 'In fact, what proof you got you see us at all?'

I stared at him while the diesels ticked softly and the sea gurgled under the hull as the yacht rolled. The inky-black shadows thrown by the searchlight swung up the bulkhead and down again, and voices speaking in Russian came up the companion. Of course we hadn't any proof. He'd almost certainly lied about the name of his ship. If we started raising hell when we got ashore we'd probably find that the *Novgorod Seversk*—if she existed at all—was halfway up the Manchester Ship Canal at the time she was supposed to be firing on us. Not that we'd be likely to raise much hell anyway, I reflected grimly. Publicity was the last thing we needed. 'All right,' I said slowly. 'But what about that?' I nodded at the Redifon Marine R/T set. 'How d'you know I haven't used it?'

'Because we listen to jam your transmissions.' He went past me and put his hand on the grey matt-painted top of the set. It was stone cold. 'But you make none, not even when we fire our—flares. We find that very strange. It makes us think that you have something to hide. From us, perhaps?' He watched me suspiciously as three seamen filed up from below. Besides the one who'd gone for'ard to the hatch on the foredeck there were two others who had evidently gone below through the cockpit door that led to my quarters. The first one reported briefly to the officer, who, judging from the tone of his voice, said, 'Good God! Are you sure?' There was an impassive '*Da*' from the sailor. The other grunted, his eyes on me again, and the men went out into the glare, their boots clumping loudly on the deck.

'So!' The Russian was still edgy, but his attitude had relaxed from suspicious hostility to contempt. 'My men find the cargo you carry. Very interesting. Cases of the new Australian currency. One-, two-, and ten-dollar notes—all freshly printed.' The boot-button eyes travelled slowly round the chartroom as if seeing it for the first time. 'So that is why you run away and do not use your radio. Small-time capitalist private enterprise, yes? It is good for my men to see such an example of Western decadence with their own eyes.' He looked at Lorelei, who cut him dead, then his gaze took in the bulbous blonde on the whisky firm's calender that Two-tooth had pinned to the bulkhead. 'Do you people think of nothing but dollars and blondes and whisky?'

Two-tooth looked up at him from where he sat sprawled behind the table. 'Too right we do,' he drawled. 'With me, it's dollars, redheads and beer.' He added matily: 'You'll be a rouble, brunette and vodka man, I reckon?'

The other declined to follow up this fascinating line of thought. 'Smugglers,' he snapped. 'Petty criminals, parasites. In the Soviet Union you would be shot for this. It also explains another mystery—the meeting you had with a small Japanese fishing boat, the *Haraguro Maru, nyet*? Two hundred and fifty tons. Port of registration, Kobe. A tuna-fishing boat.'

'If you know so much,' I said sourly, 'perhaps you could tell us poor decadent smuggling capitalists what the hell it is you're looking for?'

I might as well have saved my breath, of course. 'You mind your business,' he said curtly, 'I mind mine, eh?' He gave us an ironical clenched-fist salute with the hand holding the gun. 'A good journey, comrades. In your small way you serve the Soviet Union also. For it is you and your kind who will one day bring about the collapse of your corrupt imperialist society. I wish you every success.' He went out and over the rail without looking back.

Two-tooth and I stood watching the Indian-ink blob chug out into the aching sunburst of light. He said dourly, 'Stuck on the wrong end of a gun by a fat little commo. And all we can do is thank our lucky stars it was the wrong navy. Funny in a way.' He grunted. 'Once you go outside the law, anybody bigger than you can push you around and you can't do a thing about it. You're on your Pat Malone, back in the jungle with the big crooks eating the little 'uns.' He screwed up his eyes, trying to see behind the light. 'What d'you reckon they were after, Tallon?'

I was trying to get a look at the *Novgorod Seversk*, too, but the Russians had other ideas. They kept the light trained right in our eyes and we couldn't see a thing. 'I don't know, except that it was something worth risking an international incident for. Something he thought we might have brought in off the *Maru*, perhaps.'

The outline of the motor-boat had been absorbed into the dazzle for some minutes. Two-tooth said suddenly, 'Let's get the hell out of this. I keep thinking about the last crack that bastard made—about us working for their mob.' He added viciously, 'I'd like to sling those bloody cases over the side and get a job as a wharfie.'

'Are you serious?' I said brutally. 'We wouldn't last five minutes. This is all we're fit for, and we can't even do that properly.' Deep down inside, I knew he was right. Somewhere in the vast, friendly spaces of Australia we'd have found work with people who didn't give a damn who we were as long as we were prepared to earn a crust. But giving up working for Zaghrali meant giving up *Lorelei*, and I'd have to be pushed a long way before I'd do that. I'd carry anything this side of narcotics to keep her. It was this guilty knowledge that made me say surlily to him, 'Go and have a look at the blasted cargo and stop trying to kid yourself.' It was at that moment that the searchlight went out.

The stars were flying high among the ragged clouds, but even they were obscured by the multi-coloured balls of light that swam in front of my eyes against a background that was as black as the pit. Gradually, I adjusted to the darkness until I was able to see the dark sea and the paler shading of the sky and the line where they met. And nothing else. I stepped down to the deck and gripped the rail, peering out into the cool windy night. Two-tooth said from behind me, 'If you're hoping they've sunk with all hands, you're out of luck. That trawler was one of the underwater variety.'

I stepped up to the control position again. We ought to have guessed. Only a submarine officer could say, as the Russian had done, 'What proof have you got that you've seen us at all?' And the source of the light had been too low in the water to come from one of those big streamlined jobs that the Russians playfully call trawlers. I said, 'Even if we'd been in a position to make a fuss about this when we docked we'd never have been believed. Remember the one they saw off the Victorian coast? And the one that pilot saw off northern Queensland? Nobody believed them, either, and they were seen in broad daylight.' I glanced at the lighthouse as I slid into the control seat and stretched out my hand to the throttles. As I did so, the cry came out of the sea—a thin cry, like that of a seabird, from out to starboard.

I'd torn my shoes and sweater off, climbed on to the rail

and jumped before I could ask myself whether the pale, ghostly blur I'd seen momentarily against the dark, restless blackness had been really human or not. The water was like black ice, a reminder that there was nothing between me and Antarctica except a few thousand miles of heaving desolation, and after the warmth of the bridge the numbing cold hit me like an iron-fingered hand clutching at my heart. I nearly gasped underwater with the shock. Then I kicked out and surfaced, looking for the green starboard light of the yacht to give me a bearing. The eerie cry still rang in my ears—a sound that had had the sinister bubbling quality of air being expelled from lungs that were already half full of seawater.

What had seemed merely a gentle swell from the bridge turned out to be a very different proposition when I was down on the mat swapping punches with it. Waves with the momentum of thousands of miles of landless ocean behind them hauled me up by the scruff of the neck, kicked me in the teeth, and then threw me down again—as if searching for a drowning man by the light of a few flat-batteried stars wasn't hard enough anyway. It was the second cry that gave me the fix I needed. It came from behind me, a despairing croak fading into a watery gargle that brought me round like a homing torpedo to where he was lying half submerged in the trough of a wave.

The waterlogged life-jacket that was slowly drowning him was a dead-weight that nearly finished the pair of us by the time I got him to the yacht. It acted like a sea-anchor, so that I had to kick away like an epileptic grape-treader to make any sort of headway at all. I didn't dare try to get it off him. If I'd as much as let go with one hand he'd have gone to the bottom like a stone. He was a big man who took plenty of towing, and he was far gone—slack and sluggish in the water like a ship near her end. I battled on, with the sea doing its damnedest to tear him away from me, until I sensed that we were under the yacht's lee. Her hull towered above me like a cliff with a green lighthouse on top of it, far up in the flying clouds. It made no difference that her deck was only six feet from the sea. As far as my chances of getting him aboard were concerned it might just as well have been six miles.

But once I'd got Two-tooth's line under his armpits my job was over. The limp figure, streaming water, went up out of the sea like a leaping porpoise. There was a pause during which I had nothing to do except admire the way our resin-glass hull kept the barnacles out of business, then I went aboard too, Two-tooth hauling my twelve stone out of the water with as little effort as if he was taking soundings with a ten-pound lead. I wedged myself between the rail and the bridge, spitting out Southern Ocean while Two-tooth picked the man up in a fireman's lift and staggered off below through the deck saloon door.

I pulled myself up on to the bridge. The sea still seemed as empty as ever, but I couldn't rid myself of the feeling that we were being watched. Somewhere not far away there could be men sitting at their consoles, their Slav faces illuminated by the glow from the radar screens, watching the small blip that was *Lorelei*. Or they could be nearer still, submerged, peering through a periscope. Either way, they would soon be asking what we were hanging around for.

Shivering in my dripping clothes, I eased the throttles forward, letting the revs build up for ten knots, and swung the yacht on to a westerly heading where she'd be out of harm's way until I could work out a fresh course for Storm Bay and Hobart. Then I set the Martinet auto-pilot and dropped down the companion into the saloon, leaving a trail of seawater on the jade-green carpet as I went for'ard and down the ladder to the galley.

The light was on, showing me a broken teapot that lay on the green rubber-tiled deck in a pool of brown liquid. A door led off to the fo'c'sle, at present untenanted, and another opened off on the port side to the cabin Two-tooth used. He had his patient, minus the life-jacket, face down on the lower berth and he was leaning over him, pumping him dry in the Schafer's method, his big hands in the small of the man's back and his body swinging backward and forward rhythmically. Water gushed sluggishly out of the man's mouth and dripped on to the midnight-blue carpet. I said, 'Will he make it?'

He was a big man in his forties, wearing a grey zip-fronted jacket and blue serge trousers, sodden and gleaming with seawater, and there were blue-and-white canvas sneakers on his feet. He had dark-brown, close-cropped hair, and the face that was turned towards me was probably craggy and tough when he was conscious. Now, with the eyes shut and the mouth dribbling, it looked like the face of a drunken swagman. But I noticed that the nails of the hand that hung down from the side of the bunk were clean and clipped, and that the hand itself was broad, capable and as scrubbed as a surgeon's. Two-tooth said, still pumping. 'He'll be right. He's breathing by himself and I'm only doing this to clear his lungs. Tough bastard. With that bundle of rags he'd got slung round his neck, it's a wonder he ever kept afloat.' He paused, noting with satisfaction that the water had stopped coming out of the man's mouth. I picked up the life-jacket that Two-tooth had cut free. It was—or it had been—self-inflating, one of a type I'd never seen before, but it hadn't stayed inflated very long. I looked at the words stencilled neatly across one of the panels, and they told me everything and nothing, both at once. They were in Russian.

Two-tooth nodded when I looked up at him. 'I saw it too, mate. I only speak two languages—bad, and plain bloody filthy—but I reckon that don't say "Made in Hong Kong". This is what our Volga boatmen were looking for.' He struggled with the zip and removed the man's windcheater with a gentleness that would have surprised anyone who hadn't seen him re-set a seagull's broken wing. I'd always thought him ham-handed myself until I'd watched him—from half a mile away—defuse an old 200-kilo Jap aircraft bomb up in Rabaul for a bet. It was his naval training in bomb disposal that had made him one of Australia's most distinguished safe-breakers. He said, 'Gimme a hand to get him under the blankets, will you? And then you'd better get changed. I'm the one who'll have to clean up the carpet when you've finished dripping all over it.'

We stripped the stranger to his hairy, muscular pelt and got him between the sheets. He was semi-conscious and trying to fight us by that time. Two-tooth scooped up his clothes and the life-jacket and I followed him into the galley. He hung the soaking wet clothes up to dry and took two rubber hot-water bottles out of the first-aid cupboard. 'Yer better get on deck,' he said, filling a bottle with steaming hot water from the tap, 'when you've got changed. With your navigation we could be off Vladivostok. Explain a lot, that would.' He squeezed the bottle against his barrel of a chest to expel some air. As he screwed the top on he said casually, 'Now you've landed him, what are you planning to do with him, Tallon?'

It was a good question. I got the medicinal-purposes-only brandy down and dosed myself with forty millilitres. I felt it boring down my gullet like a red-hot scalpel on its errand of mercy and said, 'Hoist him up on the block-and-tackle and have my picture taken with him, what else? What the hell can I do with him—throw him back?'

'You may wish you had, later.' He watched me grimly. 'You better start thinking, mate. If he's as Russian as his life-jacket, we got problems.' He went back into the cabin and put the hot-water bottles in the bunk. Through the open door I saw the man lying with his eyes wide open, staring up incomprehendingly into Two-tooth's piratical face.

I took the brandy bottle with me and went aft to change my trousers and shirt. I put my sweater back on, and went up on to the bridge. I parked my medicine glass and bottle on the chart-table while I turned the yacht north-east. The wind was steady from the west and the sky had cleared. Astern, the Southern Cross hung low in the sky like an illuminated kite, but there was nothing else. No low, sinister silhouettes trailing us, no white feathers of spray from periscopes. Just the sea and the stars and the white train of frothy lace that *Lorelei* trailed hissing behind her across the black marble floor of the ocean.

Two-tooth came up the ladder with two steaming mugs of tea. He gave me one, sat down behind the chart-table and started ramming what looked like seaweed into his lethal little pipe.

'Yeah, problems,' he said, continuing—as was his habit—the conversation from where he'd left off, 'is what we've got if we sail into Constitution Dock with him on board.' He looked up at me. 'Police,' he said with loathing. 'Immigration blokes. Newspaper reporters, radio newshawks and the ABC fighting the commercial telly for pictures. And Customs, Tallon.' He struck a match. 'After that,' he said, between puffs, 'we might just as well turn ourselves in. Think of the grilling we'd get.' He impersonated an official of the Department of Trade and Customs interrogating me, for some obscure reason choosing one with a squeaky falsetto voice. ' "And what, may I ask, were you two mugs doing when you found this poor bastard with his hat floating? Fishing, was you? Well, well. Funny yer didn't catch nothing except a cold, isn't it, Mr. Tallon? Here, you wouldn't be in on this currency-smuggling lurk we've been trying so hard to stop, now would you?" ' He reverted to his normal gravel-sifter voice to say dourly, 'You know bloody well that, with our form, they'd shop us before you could spit.'

I drank some more of the brandy that was becoming more medicinal every minute. He was right, of course. Our deep-sea-fishing cover went just as far as the point where the Criminal Investigation Branch started asking questions about it. As long as we kept out of their hair we were reasonably secure. But once we attracted their attention, and they put through an overseas call to Criminal Records in London . . . I said bitterly, 'God, why do these things always have to happen to us? Last time, it was you having hallucinations off the south-west coast. Now this!'

'All right, all right.' He waved his pipe huffily at me. 'I'm sorry I ever said a word about that. But you were below at the time, so how the hell would you know what it was? It was no hallucination, mate.'

'We've been through all this before,' I said wearily. 'There could be a hundred and one explanations. It could have been a reflection on the window. It could have been a cloud, or a plane. Or it could have been your liver. Whatever it was, this is no time to . . .'

'There's nothing crook about my bloody liver,' he snapped. 'I stick to beer, not that rotgut you got in your hand.' He leaned forward, his beard bristling. 'What about that report in the papers, that the Space Tracking Station at Tidbinbilla had picked up something it couldn't identify? Anyway, it's there on the chart, Tallon, you can't get round that. I put the glasses

23

on it and there was this thing hanging in the sky, as plain as I'm seeing you now. It was real enough to take a bearing on, so . . .'

'All right. Don't run it into the ground,' I said impatiently. 'The point is, are we going to get on the radio now, or . . .'

'No. You must not do that.' It was a good job my glass was empty. I must have cleared six inches off the deck when the slow, deep voice came from down on my left. He was standing at the foot of the companion, wrapped in the brown blanket he'd taken off Two-tooth's bunk. Two startling green eyes stared up into mine out of a face that was just as craggy and tough as I'd thought it would be. 'They may be waiting for you to report that you have picked me up. If you do, they will be back before your authorities can reach us.' He came up the steps of the ladder slowly, immense and bear-like in the hairy blanket. At any other time I'd have been amused by the way he clutched it round him when he saw Lorelei in her corner. He stopped and said, 'Excuse me. I did not know there was a lady on board.'

'There isn't.' I got ready, a trifle wearily, for the dolls-for-men routine. 'It's our ship's mascot. A shop-window dummy.'

'So?' he said politely. He spoke slowly but with very little accent. He dismissed Lorelei instantly as his eye fell on the brandy bottle. 'I should very much like a drink. Some of your brandy, perhaps?'

'Jeez, you bounce back fast, don't yer?' Two-tooth stared at him with respect. 'Crook as Callaghan's cat one minute, knocking back the grog the next.' I went down to the saloon and got another glass out of the cocktail cabinet. As I came up the ladder again I heard him say, 'Just how long were you in the water, mate?'

The man thanked me gravely as he took the drink, his eyes on Two-tooth with the wary look of one toughie touching gloves with another. 'I do not know,' he said briefly. He slung the brandy down like cough-mixture and took a refill. Then he said, looking at my hair which was still plastered down on to my skull, 'I must thank you for saving my life. My name is Nicolai,' he gave me a little bow from whose dignity not even

24

the blanket could detract, 'and I offer you my sincere gratitude.'

'That's all right,' I said awkwardly, hoping he hadn't heard what I'd said earlier about throwing him back. I noticed he hadn't supplied us with a surname. 'My friend here,' I said carefully, 'looked after you when you came aboard.'

He gave another, stiffer, bow in the direction of the chart-table. Two-tooth waved his pipe gracefully. 'Plistermitcha, Nick,' he said genially, not to be outdone in old-world courtesy. 'Must have been bloody freezing out there, eh? What happened, mate? Fell off your surf-board, did you?'

'I have defected,' said Nicolai evenly, 'from a Soviet whaling vessel.' He looked from one to the other of us. 'You have probably guessed as much already. It was not difficult. To jump overboard twenty miles from land is not a thing to be expected. But to be picked up,' he shrugged, 'that is a different matter. I was lucky you happened to be where you were.'

'Too right you were.' Two-tooth turned to me. 'Didn't I say he was tough?' he said admiringly. ' "Not difficult," he says. Just like that.' He drew on his pipe, watching the Russian. 'Now, if it had been me,' he said reflectively, 'I wouldn't have said jumping out of a submarine was all that easy. How did you manage that bit, Nick?'

The diesels throbbed effortlessly in the silence while Nicolai stared back at him with that dog-meets-dog look in his eyes again. 'I am very grateful for what you have done for me,' he said at last. 'But, please, do not let us ask too many questions. After all, what I have done is my own business. And so . . .' He finished the remainder of his brandy, leaving the rest of the snub hanging in the air.

I said bluntly, 'I'm afraid it isn't as simple as that. You became my business the minute you came on board this ship. There are one or two questions I'll want answered whether you like it or not. For a start, I take it you're going to apply for political asylum in the usual way?'

The green stare switched from Two-tooth to me. For a moment I thought he was going to tell me to go boil my head too, but instead he shrugged. 'You have a right to know that. And the answer is, no. I am not.'

'You're not?' I said sharply. I heard Two-tooth's teeth clench on his pipe stem as I said, 'Now, look. I'm not getting mixed up in . . .'

'I know what you are thinking. That I am a spy, an agent—something like that, yes? But I give my word it is not so. I could have lied to you just then, and said I was going to hand myself over to your police. But I prefer to tell you as much of the truth as I can.' He put his glass down with a click that sounded very loud. 'I am, as you say'—he nodded at Two-tooth—'from the submarine that, it appears, has already stopped you tonight. They are out there now, looking. for me, which is why you must not—for your own sake, as well as mine—use your radio. I know certain things,' he paused, choosing his words carefully, 'that make it vital for them to find me. So vital that I should not be safe from them even in your strongest prison. That is why I cannot go to the authorities here. As soon as the announcement of my arrival appeared in your newspapers they would find a way of silencing me. They have contacts in so many unexpected places. And so—I must just disappear. All I want is to be put ashore quietly and for you to forget that you have ever seen me.'

I was a fool to give him that second drink, I thought. He was swaying far more than the even motion of the yacht warranted and his face was shiny with sweat.

'You must see that I can't do that,' I said reasonably. He stared back at me with eyes that were unnaturally bright as I said, 'If you don't go to the authorities what are you going to do when you get ashore? If you go off on your own you're going to need money. And there wasn't a cent in your clothes. This is a small island with three hundred and fifty thousand people in it. They don't pry into your private life, but you've got to have a background of some sort. I don't think you'd last very long. And if you've got any ideas about hiding in the bush you can forget them. The Tasmanian bush is like nothing else anywhere in the world. In the south-west, for instance, it's just one vast, vegetable barbed-wire entanglement that's never been fully explored to this day. It's got a rainfall of over a hundred inches in parts, it's alive with venomous snakes at this time of the year, and there's nothing there to support life at all. You'd die of snakebite, starvation or exposure inside a week.'

He rubbed a hand across his forehead. 'I cannot give myself up,' he said stubbornly. His face had gone a dirty shade of grey. 'I have friends here who will look after me. Once I am ashore . . .'

'We can't do it, mate,' said Two-tooth regretfully. I knew what he was thinking—that if we agreed, everybody would be happy. But it was out of the question. Illicit currency was bad enough, but illicit tourists from behind the Iron Curtain . . . I shook my head.

He seized my arm desperately. 'But you must. It is not for myself alone that I ask—beg—you to do this. There are others whose lives depend on my . . .' His voice had a harsh edge of strain that brought Two-tooth to his feet, but I was the one who caught the Russian, staggering under his weight as he folded at the knees in front of me.

Getting him below wasn't one of the easiest jobs I've ever tackled, but we finally got him back in his bunk and tucked him up. He was sweating like a ton of badly set concrete and he had a temperature that was probably well into three figures. He thrashed about as we arranged the blankets, mumbling incoherently to himself, and the same phrase kept occurring all the time—what sounded like 'Solnishko Odno, Solnishko Odno', as if he was using an R/T call-sign. It could have been Yiddish for all I knew. But just as we were leaving him he said clearly in English, 'You must help me. Igor and the others will die if . . .' and then he started off about Solnishko Odno again.

We were very silent on the way back to the bridge. I took out the auto-pilot and sat at the wheel, staring out unseeingly while *Lorelei* surged through the sea towards the faint glow in the sky ahead of us. Two-tooth stood balanced against the slight roll and drank some lukewarm tea, staring at the Redifon. 'By rights,' he said, half to himself, 'we ought to be radioing for an ambulance to stand by, as well as the police.'

'How the hell can we,' I said liverishly, 'with a load of slush on board? They might come out and meet us. He'll be all right until we dock. Once we've met Zaghrali and got rid

27

of the stuff we can start thinking what story we're going to tell them.' I glanced back at him. 'You think he's lying? About being a defector, I mean?'

'I think he's as phoney as a Hebrew haggis. "Just put me ashore quietly, I only want to visit me cobbers." ' He snorted derisively. 'Jeez, he must think we came down with the last shower.'

'You think he's an—you think he's been put ashore, then?' The word 'agent' sounded like something from a television serial. I said, 'But he can't have been. Those sailors wouldn't come looking for him if they'd . . .'

'Oh, yes, they would. But not because he's been put ashore. They were looking for a deserter from their bloody navy, Tallon. And that's what he is. Stands to reason, doesn't it? Only bloke who could get out of a sub. would be a lookout, or somebody who'd been given a job on deck when they surfaced. He's jumped ship, and now he's scared stiff that if the Immigration Department grabs him they might shoot him through to the Russian Embassy in Canberra.' He grinned, showing the two white protruding fangs that, together with his surname, had inspired some lower-deck wit to call him Two-tooth—an Australian term for lamb. 'That officer with his four offsiders brought back happy memories. I've been a deserter myself, don't forget.'

'He could be a Red agent,' I said uncomfortably. 'They could have planted him on us and then tried to make it look authentic by . . .'

'Aw, for crying out loud! Who'd want to impress us? And what the hell would they unload an agent off Tasmania for? There's nothing here for them to be interested in. Now if it was South Australia, with Woomera to go for, it'd be different. No, mate, he's deserted. Whatever AWOL is in Russian, he's done it.'

'I'd like to know what that Solnishko thing was he kept saying.' There were so many holes in Two-tooth's argument you could have used it for miniature golf. Russian deckhands do not, as a rule, speak flawless English, nor would a deserter jump overboard from twenty miles out in the dark. But I shut my mind to them. I wanted to be convinced that there'd

28

be no harm in an idea that had crossed my mind—that perhaps we might be able to bundle our unwanted visitor off the ship and dump him anonymously on a hospital doorstep when we docked. 'The name of his ship, perhaps?'

'Could be a nasty word for his ma-in-law, for all we know.' He picked up his pipe from the ashtray where he'd parked it and stuck it in his mouth. 'He's pretty crook,' he said hopefully. 'You never know, he might have that loss of memory thing, and forget all about us when he gets better. Anaemia, they call it.'

'Amnesia,' I said mechanically. His solution to our difficulties was no crazier than mine. I stared through the windscreen at the reflection of the lights of Hobart in the night sky. A light dipped on the horizon, then rose above it to flash in groups of three every nine seconds. We were about ten miles south-east of the Iron Pot, the unwatched light that marks the estuary of the Derwent. 'Better get below and make sure he doesn't die on us,' I said. 'They say it's unlucky to have a corpse on board.'

Three

WE WERE twenty minutes late at the pick-up point, and
Zaghrali was getting scared. He came on board with all the
vicious temper of a frightened man, nearly stamping his high
heels through the rotten planking of the disused jetty as he
sprang on to *Lorelei*'s deck. 'Where the hell you been, Tallon?'
he snarled. His gigolo face with its black, hairline moustache
looked devilish, lit from beneath by the torch he had in his
hand.

We were showing no lights, and neither was the truck that
waited twenty yards away with its engine turning over quietly.
The road ran in a convex curve parallel to the water's edge—a
dirt road, that ended here where a long-abandoned sawmill
crouched against the stars. The nearest house was three miles
away and was owned by an elderly couple who invariably went
to bed at sundown. Ours was a very simple set-up. We ferried
the contraband—small, easily disposable items such as watches
and transistor radios, as a rule—from the tuna boat to an un-
loading point such as this. We never used the same one too
often, and we ran to a timetable that meant no hanging about
for anybody. Which was why the Egyptian had got the wind up.
We'd never kept him waiting before. 'We been waiting all
bloody night for you,' he hissed, his thin five-foot-three outlined dimly in the bridge doorway and his Cairo accent getting
the better of his Australian in his excitement.

This was the first slush run we'd done. As he'd said, decimal
currency was then so new to Australia that most people hardly
knew the difference between a one- and a ten-dollar bill, let
alone whether they were genuine or not. In fact, there had been
a case in the papers of somebody getting stuck with the

coloured picture of one of the new notes that had been cut out of a magazine. It could be a very profitable investment. And Zaghrali had the contacts to get rid of the stuff. There is a Zaghrali in every seaport in the world, somebody with as many contacts as an octopus, and that was the sole reason for the uneasy partnership we had. A big disadvantage of working outside the law is that you have even less choice of business associates than you have inside it, and in any other circumstances I'd just as soon have done business with a carpet snake. Zaghrali thought that scruples were Russian currency. 'What if the police had come to ask questions?' he asked, sticking his face into mine.

'Then you'd have had to think up some good answers,' I said curtly, getting a whiff of the street-walker perfume he used. 'But they didn't, so let's get the stuff unloaded, shall we?'

'That's right, Gyppo, we haven't got all night, yer know,' said Two-tooth reprovingly from the darkness behind me. 'So how's about a little action, instead of standing there like a tart at a eunuchs' convention?'

Zaghrali's voice rose to a yelp of fury. 'Alla time I tell you not to call me Gyppo. Perhaps one day I kill you for that, bastard, pig, dog. I spit on you, English offal . . .'

'Here, just a bloody minute!' I could hear the grin in Two-tooth's growl as he said, 'Who're you calling English, you miserable little ratbag? Tallon's the only one who's English around here.'

'Stop needling him, Two-tooth,' I snapped. I was thinking of the man we had below. The sooner we got rid of Zaghrali the better. 'And you get on with your side of the job, Zaghrali, unless you'd rather do it in broad daylight.'

He spat something at me that was probably not socially acceptable round the Pyramids and went back to the jetty, where I could hear him taking it out of the two burly characters who were waiting by the truck. I noticed he didn't risk spoiling the fit of his Italian suit by carrying anything himself. He stood at the tail-board without saying another word to us, and five minutes later I could still hear his high-pitched voice, this time bawling out one of the men for taking his time with the last case. As Two-tooth jumped down on to the rickety pier to cast

31

off there was a renewed outburst of angry shouting from over by the truck and I could see Zaghrali's torch flashing like an Aldis lamp as he waved his arms about. Then his shrill voice was drowned by the slow thump of our diesels as we swung out into the estuary of the Derwent, and I gave all my attention to manœuvring the yacht in a fathom and a half of water.

Two-tooth went below and came up a few minutes later to stand on deck, leaning against the bridge doorway with his arms folded. Over his shoulder he said, 'Jeez, he's just about ropeable, that Gyppo. Why one of them blokes doesn't take a poke at him I don . . .' He stopped. Above the beat of the engines I heard the truck roar as it was revved violently and Two-tooth burst into a bellow of laughter. 'Aw, look, Tallon! They've ditched the poor little bludger.'

I took a quick look. Headlights were flickering behind the screen of trees that lined the bank, travelling fast in the direction of Hobart, and the torch was winking wildly from the jetty. 'They've gone off in the truck and left him to walk it. And in those bloody winkle-pickers of his, at that.' He guffawed again.

I grinned. 'And we can't offer him a lift, can we, not with . . .?' My grin vanished as I remembered our passenger. 'How's Nicolai? Did you get a look at him just then?'

He stopped chuckling and came inside. 'Yeah. I didn't put the light on—just put my head round the door—but he's pretty bad, Tallon. I could hear him mumbling away to himself, and he's tossing and turning still. We'll have to bring a doctor on board to him. I reckon he's got pneumonia.'

'And that means blowing the whole thing sky high,' I said flatly. 'Well, that's the way it has to be, I suppose. God, why couldn't this have happened when we were trying to earn an honest living up in Queensland? When you want the blasted publicity you don't get it. And now it's going to put us behind bars.'

'Maybe she'll be right,' he said unconvincingly. 'Maybe we'll get away with it. After all, we've got nothing on board now.'

'For God's sake, Two-tooth, stop trying to cheer me up,' I exploded. 'They're not idiots, those people in the Customs House, you know. First thing they and the police will be asking is where we get the money from to run *Lorelei*. We haven't had a client since we came here.'

There was one of those silences that creep up on you and breathe down your neck. *Lorelei*'s mast swung in front of me against the twinkling lights from the land like an admonitory finger and her engines rumbled sombrely like the roll of muffled drums. Two-tooth said unhappily, 'We could put about and beat it for the mainland. Refuel somewhere, and try to make New Zealand.'

I didn't bother answering that one. He knew better than I did that we hadn't got enough in our tanks to take us the length of Tasmania, let alone across the Bass Strait. And with a sick man aboard we were tied to the nearest port.

It was close on midnight when we reached Sullivan's Cove, the site of the first settlement and now the principal port area of Hobart. They raised the small bascule bridge to let us pass into Constitution Dock, then it was lowered again—like a cell door, I thought morbidly, closing slowly and with finality behind us. In Hobart, as in Naples, the docks are at the ends of the main streets. Road and sea transport are in such close juxtaposition that you get the impression that you're liable to be pinched for a parking offence when you tie up under the yellow Restricted Parking signs that line the docksides, and we were almost in the city itself where we were berthed. The long façade of the Customs House watched us expressionlessly from across the dark water of the dock, and the murmur of late-night traffic took the place of our diesels when I switched off, mingled with the chug of a donkey engine from a Norwegian freighter moored at King's Pier fifty yards away. The black bulk of Mount Wellington, carrying the highest television station in Australia, loomed against the stars, and the city sprawled sleepily at its foot, spangled in neons and streetlights. I snapped off the lights on the bridge and I was climbing wearily out of the control seat when a voice like that of Hamlet's father calling from the cellerage said hollowly, 'Tallon. Come down here a minute, will you? We won't be needing that doctor after all.'

I went down the ladder in one jump, my mind leaping ahead of me to the obvious conclusion. I'd said it was unlucky to have a corpse on board, without thinking just how unlucky it would be. Producing a live Russian would have been bad enough, but a dead one didn't even bear thinking about. I went below with the accusing voice of the Soviet delegate to the United Nations ringing in my ears while I fended off the unpleasant thought that if we hadn't had a load of contraband to dispose of, Nicolai could have been in hospital by now.

But there was no corpse. Two-tooth stood at the head of the bunk while I looked down in a daze at the figure lying on it—at the big, fat man who was struggling to free himself from the strips of sheet with which he'd been lashed to the berth. His enraged eyes glared savagely up at me from above the gag that was jammed into his mouth. He was stark naked. And I'd never set eyes on him in my life before. But Two-tooth had. 'It's Hydraulic Herbert,' he said. 'Zaghrali's truck-driver.'

Even Two-tooth was staggered by the stream of obscenity that blasted us when we took the gag out. The stranger cursed and swore without repeating himself once while we cut him loose and started massaging the white, criss-cross weals on his wrists and ankles, and it was only when the circulation started to come back that we were able to get a word in. He'd been lifting a crate—the last one—when somebody had knocked him cold from behind, and he wanted to know, very badly, which of us it had been. When he'd come round he'd been lying in this bunk, tied hand and four-letter foot, and when Two-tooth had looked in at the door he'd tried to shout and kick. He glowered at us malevolently, his unshaven face twisted with cramp. 'But all you did, you bastard,' he said to Two-tooth, 'was say, "Poor old Nick. You'll be right, mate." And then you sugared off and left me to it. What's Old Nick got to do with it? Where the hell are my clothes? What are you jokers running, anyway, a sex-orgy on a floating bloody madhouse?'

We calmed him down eventually after I'd got a slug of brandy into him that would have petrified an ostrich, fixed him up with some of my clothes, given him a ten-dollar bill—one of the real kind—and spun him an improbable story about mistaking him in the dark for a Customs spy who'd tried to sneak on board. We promised to fix him up with a meal, and we said he could stay the night if he wanted. He said surlily that he wasn't paying for no flaming taxis, so I left the bottle with him and told him to keep out of sight.

In the saloon Two-tooth said disgustedly, 'So that's what poor little Gyppo was doing his block for. That bloody commo bashed Hydraulic, pinched his gear and walked off humping a crate. In the dark who'd know the difference? And we just stood there like a couple of dills while he drove off with the truckful of slush. I told you he was worth watching, Tallon. My oath, if I ever meet up with him again . . .'

'You won't. He'll be picked up as soon as he burgles his first house. I only hope he keeps his mouth shut about us when they grab him, that's all.'

'Why should he? And what's going to happen when the police find the truck? If they trace it back to Gyppo we're cooked. He'd grass on his own grandmother if it'd get him a few days' remission.'

'I don't think Zaghrali'd be such a fool as to use a truck that could be traced.' Both of us were edging round the question that neither of us was willing to bring into the open—whether, having turned a Russian loose in Tasmania, we ought to take the irrevocable step of going to the police. If he was a secret agent . . . But that was going to melodramatic extremes. As Two-tooth had said, what would an agent be doing here? 'Who's making the supper,' I asked, 'you or me?'

He was, so I sat on the L-shaped settle in the saloon and smoked a cigarette. Our system was that whoever did the cooking had the galley to himself. Whoever didn't do the cooking washed up, so that was something else for me to look forward to. After a while he came back in an aroma of bacon and eggs, dumped the plates on the table and said, 'I made three lots, but we'll have to eat them ourselves. That plonko won't be needing any.'

My mind was still full of men in raincoats with snub-nose automatics in their hands. 'Plonko?' I said absently.

'That joker with the brewer's goitre. He's out to the wide in my bunk, shickered, with the empty bottle on his chest. Full as a bloody boot, he is.'

I shrugged. 'At least somebody's got something out of tonight's little shambles. You'll have to sleep in . . .' I stopped, looking through the plate glass window at the Yellow Cab that had pulled up on the dockside above us. And at the legs that were getting out of it.

They were long and slim and there was quite a lot of them. Nylon flashed briefly in the light as the girl slid out of the car and stood for a moment pulling her skirt straight. Then I got a repeat performance as she jumped across from the concrete steps on to our deck. I recognised those legs. They were one of the many qualifications that had got Lucky Silvera her job as private secretary to an elderly, but loaded, pickle manu-facturer, who had been led to believe that she was a member of the Italian Royal Family who had sacrificed a career in films to work for him. He would have been disillusioned to hear that her father had been an Italian migrant who had lived off his wife's dubious earnings in Footscray, Melbourne, where Lucia Teresa Sandra Margaret Silvera had been born.

She came through the door in a cloud of expensive perfume that was more than a match for the bacon and eggs, looking as if she was modelling the cream linen suit she was wearing under her open pillar-box-red summer coat. There were blue lights in her short, jet-black hair and her skin was the colour of cinnamon. She had large, dark, childishly innocent eyes, a wide, full-lipped mouth and a figure that would have quelled a riot. She came right up to me and said, in that fascinating Italian accent it had taken her months to acquire, 'Patreeck, *carissimo*, how lovely to see you again.' She slid her arms round my neck and kissed me uninhibitedly, putting quite a lot of work into it. I felt the hard pressure of her breasts and thighs as she stood on her toes and leaned against me and I wondered briefly how her pickle-packing employer stood the pace.

'*Ciao*, Lucky,' I said, as soon as I could tear my face away. 'What are you doing out of bed at this hour of night?'

She tightened her grip round my neck and moved her body gently against mine, leaning back to give me the full effect of her wickedly innocent eyes. 'We could do some research on that,' she said softly. 'Why don't you kiss me properly and take it from there?'

'Because,' I said reasonably, 'I don't like cold bacon and eggs.' I unpeeled her and sat down at the table⁕ This come-and-get-it act was a game she liked to play, and meant, I knew, absolutely nothing. It kept her technique up to date, and that was all. Behind all that warm, scented sex there was a mind as coldly calculating as a cash-register.

Two-tooth's knife and fork had been clinking away steadily throughout this performance. Now, he looked up at Lucky, inserted a forkful of egg—none too accurately—through his beard and said, champing, 'How yer going, Lucky, girl? Wanta bit of fried bread? All we got left.'

She shook her head and draped herself elegantly on the edge of the table, allowing her short skirt to ride up just the right amount. 'No, thanks, mate,' she said, the Italian receding rapidly. 'Could do with a cuppa coffee, though.'

Two-tooth waved his fork politely to indicate that his mouth was more than usually full. When he could speak he said, 'Haven't made it yet. Gimme time to finish this, will you?'

She slid to her feet again. 'I'll make it,' she said. 'I know how I like it. I want it freshly ground, not out of a bloody tin.'

I stared at her, dumbfounded. She'd once told me she hated cooking of any sort so much that she lived off milk and biscuits when there was nobody around to wait on her. As far as I was aware, she didn't even know how to boil water. I said coldly, 'Wait a minute, Lucky. Whatever it is you're after, you won't get it by making the coffee. Even if you know how.'

She turned her lovely liquid eyes on to me. 'You are becoming hard and not very nice, Patreeck *mio*,' she said reproachfully. 'I want nothing. Nothing at all, except a little cup of coffee. Now I go to make it, yes?'

I sat with my knife and fork poised, watching her smooth dark head disappear down the ladder. 'She's up to something or other.' I looked across at him. 'Your cabin. If she goes in there, she'll find him.'

'So what?' He wiped his mouth and beard with a limp khaki handkerchief. 'He's out cold, isn't he? And we've had drunks on board before now.' He leered horribly at me. 'Anyway, it's your bunk she seems to be interested in, not mine.'

I gave him the hard eye and got on with my meal, listening

37

to the whirr of the electric coffee-grinder from the galley that accompanied Lucky's slightly husky voice singing 'Mi chiamano Mimì' from *La Bohème*, a rendering she'd learnt off by heart for the enslavement of the pickle king. When I'd finished I lit a cigarette. 'Are you sure,' I said quietly, 'you really think he's a deserter?'

He looked up at me, his pipe and pouch in his hand. 'Sure,' he said, surprised. 'Why, you aren't still stuck with your Russian-spy theory, are you? I thought we'd sorted all that out.' He leaned forward. 'Forget it, mate, she'll be right. When in doubt, do nothing. They'll pick Ivan up without any help from us, and so . . .'

'Ivan?' Lucky came in with the tray. She'd put a cloth on it and served the coffee in the harlequin cups with triangular saucers instead of the chipped mugs we usually had. She put the tray down on the table and gave Two-tooth his. 'Who's Ivan?' she asked.

'Russian who runs a café up on Elizabeth Street,' he said, without batting an eyelid. He slurped some coffee. 'Doesn't turn out a beaut cuppa coffee like this, though.'

'I bet he doesn't,' Lucky agreed. She sat down on the end of the settle next to him and smiled across at me. 'I bet,' she said silkily, 'he doesn't leave his life-jacket in the galley, either.'

Two-tooth's cup clinked loudly as he set it down and a little coffee slopped over into his saucer. She said calmly. 'But, of course, that's got nothing to do with me. I'm not going to ask any questions about who the Russian is you're smuggling into the country, or why he should be boozed to the eyebrows in the cabin off the galley. But I'd get rid of the life-jacket, if I were you. Unless,' she added, 'your cobber up on Elizabeth Street wants to borrow it for when he goes for a swim in his samovar.'

'Now listen, Lucky,' I said quietly. 'It's much better if . . .'

'All that,' she said, raising her voice slightly, 'isn't my business. What I'm interested in is where I'm going to sleep to-night.'

'Well, you won't be sleeping here,' I said, staring at her. 'What's the matter with your flat? And what about Pickles?'

'Pickles' wife,' she said bitterly, 'found out about the flat. I

38

had to leave in a bit of a rush. And I can't go to an hotel at this time of night with no luggage or anything. They might think,' she said coyly, 'that I was after men. Let me stay here, Pat. Please.'

'My bloody oath,' said Two-tooth, grinning. 'So that's why you were breaking your neck to fix the coffee.' He turned to me. 'I said it was your bunk she was after, didn't I?'

'You can't stay here, Lucky,' I snapped. 'Isn't there some girl you can go to?'

'I don't know any girls, Pat,' she said pathetically. 'I haven't got anybody to turn to.' She looked down at the table and drew a little pattern with a scarlet-lacquered fingernail. 'Except one or two boys I know.'

'O.K., go to one of them,' I said brutally. 'But give him a ring to make sure his wife's away first.'

She looked up at me with huge, tragic eyes. 'That's not a nice thing to say to a girl, Pat. But I can see you're upset, with this commo on board and everything. Still,' she brightened, 'I could always go and ask the police what to do, couldn't I? They'd help me.'

'So that's it,' I said slowly. 'You crafty little blackmailer. Well, this time you're a bit off course, Lucky. The man in Two-tooth's cabin's no more Russian than you are.'

'And I suppose the life-jacket isn't Russian, either?' She stared at me for a long moment, without the fooling this time. There was something in her dark eyes that I'd never seen there before as she said, 'Why do you have to do these things, Patrick? I'd hate to do anything to hurt you, but . . .' She stopped and then said, 'But I've got to have somewhere to sleep, haven't I? I won't get in your hair, and it'll only be for tonight. Hell, you'd do as much for any other stray cat, wouldn't you?'

When I didn't say anything Two-tooth stood up. 'Nobody gives a monkey's where I sleep,' he said sourly. 'I'm going to fix meself up with a berth while there's still one going, and I might even have a nice hot-water bottle.' He looked at me expressionlessly. 'You won't be needing one, I reckon?'

Four

THERE wasn't much of the night left for sleeping, and what there was I didn't make much use of. My cabin was the only one with a single berth, so Lucky got it after all, while Two-tooth and I moved into the guest cabin next door. He'd refused, understandably enough, to take the spare bunk in his own cabin, and the fo'c'sle was too reminiscent of a prison cell to be comfortable. So he took the lower berth and I lay awake for a long time listening enviously to his steady, untroubled breathing from below me, and to the cluck of dock-water under *Lorelei's* hull. The thought that this might well be my last night aboard her nagged like an aching tooth. I wondered what had happened to the Russian, and whether he'd been picked up, and what would happen to Two-tooth and me if he was, and whether we'd ever go out into the wide freedom of the sea together again.

I thought of that other time when I'd waited for the police to come for me—a cool, quiet, late-summer night like this, in England, when the leave-roster had been altered unexpectedly and I'd flown in from Malaya to find that the anonymous letter I'd torn up had been true after all. But it had been my fault, not hers. I was the one who'd pestered her into marriage, knowing all along that it wouldn't last. As for him—I frowned into the darkness. I couldn't even remember the name of the man I'd killed. I kicked the blankets off and pulled them on again. The realisation that you've made a complete mess of your life isn't very nice to live with at the best of times, but in the small accusatory hours of the morning when the church clocks toll only for you there's nothing like it to bring on a chronic attack of insomnia. I dropped off eventually, to dream of dead faces that came up out of the dark sea to stare at me accusingly.

But it seemed that I'd only just closed my eyes when the scream shattered the silence like a steam-whistle.

I was out of the bunk in a flash—and fell a sickening four feet to the deck with an impact that woke me up completely. I heard Two-tooth's startled oath, but by that time I was out of the door and limping forward to where the pandemonium of shouts and crashes was coming from. I went up the companion, across the saloon with its smell of stale tobacco smoke, and down to the galley. The slamming of doors and a thump that I couldn't identify had given way to a sort of gibbering howl that was coming from behind the closed cabin door that led off the galley. I tried the handle, but it was locked. 'Open the door,' I shouted, rattling it. 'What the hell's going on?'

'Keep away from me!' The voice from inside was almost inarticulate with terror. 'I've got your knife, and the first one through the door gets it. I'm warning you, keep away from me!' The high-pitched voice cracked and he started to laugh insanely.

'Don't be so bloody stupid,' I said, lowering my voice with an effort. 'It's me, Tallon. Open the door. What's the matter with you?'

'What isn't?' Two-tooth said from behind me. He was wearing his black leather jacket over his striped pyjamas. 'He's got a touch of the green lizards, that's what. Jeez, this is all we needed, Tallon, a grog artist who's slipped his bloody trolley.' He gave the door a thump that nearly unhinged it, and drew a bedlam of shouts and obscenities from within. 'Delirium tremblings,' he said disgustedly. 'That's what he's got.'

It took us about ten minutes to talk the man into opening the door. When he finally let us in we found him backed up against his bunk, a wicked-looking long-bladed knife in his hand and his face the colour of an old tennis ball. 'By God, I'll get even with you for this, Tallon,' he snarled. 'And you, Harry Lamb. Bashing me over the head, and now sneaking in here dressed like Ned Kelly trying to scare the daylights outa me.' His voice slipped its clutch. 'What's it all for?' he shrieked. 'What have I done to you? You're mad, the bloody pair of you. Mad, that's what . . .'

'Told yer,' said Two-tooth with gloomy satisfaction. 'He's as crazy as a two-bob watch. They always think everybody else is nuts.' To the truckie he said reassuringly, 'Put that knife down, yer stupid nong, before I use it to cut your tripes out. What would we want to dress up for to frighten you? We could do it just as well by offering to give you a wash.'

Hydraulic lowered the knife point and gaped at us uncertainly, a balding, fat, frightened man on the wrong side of fifty, with flabby, unshaven jowls that were mottled yellow and dirty grey and trembling like a pair of decaying custards. He stank of sweat and booze and he looked terrible. 'Just take it easy,' I said to him quietly. 'Nobody can get at you here.' To Two-tooth I said, 'There's a bottle of White Horse in the cocktail cabinet. Fix him up with a tot, will you?'

He shambled out, muttering something about the poor view Alcoholics Anonymous would take of this, and Hydraulic sat down groggily on the bunk. He put the knife down on the blankets. 'Fair dinkum, Tallon,' he said weakly. 'Was it you or not?'

'Of course it wasn't.' I said it as matter-of-factly as I could, trying to bring him back to normal.

It was the worst thing I could have said. He stared at me in horror, gripping the side of the bunk. 'You mean,' he croaked, the whites of his eyes showing like those of a startled horse, 'he was really trying to do me in, that bloke?' He picked up the knife again and clutched it convulsively, his eyes darting to the open doorway behind me.

'There wasn't any bloke,' I said liverishly. By now I was convinced that Two-tooth had the right idea after all. The temperature goes down fast at night in Tasmania and I was only wearing pyjamas. And I'd had hardly any sleep. 'You were having a nightmare, you fool. Who'd want to kill you?'

'It was no nightmare, mate.' He shuddered, his eyes still on the door. 'Where d'you think this knife came from?' He switched his eyes to me suspiciously. 'Or does it belong to that black-bearded baboon out there?'

I'd forgotten that he'd been stripped to the buff when we'd found him. I took the knife out of his clammy hand. It was a vicious-looking piece of cutlery, with a carved and polished haft made of some sort of reddish wood and a blued-steel blade that was cruciform in section and pointed like a surgical needle. 'No,' I said thoughtfully. 'It's not one of ours.' I looked up at him. 'What was he like, this character you saw?'

'Bloody horrible.' He shuddered again. 'Jeez, I don't ever want to go through that again.' He looked at me like a sick monkey. 'I came to, the way you do when you got a feeling there's somebody in the room. It was dark, sort of, but there was enough light through the porthole for me to see this black shape. Gawd, that woke me up all right, I can tell you.' He wiped his forehead with the back of his hand. 'He was about eight feet tall, all sorta shadowy and black, and he hadn't got no face.' He stopped and put his head in his shaking hands.

'But you could see he had tentacles and he was riding a motor-scooter,' growled Two-tooth unsympathetically, coming in with a glass that contained a good quarter of an inch of whisky. 'Look, mate, you want to lay off the hard, and stick to beer. I've seen blokes . . .'

'Pack it in, will yer?' shouted Hydraulic desperately. 'I tell you, I saw him. It was only when I woke up I thought he hadn't got no face. But then I saw he had some sort of hood over his head. Like those Ku Klux Klan blokes, only black, see?'

'Here, get this down,' I said quickly, before Two-tooth could send him off again. As I gave him the glass I said, 'Did he say anything?'

'Not a bloody word.' Hydraulic drank the whisky down, his teeth chattering against the glass. 'That made it all the worse. Silent, he was—didn't even seem to breathe. He just went for me with this knife. I grabbed his arm, but it was like trying to wrestle with a parking meter. He did something to me arm that nearly paralysed it and then I saw the knife going up over me chest. So I lashed out with me knee and let out a yell. I must have got him in the goolies, because he let out a grunt and backed off. Then there was a hell of a crash from the other end of the boat and he just seemed to vanish. I put the light on and locked the door. When I heard you jokers, I thought it was him coming back, but then I remembered that bash on the head, and I thought it was you lot who'd been trying to put the wind up me.' He gave me the glass. 'Gawd, I wish now it had been.'

I stood up and exchanged a look with Two-tooth. 'Well, whoever it was, he won't be back tonight,' I said soothingly. 'So why not just get your head down and we can . . .'

'Not flaming likely, mate.' Hydraulic jumped to his feet. I dunno what lurk you blokes are up to, but whatever it is I'm not getting mixed up in it. You can have your gear back one of these days, but right now I'm off.'

A couple of minutes later we were on deck, watching him heading at a fast shamble for Dunn Street, looking back over his shoulder as he flitted from one patch of lamplight to the next. The stars were paling among the mastheads and aerials of the shipping whose jumbled outlines were beginning to show clearly against the dove-grey sky to the east, and I shivered as a chilly dawn breeze sneaked off the Derwent. As the truckie disappeared into the deserted city I said to Two-tooth, 'You don't think he'll go to the police?' Quite a lot of men like Hydraulic make a steady income on the side that way.

He grunted. He'd been very quiet during the last few minutes. 'Not him. Don't you know why they call him Hydraulic?'

'No.' I turned to go below.

'Because he'd lift anything.' He snorted briefly. 'No, he and the dees don't get on.' He paused and then said casually, 'Reckon I'll just have a bit of a look round, O.K.?'

I nodded, my teeth chattering. 'I'm going to see if the girl's all right.'

He didn't make any of the cracks I might have expected about me dropping in on Lucky in my pyjamas. He padded away forward, moving like a cat—as he could when he wanted to. I went aft to the cockpit where the two fishing chairs sat under the pallid stars like empty judgment seats. The owner's cabin had two doors, one opening off the cockpit and the other a sliding door leading forward. The cockpit door was locked, as it should have been, so I went below via the bridge and moved the sliding door back an inch, listening to the girl's calm, regular breathing. When I turned round, Two-tooth was standing outside the door of the guest cabin, the knife dangling in his hand. 'She asleep?' he asked softly. I nodded and followed him into the cabin. He shut the door and put the light on. 'You sure?' he asked, watching me.

'I didn't examine her all that closely,' I said coldly. 'Did you find anything?' I pulled myself up wearily into the bunk and got under the blankets.

'Fo'c'sle hatch-cover's unclipped.' He sat down on his bunk. 'He must have got out that way.'

I remembered the thump I'd heard after Hydraulic had yelled out. 'He did. I heard him. You've abandoned the theory that Hydraulic was seeing things, then?'

'Hell, yes. The knife proves there was somebody here. We wouldn't keep a pigsticker like this on board. Last time I saw anything like this was in Yokohama when I was living with that kid in the Yoshiwara and the naval cops were after me. That bloke could have stuck it into Hydraulic's heart and there wouldn't even have been a drop of blood to show for it.' He snapped the light off and I heard him scrambling into the bunk beneath me. 'If it comes to that,' he said thoughtfully in the darkness, 'it didn't have to be a bloke at all. Could have been a sheila, for all our friend knew. Didn't speak or anything.' He was silent for a minute, then he said off-handedly, 'That Lucky's a pretty sound sleeper, isn't she? You'd think with all the row you and Hydraulic were making between you she'd have been out to see what was going on?'

'You'd think so. But she's probably . . .' I stopped. 'Lucky!' I said incredulously. 'Good God, Two-tooth, you can't seriously think she . . . You must be out of your mind.'

'Wouldn't be surprising if I was, the things that go on around here. But she was sneaking round the ship earlier on, while you were snoring your head off. I was on me way to the heads when I saw her rooting around in the saloon. Strewth, did she give me a look. Came about as if she'd been lassoed and said she was looking for another blanket.'

'Perhaps she was. I didn't think of asking her if she wanted extra blankets. I just fixed her up with a pair of my pyjamas.'

'I know, mate. She was wearing them—the top half, anyway. Just about covered her requirements.' For some reason he seemed to find this very witty, for I heard him guffawing to himself down below, thrashing about and yuk-yukking in the dark until I thought his mattress was going to bust a spring.

45

When he'd finished he said, 'But the point is, Tallon, who was supposed to be done over tonight? Not Hydraulic, that's for sure.'

'No.' The bunk was beginning to warm up and I thought that, given the chance, I might be able to put in another couple of hours' sleep. The rectangle of sky through the porthole just above me was flushed with a delicate wax-flower pink. I said sleepily, 'Not Hydraulic. Nicolai. He said there'd be somebody after him sooner or later.'

'Right,' said Two-tooth energetically. 'And who knew we'd picked him up? The Russians didn't. Zaghrali might have known there was something funny going on, but if he did, he'd know the bloke had got away, wouldn't he?' He was silent for so long that I thought he'd dropped off. Then he said, exasperatingly wide awake, 'No, mate. The only soul who knew we'd got a passenger was Lucky. Take it or leave it.'

'I'll leave it.' I was getting fed up with this. 'But there's another possibility you haven't thought of yet. Wouldn't it be a laugh if our visitor had been after the fellow who usually sleeps in that cabin? And all he got was the boot from Hydraulic instead?'

He chuckled. 'My word. I'd like to have seen his face when . . .' He stopped laughing all of a sudden. 'Now you're being bloody ridiculous,' he said stiffly. 'That's my cabin. Who'd want to murder me?'

'Who wouldn't,' I said, grinning in the dark, 'when you go on yabbering all night? Now shut up, will you, and let's get some sleep.'

Five

WHEN I opened my eyes again the porthole above me was a
brassy, aching blue and a dazzlingly white rectangle of sunlight was reflecting off the bulkhead opposite. I climbed down
stiffly from the berth, noticing that the sheets and blankets of
the lower bunk were already folded neatly on its mattress, and
went out into the passageway. My quarters, now infested by
Lucky, lay at the end of it behind the bird's-eye maple sliding
door. Forward, the short companion led up to the bridge, with
the fireproof, watertight door of the engine-room beside it.

There wasn't a sound from my cabin, but I could hear Two-
tooth clinking plates in the galley as I went into the cool of the
bathroom. I showered and shaved and then went along the
passage to my cabin, where I sneaked a clean shirt and a pair of
grey flannels out of my wardrobe. I pussyfooted back to the
one I was using, grinning to myself at the thought of Two-
tooth's face if he'd caught me leaving Lucky's boudoir with my
trousers in my hand. She'd looked oddly different asleep, with
a quality of tranquil candour on her face that made me admire
her acting ability more than ever. When I'd dressed I went up
through the saloon, where last night's coffee-cups still squatted
unhealthily on the table, and on to the bridge.

It was a hot, blue-and-gold enamelled morning. The sun
blazed down out of a sky the colour of copper sulphate, making
the glittering brasswork of the bridge handrails hot to the
touch although it was only just after eight o'clock. On the starboard side the flared, tomato-coloured bow of the Norwegian
freighter towered over the green-and-white Marine Board
sheds on King's Pier, the Blue Peter fluttering at her foremast in the warm morning breeze and her winches clanking

47

busily. A big scarlet International semi-trailer, stacked with apple-boxes, ground past in low gear and a few cars were moving on Davey Street across the dock where the cuboid modernistic museum extension glowed salmon pink in the sunlight. Along the waterfront, like a row of prosperous burghers turning their backs uncompromisingly on upstart newcomers, the sober Victorian buildings stood foursquare and solid with the glittering, concrete-and-glass office blocks peering impudently over their shoulders. And Mount Wellington, who had been here longer than any of them, basked serenely in the sun, as befitted the oldest inhabitant, with the red-and-blue roofs of the western suburbs spread across its knees like an Indian rug, and a wisp of powder blue, like the smoke of an after-breakfast pipe, rising lazily from a small bushfire halfway up its soaring, grey-green flanks.

It was hard to believe, looking at this prosperous, sunlit city, that it had once been regarded as the bridgehead to hell on earth. For that is how it had seemed to the pallid, half-starved convicts who had stumbled, clanking their chains and blinking owlishly in sunlight just like this, off the wooden ships that had brought them from England to Hobart Town a little more than a century ago—the doomed felons who had been sentenced to the penal settlements and the labour gangs of Van Dieman's Land, the old name for Tasmania. Demons' Land, they had called it, with the macabre humour of the condemned. For this had been the Devil's Island of the Southern Hemisphere, the 'Gaol of the Empire', to escape from which men had been known to commit brutal murder solely that they might qualify for the merciful oblivion of the gallows. Others, less fortunate, had escaped into the savage bush country of the south-west, to die in a subhuman extremity of hunger—or to be found, as one of them had been, wandering in circles with a half-gnawed human arm in his pocket. A man can be brutalised to the point where even murder and cannibalism are infinitely preferable to a screaming insanity of pain on the whipping triangle where the flesh would be slowly and scientifically shredded from his bones.

And if I'd been born a hundred years earlier I could have been one of them. I could have been sentenced to the chain

48

gangs of Port Arthur instead of to the luxury of the Scrubs. Or would they have hanged me? I shivered in the warm sunlight and turned to go below, conscious of Lorelei watching me composedly from her corner, her primrose dress glowing in the reflected light off the dock and her short dark hair immaculately groomed. She reminded me of the Soviet officer and the events of the night before. Perhaps, I thought morbidly, I might end up in a Tasmanian gaol yet.

Two-tooth was in the saloon, putting away a mound of grilled sausages and ham and looking as if he'd had eight hours of the sort of sleep they recommend in the malted-milk advertisements. I never eat breakfast, so I sat and drank a cup of black coffee and watched him until he chased the last fugitive bit of sausage round his plate, put his knife and fork down contentedly and sat back. Then he winced and leaned forward again, his hand going to his stomach.

'The bicarb,' I said vindictively, 'is in the medicine cupboard.'

'It's not me guts.' He reached inside his blue denim trousers, half rising, his eyes bulging with the effort. 'Bloody foresight's like a razor blade,' he said censoriously. 'Thought I'd done meself an injury that time.' He pulled a flat, blued-steel automatic out of the waistband of his pants and put it on the table beside his empty plate.

I stared at it. 'What the hell,' I said disbelievingly, 'are you carrying that around for?' I reached across and picked it up. It was a .32 Scott & Webley MP, loaded and ready to go. I looked up at him, expecting to see him looking sheepish, but his grey eyes stared back at me without a flicker.

'What d'you think it's for? Encyclopaedia salesmen?' He poured himself another cup of coffee. 'It's for the ratbag who was after me last night, that's who it's for. And if it so happens that it was Flash Annie, then she'd better be wearing a bullet-proof brassière next time.'

'For God's sake,' I exploded. 'Leave Lucky out of it, will you? We had enough of that last night. And nobody's trying to murder you, you idiot. I only said that to shut you up. It was the Russian they were after. Nothing's going to happen now he's gone.'

'You go on thinking that.' He added milk and about half a pound of sugar to his coffee and stirred it, watching me grimly. 'And when you wake up one morning with a knife in your ribs don't say I didn't warn yer.' He drank some coffee and then put his cup down and leaned forward. 'I did a lot of thinking last night. I reckon you were right about it being me they were after—but not only me. You as well. That Ivan said they were after him because he knew something, didn't he? All right. Maybe they think he talked to us about it. We might know more'n's good for us, mate. So they got to arrange for our life assurance to become payable as well.'

I stared at him dazedly. 'So they're going to murder everybody Nicolai comes into contact with? And Lucky's the one with the double-O number? Isn't she going to have rather a full programme? There's you and me, and the truckie and Zaghrali . . .'

'I never said that. But better people than Lucky Silvera have turned out to be Reds,' he said sententiously. He took the gun out of my limp hand. 'Anyway, I'm not taking any chances. And if you sit there with that in your fist, you're going to attract a crowd.' He jerked his head at the sunlit dockside as he half rose to stow the gun away, stuffing it into his hip-pocket this time. 'We got girl trouble again, Tallon. Go and do your stuff.'

I twisted round in my seat. There was a red-and-white taxi standing above us on the dockside, a Toyota Crown de Luxe. Through the green anti-glare windows of the car I could see the girl beside the driver, looking out at the yacht. Then she opened the nearside door and got out. 'Oh, no!' I said wearily. 'Not this morning.' I jumped up to head her off. We got them all the time—the joy-ride girls, teenagers straight out of school mostly, who wanted to air their bikinis on our sundeck. Sometimes they wanted to try out our spring mattresses as well, but whatever they were after they all worked on the assumption that if you had a big expensive boat you had a big expensive bank account to go with it.

This one stood by the car putting on a pair of sunglasses, a small girl with a figure like a prima ballerina and long, strawberry-blonde hair that gleamed like gold in the sun, with a touch of copper to put the red lights in it. She was wearing a jade-green Thai silk shirt, and her slim, dancer's legs were encased in stone-coloured stretch pants that fitted her the way butter fits a slice of toast. She stood for a moment, outlined against the dramatically blue sky, then she started down the steps. She came right down to where I was glowering at her and said, 'Mr. Tallon? Good morning. May I come aboard?' She had a clipped, expensively educated voice, and her makeup wasn't like that of our usual applicants for a weekend afloat. But whatever she was, I thought grimly, she wasn't getting any gangplank rigged for her. We'd had all the visitors we could take already.

But, without breaking her stride, she put a moccasin-shod foot on the rail, stepped down to the deck beside me and said, 'My name's Barbara Mackail. I'd like to talk to you about hiring your boat.' She flashed her sunglasses at me and before I could throw her overboard she'd slipped under my guard and was in the saloon, where I could hear her in her head-prefect's voice introducing herself to Two-tooth.

I followed her in a fury. Two-tooth's face was wreathed in a beaming smile as he lumbered round the table to swallow up the slim hand she gave him in his enormous paw. I remembered with foreboding his partiality for girls with red in their hair as he said, 'Call me Two-tooth,' fondling her hand as if it was another helping of sausage and bacon. And this one was certainly worth having a partiality for. Her face was between heart-shaped and oval, with high cheekbones and a wide, shapely mouth. The smooth café-au-lait tan that she wore, with the minimum of make-up, gave her a clean, appealing look, and the red-gold, shoulder-length hair was caught up in a green ribbon at the nape of her neck. But she didn't smile. There was a curiously dead-pan look about her that gave her beautiful face the look of Lorelei, the mascot we had on the bridge. Her eyes, blank behind her Zeiss Umbral sunglasses, had gone on a tour of the saloon, taking notes, and her expressionless stare annoyed me more than ever. Neither Two-tooth nor I was very fond of housework, and the bright sunlight pouring in on the starboard side highlighted unmercifully the film of dust that made the expensive furniture look pretentiously

51

tawdry. The cocktail cabinet with its solid silver fittings looked as if it might have 'Best Quality Tasmanian Apples' stencilled on the back, and an ashtray that hadn't been emptied for days had spilled a mess of cigarette ends and ash on to its figured walnut top.

I snapped the venetian blinds shut to keep out the sun. 'O.K., Miss MacTavish,' I said unpleasantly. 'You've shaken hands with the bearded lady. Now beat it, will you? We're not in the market for free trips round the harbour this morning.'

'Free trips?' she asked calmly. She took off her Zeiss Umbrals and stared at me. She had the greenest eyes I'd ever seen, the green of a breaking wave, and they looked at me without any expression whatever. 'I don't want any free trips, Mr. Tallon. I'll pay for the charter, naturally. And my name,' she added without heat, 'is Mackail.'

I remembered the blonde, self-possessed sixteen-year-old who, with her long-haired friends of both sexes, had commandeered *Lorelei* for twelve hideous hours by posing as the daughter of a millionaire grazier. That had been up in Cairns, and it had cost me a new saloon carpet, over a hundred dollars in fuel oil, and had nearly brought the local police down on us. 'It's been tried before,' I said. 'Next time, try something more original—like disguising yourself as the Man from the Prudential. Good morning.' I jerked my thumb at the door.

She didn't lose her temper, weep, or even show any sign of embarrassment at my uncouth behaviour. She stood perfectly still, looking at me as placidly as ever as she said, 'I don't think you understand. You advertised in the Queensland papers that you were willing to hire your yacht. Well, I want to charter it. I can give you a banker's reference and put down any deposit you care to name. You're not already engaged, are you?'

I avoided that question. 'I see,' I said expressionlessly. 'And what sort of fish would you be interested in, Miss Mackail? Mackerel? Blue-fin?' She didn't look big enough to cope with a sardine.

She sat down composedly in the armchair by the cocktail cabinet. 'I'm not interested in fishing at all. You see, I'm a writer. I want to take a trip up the west coast for a book I'm working on.'

I leaned back against the table opposite her, my attitude undergoing a marked and rapid change. Far from being a pest, this girl could be God's gift to the unlicensed import business. It would give our credit rating a tremendous lift if we could tell the police, or anybody else who came asking awkward questions, that we were on a bona-fide hire job. And a contract with an author could be used to explain away all sorts of irregularities—even our reason for being out last night, perhaps. It could be that we'd turned the corner at last. This coolly composed customer might have contacts in Hobart who might even want to go fishing—not only writers, but people with money. I offered her a Player's and a drink and she refused both. She looked at me with eyes as clear and candid as green traffic lights as she said, 'I'm collecting material for a book on shipwrecks on the south-west coast. I'm calling it *Where the Devil Meets the Tiger*. After Tasmanian devils and tiger-wolves, you know.'

I wondered if she knew that the thylacine, the unique tiger-striped marsupial wolf of Tasmania, was supposed to be extinct, but before I could bring that controversial question up Two-tooth said enthusiastically, 'Jeez, Miss Mackail, that's a beaut name for a book.' The combination of red-gold hair and a charter fee had obviously won his heart. 'So it's the south-west you're interested in, then? I can give you all the dope you want on that, my word I can.' I knew for a fact he'd never set foot in the place in his life.

'A man of your experience could, I suppose.' It was a clinical statement of probability, not flattery, but he smirked just the same and leaned forward with one elbow on his knee in a Boyhood-of-Raleigh attitude. She said to him, 'There are some wonderfully dramatic names along that coast, aren't there? Those islands in Macquarie Harbour, for instance—the Isle of Condemned, and Dead Island.' She turned to me, 'Do you know the coast too, Mr. Tallon?'

'I've sailed as far as Strahan, in Macquarie Harbour,' I said cautiously. 'I think I could get you wherever . . .'

'Good.' She nodded, satisfied. 'I think places like that are just made to be written about. And the entrance to the harbour —what's it called?'

I realised I was being tested out. 'Hell's Gates,' I said obediently. 'It was named by the convicts.' And, I thought, they'd called it Hell's Gates with good reason. Exposed to the almost incessant rains and howling gales of the Roaring Forties, the convict settlement in the huge inland sea called Macquarie Harbour had been a hell of human misery and inhuman brutality. It had been a purgatory populated by fiends and damned souls, isolated from the world of men by the mountain ranges that make the climate of the south-west so different from that of the rest of Tasmania. The convicts had built their own hell at Macquarie, standing up to their necks in ice-cold water from dawn to dusk while they manhandled into position the huge logs that had been floated down the Gordon River by the felling gangs, working like teams of two-legged bullocks under the whistle and crack of the overseer's lash. They'd eaten their flour-and-water porridge at nightfall with their numbed and splintered fingers, since cutlery of any sort was forbidden, and then they'd been herded, still chained and soaking, into their leaking, draughty shed with the perverts and the half-crazed for company. 'Yes,' I said heavily. 'You'd get a good story out of a place like that.'

'I did a year's research on Macquarie Harbour alone,' she said. 'But it's the area south of that I'm interested in now.' She gazed at me speculatively. 'You'll want to know where we're going before you can name a fee, I suppose?'

'I'll get the chart,' said Two-tooth with alacrity. He clambered up the bridge ladder and a moment later he was back with a yard-long roll of white cartridge paper under his arm. It crackled like a miniature thunderstorm as he flattened it out on the table, pushing his greasy plate to one side. 'Admiralty Chart 1079,' he said over his shoulder. 'This should do for a start.' The girl went to stand behind him, looking smaller than ever against his bulk. 'And this is your stretch of coast,' he said, running his finger down it. He grinned down at her. 'South of Hell's Gates.'

I went to look over his other shoulder. He was staring down at the chart, his big hands splayed out on it. 'It's as bad a stretch as any in the world,' he said thoughtfully. 'Breakers, shoals, uncharted rocks and fog. A wrecker's coast.' As if drawn by a magnet, my eyes followed his to the neatly-pencilled line that was drawn at an angle to the coast and labelled 'UFO 1830' followed by the month and day—Two-tooth's sole evidence that he was one of the happy breed who have been privileged to see a flying saucer. I stiffened. Surely he wouldn't be fool enough to mention that? If he did, then we could say goodbye to our chance of getting a client. Who'd want to entrust his life off a wrecker's coast to people who took bearings on little green men? As if to confirm my worst fears he said broodingly, 'There've been some queer things happen along that coast, my word there have.'

I said quickly, trying to catch his eye, 'I think Miss Mackail might like some coffee, Two-tooth. How about it?'

'Yeah, I could do with one,' he said absently, without looking up. 'You'll find a fresh tin in the cupboard over the sink. Now where was it you wanted to go, Miss Mackail?'

'I don't want any coffee, thank you,' she said briefly. Then she put a slim finger on the pencil line. 'What'—she looked up at Two-tooth and I felt my blood run cold—'happened here in 1830? That's the sort of date that interests me very much.'

He looked down at her in surprise. 'That's the time, not the date. Half past six in the evening. And UFO,' he avoided my eye studiously, 'stands for Unidentified Flying Object.'

Well, that's the way it goes, I thought numbly. But why the hell hadn't he had the sense to say it stood for Unusual Fish Observed, or something like that? I clenched my fists, cursing myself for not having erased the damn thing, and said, clenching my voice as well, 'Perhaps we could just get on with the details of your trip, Miss Mackail. I hardly think you'll be interested in . . .'

'Oh, but I am.' She looked round at me and I was surprised at the way her face had come to life. Her cool green eyes were now full of a sort of incredulous excitement, as if she'd unexpectedly found something she'd given up for lost. 'It makes me more anxious to charter *Lorelei* than ever,' she said earnestly. She put her right hand on Two-tooth's sleeve. 'Do tell me about it. And please call me Barbara.'

I watched her, wondering if perhaps she was pulling our legs. Then I remembered that she was a writer and therefore liable to go overboard for all sorts of weird things. Perhaps Two-tooth hadn't been so ham-fisted after all. 'You don't mean to say,' she breathed, 'that you've actually seen something from outer space?'

'Aw, look, Barbara, I wouldn't go as far as to say that.' He had the grace to look embarrassed, shuffling his feet and keeping his eyes glued to the chart. 'It was something I saw a couple of nights ago, that's all. It was half past six, like I said, with no wind and the sea as calm as a bowl of soup. There was a lot of cloud over to the east, but it was well inland, all pink and white.'

Beginning to get engrossed in his story, he lowered his voice, fixing the girl with an eye as glittering as that of the Ancient Mariner. 'Tallon was in the galley, so I was on me Pat Malone, see. We were close in to the coast, but not too close, because some of the charts are a bit optimistic in patches. Well, all of a sudden, there was this flickering light out to port—over the land. A bluish-white glow, it was, coming from up in the air, but it wasn't a plane—not that you'd find a plane in that area anyway. And it wasn't a star, it was too big and too early. So I got the glasses on it. I saw'—he paused for effect, hamming it up in a way that made me long to let fly at his broad stern—'a thing like a bloo—like a blooming great lampshade hanging in the sky with this sort of weird bluish glow coming from underneath it. It seemed to lose height while I watched it, and it was coming down fast, about a mile or so inland, as near as I could tell. There wasn't time to call Tallon,' he gave me a mean look, 'and anyway he wouldn't have believed it if he'd seen it. I just about had time to take a bearing on it before . . .'

He stopped, looking straight out of the window on the port side at the shadow cast by *Lorelei*'s superstructure on the dark, calm water of the dock. 'Wait on,' he said softly. He jumped, silent in his rubber-soled canvas shoes, for the bridge ladder. He peered up for a moment, then he came back, his face apologetic. 'Sorry,' he said. 'Thought I'd left me pipe on the chart-table just now. I could smell smoke.'

I didn't say anything. I couldn't smell anything except the expensive perfume the girl was wearing, and I knew perfectly well that Two-tooth had never smoked between getting up and midday in all the years I'd known him. He said, rather tamely, 'Well, that's the bearing I took.'

Barbara Mackail said, 'But you reported this to the authorities, of course?'

He shook his head. 'If it had been a ship in distress, or an aircraft, it'd have been different. But we don't want—I mean, they wouldn't . . .'

'They wouldn't believe you?' She nodded. 'Did any of your friends believe you when you told them?'

Two-tooth glowered at me. 'I haven't bothered to tell anybody, not after Tallon as good as said I needed my head seeing to.'

'I see.' She stood silent for a moment. Then she looked at her tiny wristwatch and gave a startled exclamation. 'Do you know, I've only just remembered I've a hairdressing appointment in ten minutes. I'll have to go. But I don't think there's anything else to discuss, is there? You'll take me to this area, and I'll let you know when we get there where I want to land, and so on.' She took an envelope out of the breast pocket of her green silk shirt. 'If I give you this as a deposit I can consider the yacht hired, can't I?' She passed it across to me and I nodded as off-handedly as if we were doing this all the time.

'I'll give you a receipt,' I said. I opened the envelope, took out the cheque and looked at it. I raised my eyebrows. 'Just how much,' I asked, 'were you thinking of paying for this charter, Miss Mackail?'

'Isn't it enough?' She frowned with a touch of impatience. 'It's only a deposit, you know.'

'Enough?' I stared at her, the green slip of paper between my fingers. 'Two thousand dollars is more than I'd ask as the full fee, let alone as a deposit.' Two thousand Australian dollars, I thought dazedly. Eight hundred pounds sterling. I checked the number of noughts after the two again.

'Well, you can deduct what you want and give the rest back, can't you?' she said matter-of-factly. 'I've notified the bank. All you have to do is go in and cash it. And a receipt won't be necessary.' She put on her sunglasses. When we continued to stare at her as if we expected her to wave a wand and vanish, she said quietly, 'I know what I'm buying, Mr. Tallon. You'll earn every cent of your fee before you've finished, believe me. In the first place, you'll be risking your ship on a coast that is, as you've said, very dangerous. I shall want to be put ashore at various points and it's quite likely that I may have to enlist your help if there's any bush-clearing or excavating to be done. We'll carry equipment for that sort of work, naturally.'

I nodded. 'We can manage that. When do you want to sail?'

'This evening,' she said calmly.

'This evening?' I stared at her blankly. There was bound to be a king-sized catch in a job with a price-tag like this one. 'But that's quite out of the question. We've got to refuel, take on fresh water, stock up with food, instal the radar . . .'

'Then you're going to be busy, aren't you?' she said placidly. 'That is, if you want to earn your fee. I lead a very busy life, Mr. Tallon, and I'm fitting this trip in between two other commitments. I flew in here yesterday from Melbourne after a lecture tour in New Zealand, and I'm going straight on to London after we get back. I'm sorry to give you such short notice but, as you see, I'm prepared to pay you for your trouble. I'll come aboard at about six.'

I went with her as far as the rail and stood frowning thoughtfully at her trimly trousered figure as she climbed into the waiting taxi without looking back, the hot sun striking sparks off her hair. Back in the saloon, Two-tooth was rolling the chart up, a far-away look in his eyes. 'Well, how's that, Tallon,' he said as I went in, 'for a beaut line in shipmates? Everything in the right places, including a bank account, eh? The sort of sheila,' he said, tugging thoughtfully at his beard, 'who seems to go for the more mature blokes.' He grinned through the window at a seagull that was sitting on our rail, eyeing him sardonically. 'Looks like the fishing lurk's in for a boom at last, me old cobber.'

'With us on the wrong end of the hook,' I lit a cigarette, 'as usual. All we've got to do is a week's work in about eight hours and we're made for life.'

'Wrong end?' He stared at me. Then he tossed the chart down disgustedly on the table. 'What d'you mean, wrong end of the hook? Jeez, some blokes are never satisfied. What the hell's the matter with you, Tallon? One minute you're wingeing because you're broke, the next you're going crook because you're not. You got the bloody death-wish, mate, that's what you got. I read about it in a book once. There's some blokes . . .'

'Was it a book by Barbara Mackail?' We both swung round as the voice came from the bridge ladder. Lucky was posed at the foot of it, looking the picture of sin with her short, blue-black hair rumpled seductively and her beautiful golden legs showing to their best advantage under my navy-blue pyjama top, only one button of which was fastened. But her eyes didn't look seductive. They flashed at us, as tawny-brown and hostile as those of a tigress. ' "Would you like some coffee, Miss Mackail?" ' she mimicked. ' "Jeez, that's a beaut title for a book." Ha! She certainly had you two where she wanted you, didn't she?'

'You were listening,' I said slowly. 'Why, you little . . .'

' 'Course she was,' growled Two-tooth. 'That's what I went up to the bridge for. I saw a shadow moving up there and I knew there was somebody snooping. It was Flash Annie here. I told you last night what she was up to, the two-faced little . . .' He gave a startled yelp and backed up against the table, his hands held out defensively in front of him.

Quick as a flash, Lucky had grabbed a bottle off the top shelf of the bookcase—a bottle of the purple ink I used for bringing the charts up to date. She whipped the top off and padded pantherishly across to where her prey was cowering abjectly by the table. 'Too right I was listening,' she said softly. 'And I'll tell you something else, fungus-face. I was listening to what you were saying about me last night, too. The sound-proofing on this bucket isn't all it might be, is it?' She swirled the bottle under his nose, the ink sloshing dangerously. 'You big, stupid slob,' she hissed. 'Go on. Tell me some more about my secret life with an MVD murder squad. And then you're going to get this, right in the whiskers.'

She'd do it, too. With her half-Latin temperament she'd think nothing of getting him to start an interesting new trend in two-tone beards. He was pretty fortunate it hadn't been his automatic she'd snatched up. 'That'll do, Lucky,' I said, grinning. 'Two-tooth didn't mean anything. He was thinking with his mouth open, that's all.'

'Then he ought to get his halitosis seen to,' she snapped. She turned to me. 'As for you, you stupid galah, with the things you're getting mixed up in . . .' Suddenly all the fight went out of her. She put the bottle down slowly, her eyes on me, and said quietly, 'Oh, Patrick, you're such a fool.'

'O.K. I'm a fool,' I said agreeably. 'But that's not your headache, is it?'

'No,' she said steadily. 'But if I were you I'd make a few inquiries about this Barbara Mackail before you take her money. Have you ever heard of her before?'

'No, I haven't.' Two-tooth had recovered his nerve, but he still watched her warily. 'And I could mention a couple of hundred other women authors I've never heard of, too. What does that prove?' He snorted, while I tried to work that one out. 'The trouble with you,' he said caustically, 'is that you're just plain bloody jealous, that's what.'

'Jealous?' Her voice went up to a squeak of rage and she grabbed for the bottle, her eyes flaming, but Two-tooth had already closed his huge paw round it.

'Knock it off, the pair of you,' I snapped. 'And go and get some clothes on, Lucky, before you get me run in.'

She gazed at me, genuinely surprised. 'On a day like this? Why, I didn't wear anything at all in the flat when it was hot, and Pickles never complained. Anyway, I've got something on underneath. Look.' Her hand went to the button.

'I dare say,' I said, before she could demonstrate. 'But you can't go ashore like that, can you?' To Two-tooth I said, 'I'm going to the bank and then I can start getting things moving. Perhaps you could be going over the engines. This is going to be one of those days. And in this heat, too.'

'But you can't just throw me ashore like this,' Lucky said, wide-eyed. 'Where can I go?'

'This is where we came in,' I said patiently. 'And I'm not throwing you ashore. You said yourself it was to be one night only.'

She came across to me and put a slim, cool hand on my arm. 'Take me with you,' she said softly. 'Please, Patrick. I won't get in the way, I promise.'

'I can't take you with me,' I said irritably. The thing that

60

was annoying me was that she had the same appealing look in her dark eyes that had won me over the night before. And I'd been idiot enough to think it was genuine. She always had some new trick to pull. This time there was the scent of her hair and a disturbing glimpse of white, frothy lace against tanned, golden skin where the rest of the buttons were falling down on the job. I said, 'It's out of the question. Anyway, you know damned well you'd be bored to the back teeth before you'd been on board twenty-four hours. This isn't a pleasure cruise, you know. We're on charter.'

'And Barbara mightn't like it if there was competition?' Her eyes hardened. Then she turned away. 'O.K. Don't worry about me. Go off with your bloody midget. Go and get into another racket, you damned gaolbird. But you weren't so choosy when it came to having that cool cat with the big eyes on board, were you?' I watched her slim, honey-coloured legs go up the ladder. Before they vanished she called down, her voice curiously muffled, 'I wish to God I'd never set eyes on either of you.'

I looked at Two-tooth, baffled. 'What the hell's got into her?'

He stared back at me expressionlessly. 'How should I know,' he said, 'if you don't? Now go and cash that cheque. And if it bounces, just don't bother to come back, eh?'

Six

THE mid-morning heat was coming off the concrete in waves and it was a relief to stand at the top of the steps and let the warm breeze blow through my shirt. I felt it rustling the cheque in my breast pocket and I thought what a wonderful day it was. There'd be no trouble now with the various people I had accounts with. I'd have fresh, crisp dollar bills to wave at them—Government-issue, of course, not Zaghrali's—and, with a little fast talking, it should be quite possible to meet our deadline. Whistling to myself, I turned right, towards the bascule bridge at the mouth of the dock. At the same time, somebody shouted, 'Hey, Tallon!' from behind me.

I looked back. The parking slots along the side of the dock were nearly all taken. One of them, on the far side of *Lorelei*'s berth, was occupied by a slate-grey, highly polished Holden 179 sedan that had a transmitter-receiver antenna in the middle of its roof. A thin-faced man in a grey suit had his head out of the driver's window and was grinning at me. When he saw me looking his way he shouted, above the growl of a truck that was jolting past, 'You want a lift anywhere?' He wasn't anybody I knew.

The heat seemed to go out of the sun as I walked slowly over to the car. Because, although quite a lot of firms use Holdens equipped with two-way radios, there's only one firm I know of that uses radio cars to offer free transport to complete strangers in the middle of town. They've picked Nicolai up, I thought numbly, and he's talked. I said flatly, 'How much choice do I have?'

He was a hatchet-faced character with a Surfer's Paradise tan and a pair of ice-blue eyes that grinned up at me engagingly—the sort who's a riot at the Police Orphans' Outing. He was wearing a smart grey business suit and he had a smart grey narrow-brimmed hat tilted on to the back of his head—the way American reporters do in films. His accent, too, was American when he said, 'Hell, you got all the choice in the world, Tallon. But it's a nice day, so why not let's take a little ride?'

In spite of the smile he had the unmistakable austerity in his face that they learn in police college, the air of watchfulness that stamps a copper the world over. But it was the way he spoke that puzzled me. A small minority of Australians in the radio and television business like to assume an accent that is an injudicious mixture of Brooklyn and Deep South, but I'd never met an Aussie copper with a genuine Middle West accent before. Still, I reflected, there's always a first time. And, if it came to that, I hadn't exactly gone out of my way to cultivate the acquaintance of many Aussie coppers. This one leaned across to open his passenger door. 'Get in, pal,' he said amicably. 'It's as hot as the hobs of hell standing here.'

I climbed in beside him, wondering bitterly why it had had to be me who'd pulled the Russian out of the water. If it hadn't been for him we could have made a fresh start with that charter we'd so nearly got. The man in grey started his motor, pushed the selector into 'Drive' and turned into Dunn Street between the Victoria and Constitution Docks, keeping scrupulously to the dock area's fifteen-mile-an-hour speed limit. We halted at Davey Street to allow a string of cars to pass in obedience to the give-way-to-the-right rule they have in Australia. As we moved forward again he said, 'How's the fishing, Tallon? I hear you landed a big one last night.'

He stopped for the lights in Macquarie Street. Don't admit anything, I reminded myself. Make them work for it. It kept them occupied and they appreciated it more when they got it the hard way. This was the enemy, and you gave them number, rank and name and nothing more until it was squeezed out of you like tooth-paste. I watched an old converted van clank across our bows with a surf-board on the roof and a load of tanned, shouting kids in the back and I wondered fleetingly what it would be like to belong to that other world again—the one where people had income tax problems and families and where you could take a day at the beach at weekends. You could lie on the hot sand and read in the paper how some lay-about had got ten years for smuggling Russians into the country and another ten for being involved in a counterfeit racket. I said, without much conviction, 'We're doing all right.'

'You could have fooled me.' The lights changed. 'You got rust on the swivels of those fishing chairs,' he said cheerfully as he slid forward with the traffic. 'You haven't used them in months.'

I said nothing out loud. He swung right into Collins Street, then left again, heading for the big ornamental roundabout with the sunken flower gardens and pedestrian subways that stands at the northern entrance to the city. He glanced sideways at me. 'Where d'you get the loot from to run that sea-going gin-palace of yours? Not from fishing, that's for sure.'

The sun struck blindingly through the big windscreen, uncomfortably hot on my legs as I watched the roundabout coming towards us, its forty-two-jet fountain sparkling and the glittering, multi-coloured cars swirling round it. I waited for him to take the left-hand lane that would lead us to Police Headquarters in Liverpool Street. 'It's your story,' I said tiredly. 'You can make up your own dialogue. But when you type it out in triplicate don't expect me to sign it, that's all.'

He moved over to the right, sliding in neatly between a tangerine VW 1500 with yellow-and-black New South Wales number-plates, and a big red-white-and-blue Pioneer bus. 'Aw, come on, don't be like that,' he said, grinning. He flicked a quick glance across at me and laughed out loud. 'You look like a mortician with piles. What's the matter with you? You think I'm a cop, or something?'

The flat nose of the Holden stopped swinging as he turned on to the wide, beautifully surfaced Tasman Highway that runs north along the river through the parkland of the Queen's Domain. I stared at his sharp, bony profile, shaken out of my gloom. 'Not something,' I said. 'Just a cop. D'you think I'd be sitting here if I didn't?'

'O.K.,' he said indifferently. 'If that's the way you feel.' He pulled in to the side, opposite the Olympic Pool, and stopped, the car's engine idling gently. He indicated the door. 'It's all yours, buster. Use it, if that's what you want.'

I reached for the pull-up armrest that operated the door. Then I paused. 'Wait a minute. What's going on? First you try to make out you're the law, now you tell me you're not. What for? Who are you, anyway?'

He shrugged. 'Who said anything about the law? You and your conscience talked you into that one. Impersonating a police officer,' he said virtuously, 'is a pretty serious offence where I come from, and I guess the same goes for this place too. And so is trying to detain a guy against his will. So scram out, Tallon.' When I didn't move he said, 'Go on. What are you waiting for? Blast off. Go and get yourself arrested for conspiring to harbour an alien, if that's your ambition.'

I let go of the arm-rest as if it was red-hot. 'All right,' I said angrily. 'So you're not from the Police Department. But which other outfit are you from?' Nowadays most government departments have their own private eyes. He could be from Immigration, Customs, the Treasury—even from the Taxation Department. I'd got across the lot of them during the last twenty-four hours.

'Why should I tell you that? You don't want to tell me anything.' His blue eyes crinkled as he turned on his infuriating schoolboy grin again. 'Let's say I'm just another tourist with a responsibility to pass on certain information that's come his way. About two guys who've brought a Rusk into the country, for instance.' He cocked an eye at me. 'It's a hell of a responsibility, pal. Keeps me awake nights. I was wondering if you could see your way to helping me forget about it.'

I stared at him in silence while the traffic whispered behind us and the shrieks from the nearby swimming pool sounded like the mocking laughter of fiends from the pit. 'So that's it,' I said at last. 'Blackmail.' Somebody—Zaghrali, perhaps—had been shooting his mouth off. I tried to bluff it out and dig up a mocking laugh of my own, but when it got loose it sounded more like flatulence than anything else. 'You're wasting your time,' I said. 'I haven't a cent to my name.' Which was true. The cheque in my pocket had been spent weeks ago.

'I know.' The oddly likable smile didn't flicker. 'But you'll pay up just the same, friend. Because it's information I want, not money. I want to know about the guy you brought ashore last night. And if I don't get what I want, you and your bearded buddy get the bum's push into the pen. So how'll you have it, scrambled or fried?'

'For a tourist,' I said, stalling, 'you seem to have all the information you can handle.' I had to have time to think—and time was something I didn't have a lot of, that morning. I couldn't pay him off, even if I'd wanted to. I reached for a cigarette to give me a breathing space, and I remembered I'd left mine back on the yacht. He gave me a Lucky Strike from the dispenser on the dash. I had to get rid of him somehow until we'd sailed. But not here, in the middle of the city. 'Perhaps,' I said, inhaling smoke, 'we could take that ride after all.'

He reached for the selector stick, smiling broadly. I put my hand on his left arm as if to detain him, managing to brush against the side of his jacket. 'But not,' I said, 'before I know which tourist bureau it is you're working with.' I might have known he'd be carrying a gun. A big one, in a holster under the armpit. The next move was to find out if he was working alone.

He shook his head. 'I've got you over a barrel, Tallon, and you know it,' he said pleasantly. 'I don't tell you a thing. Just fill in the questionnaire and we'll get along fine.'

'Like hell we will,' I said grimly. 'I want to know who you are and where you got your information from before I say a word. Otherwise I get out here and now. And you can go to the police and tell them what you know, but that won't get you anywhere, will it?'

He studied me for a moment, the smile gone. Then he said thoughtfully, 'All right, Tallon. Maybe it wouldn't be such a bad thing for you to know whose side you're on, at that.' He turned to face me, resting his arm on the back of his seat. 'My name's Todd Schuyler,' he said quietly. 'And I'm over here on a job for the CIA.'

I felt like laughing in his face. 'Is that so?' I said, interestedly. 'I'd never have guessed. But, since we're being so frank with one another, I've got a confession to make, too. You see, my name isn't really Tallon at all. It's Fred Karno, and I'm over here on a job for the RSPCA. And, if you asked me

66

to prove it, I'd say something like, "People in my line of business don't carry identification around with them." Now suppose you stop wasting my time, and try again?'

Without a word, and without taking his eyes off me, he reached into his inside pocket and took out a wallet. He extracted an envelope, unfolded a sheet of notepaper and hung it under my nose. 'O.K., Fred,' he said coldly. 'Read it.'

It bore the letterhead of the Department of Home Affairs, and it told whoever it might concern that Mr. Todd Schuyler was in Australia to study police methods and should be given every assistance, etc., etc. His photograph was clipped to the top with a DHA stamp across it, and there was a very impressive signature at the bottom. I looked at him, then back at the document. 'There's nothing about the Central Intelligence Agency here,' I said stubbornly. Not that it made any difference. With the police behind him, it didn't matter who he was employed by.

'We try to keep our advertising costs down.' He put the letter and the wallet away. 'What d'you expect me to have? A revolving neon on my hat?'

'But this isn't your territory. Why haven't they got an Australian working on whatever it is you're doing?'

'They have,' he said succinctly. 'Maybe you'd rather talk to one of them?' When I didn't answer he chuckled and got the car rolling. 'I'm working in with the Australian MI guys,' he said as he pulled out. 'But it's a break I got to you first, isn't it? Because I couldn't be less interested in your do-it-yourself currency racket. But if you won't talk to me I'll have to pass you on to one of my colleagues from Canberra. And they have much wider interests. So let's have it, sweetheart. The lot.'

He was a good listener. He didn't interrupt me or ask any questions as the car rolled along at a steady thirty-five and I let him have it, right from the time we'd left Sullivan's Cove the night before. After a while, he pulled in to the side again under a sign that said NO STANDING ANY TIME on a long stretch within sight of the graceful sweep of the Tasman Bridge. Even when I'd finished he didn't say anything for quite a while. He sat watching me expressionlessly while the hot engine clicked as it cooled and a bush-fly that had got into the car buzzed and banged at the rear window. Finally, he said, 'And that's all?'

I nodded. He said coldly, 'You're not exactly a mine of information, are you? We've got a submarine you never even saw and a Red sailor who drives off into the sunset leaving a stark-naked truck-driver as a souvenir. The kook with the knife you didn't see either. In fact, the only solid character in the story's the blonde—the one I saw leaving your boat. You're left with a first-class reason for getting the hell out of here, plus a cheque for two thousand dollars.' He stared at me with eyes like chips of blue slate.

I shrugged, refusing to let myself be needled by the sarcasm. Nobody connected with the law ever believed you first time round. 'All I did was tell you what happened.' I flicked ash off my cigarette. 'But if you don't like the story I know a better one about a bus conductor and a belly-dancer.'

His arm jumped at me and my wrist was gripped by a set of bony fingers that felt like pliers. 'Look, Tallon,' he said grittily. 'I'm in no mood for the comedy slot. We've got an aircraft carrier out there on the river that we think is something rather out of the way. We'd like to keep it in one piece if we possibly can, which is one of the reasons I'm over here. Because, if anything happened to it, it wouldn't be just a matter of losing about four thousand sailors and several million dollars of nuclear hardware. It would be a hell of a jolt for the whole South-east Asia Treaty Organisation and, in particular, for our relations with Australia. So when I hear there's a stray Russian on the loose I just feel I'd like to know what the score is, that's all.' He let go of my arm. 'So quit the fooling, will you? You've done enough of that already.'

'On the loose?' I stared at him. 'I thought all this was because you'd pulled him in and he'd told you how . . .?'

'If we'd pulled him in, it'd be your police who'd be interviewing you by now, not me.'

My God, I thought. We've really done it this time. I wondered, almost with a kind of awe, whether anybody else could have been so stupid as to have failed to connect the Russian with the *Fort Knox*—when Two-tooth had mentioned it only just before we'd got him out of the sea. I said, feeling as if I'd been injected with cocaine all over, 'He's a Red agent, then?'

68

'There are three possibilities—three that interest me, that is.' He took his hat off and threw it in the back. He had one of those crew-cuts that look like a worn-down shaving brush, a stiff stubble of sandy hair. 'The first is that he's a defector, that everything he's said is on the level, and that we haven't picked him up because the MVD have knocked him off since he came ashore. The second is that he's an agent, and that the whole thing was planted on you from the start. It might have been that way, too, if that sub. had known where to find you last night. Maybe the Egyptian tipped them off, maybe it was that sidekick of yours . . .'

'You can kill that,' I said curtly. 'Two-tooth's as straight as a die.'

'Sure.' He grunted. 'He's got a record, hasn't he? Like you? And that brings us to the third shot. That this Nicolai's not only a Red saboteur, but that you were paid your two grand to bring him in, and that you've organised the whole thing between the lot of you—including the blonde. Which d'you like best?'

'I don't like the last one at all,' I snapped. 'And your second guess seems crazy to me. Why should the Russians go to all that trouble to put a man ashore when they could pick a deserted stretch of beach? And Nicolai was half drowned when we got him aboard. He wasn't faking. And what about the man with the knife?' I'd forgotten about him. 'No,' I said, trying to convince myself, 'I'd say he's a genuine refugee, if unorthodox. I've done some pretty unorthodox things myself in my time,' I said evenly, 'but working for the Russians isn't one of them.'

He studied me in silence. Then he grinned faintly. 'O.K., Tallon, I'll go along with that. A sucker you might be, but not a traitor. But I can't take any chances with Nicolai. Not with a flat-top at stake. To me, he's guilty until he's proved innocent.'

'There's one way of finding out. Why don't you pull him in? On an island this size it oughtn't to be all that difficult.'

He shook his head. 'That's the line the Aussies are taking, but it hasn't got them very far up to now. Me, I've got other ideas. I don't care if this Russian's an operative with a dossier as fat as the *Britannica*. It's what he's trying to do that in-

69

terests me, not who he is. Picking him up won't stop whatever it is the other side's trying to pull. They'll just send somebody else in, with instructions to take a hell of a lot more care next time.' He drew on his cigarette, watching a couple of cars go past. 'This Mackail frail,' he said thoughtfully. 'Where does she fit in?'

'Does she have to? Just because she chartered the yacht? If she were a Communist reception committee surely she'd have had a boat of her own all ready and waiting?'

'That's right.' He gave me a sly sideways look. 'She's got a hell of a shape, too, hasn't she? You wouldn't have to take lessons to fall for a lulu like that.' When I shrugged he chuckled and said, 'O.K. So you're just good friends. But this south-west she's so interested in. Could there be these old wrecks there?'

'There could be anything. Nobody knows enough about it to say. It's some of the roughest country in the world. Rocky, inaccessible beaches, swamp, button-grass plains—that's a kind of sedge that can grow to a height of six feet—a maze of streams and rivers and impenetrable rain-forest lashed together with horizontal.'

'Horizontal? Horizontal what?'

'Just horizontal. Its botanical name is *Anodopetalum biglandulosum*. It's a tree with a stem that's as tough as spring steel but too slender to support its growth. So when it's grown twenty or thirty feet it keels over and goes on growing horizontally. It puts out branches that grow downwards and intertwine, so that you get a barrier in depth of springy, interlaced wooden poles. It can cover square miles. The only way to get through it is over the top, walking on a platform of woven, one-inch stems. They'll hold your weight all right—until you put your boot on one that's rotten. Then you fall through, and if you don't break your neck you've had it anyway, because not even a helicopter could get you out again.'

'Real jungle country.' He looked at me thoughtfully. 'You've been there?'

'Only the fringe of it, round Macquarie Harbour. But I've seen enough of it to know that it's worse than any jungle. I've been in tropical jungle, and as a rule you can get through even the densest stuff if you can crawl along the game tunnels. But there's no game in the south-west. Just tiger-snakes, whip-snakes and copperheads. There's bauera, too. That's a kind of bush-rose that puts out thorny tentacles yards long. Going through that's worse than tackling barbed wire because it's so tough an axe just bounces off it. The convicts used to call it leg-rope.'

'It sounds a hell of a place. And nobody lives there? No natives?'

'The last Tasmanian aborigine died in 1876. They're an extinct race.' I crushed out my cigarette. 'Prospectors go in. There are some people who say you can't stick a spade in the ground down there without hitting practically every mineral you can name. There's gold on the Spero River, but not in workable quantities, and a fellow I met once in Strahan showed me an opal he'd picked up on the beach. There could be oil, uranium, anything. Bush-walkers go in every summer, supplied from the air, and the Hydro-Electric Commission does surveys and so on. But a good part of it's still completely unexplored. It's been called Tasmania's Lost World.'

He sat drumming his fingertips on the wheel, staring absently at the white concrete bridge that soared a hundred and fifty feet above the river. At last he said, 'And you're sailing this evening?'

'We were, until half an hour ago,' I said, without letting him see how I felt about it.

He switched on the engine abruptly. 'O.K. Now this is what you're going to do, Tallon. You're going to go ahead as if nothing had happened. If that blonde wants you to ferry her to her overgrown vegetable patch you'll do it. It might be interesting to see what happens when she comes on board.'

I sat up. 'You mean—you're going to let us leave Hobart?'

'I've got no jurisdiction to stop you. You can all leave—you two, and the girl, and that new crewman you've got.'

'New crewman?'

'Sure.' He grinned at me, then checked that the road was clear before he pulled out. 'Me,' he said.

Seven

THE clock on the GPO building was chiming half-past three when I got back to the yacht with my shirt sticking to my back and a thirst you could strike a match on. Schuyler had dropped me outside Police Headquarters and disappeared inside while I'd scuttled away like a somnambulating mouse who'd woken up outside the Cats' Home. Now, I was hot, hungry and bewildered by the series of interviews I'd had since then with the people who supplied me with stores. Because they'd all told me the same thing—that not only had my outstanding account already been settled, but most of the things I wanted had been ordered and paid for as well. Some of them, including the fuel, were already being delivered at the docks. And no two descriptions of my unknown benefactor tallied. He seemed to range from an elderly man who walked with a stick to a young Greek who drove an Austin Healey.

But the activity that was going on at our berth drove it out of my mind. A utility bearing the name of the marine electrical firm that was servicing our radar was parked alongside *Lorelei,* and a three-ton Bedford was just pulling away. I could see a mound of packing cases stacked in the cockpit and Two-tooth was standing in the grilling sun at the foot of the gangway signing a work-docket for a man in overalls. As the electrician took it, Two-tooth looked up, saw me, and scowled. He was stripped down to his singlet and jeans and his face was brick-red where it showed above his dishevelled beard. 'Well, well, if it isn't Captain Bludger Bligh,' he said caustically. 'My oath, when you said there'd be a week's work in eight bloody hours, you kept quiet about who'd be doing it, didn't you?' He watched the ute drive away. 'How the hell did you organise this lot? I've been jumping around like a flea on a flaming hot-plate ever since you left.' He jabbed a filthy thumb at the packing cases, all neatly lashed and stowed. 'While you've been sitting with an ice-cold grog in front of you, I've had to pass the time by taking the fishing chairs out to get all that stuff of Barbara's aboard, apart from one or two odds and ends like rigging the gangway and going over the engines and supervising the refuelling and hosing down the decks and checking groceries . . .' He paused for breath, wiping his forehead with a grey handkerchief. 'Jeez, I'm just about bushed. And having that Egyptian lily on me back for the last hour hasn't helped, neither. He's in the saloon now. Says he's . . .'

'Blast.' I'd forgotten about Zaghrali. It was, I supposed, only to be expected that he should require some explanation of the fun and games of the night before, but at that particular moment he was every bit as welcome as a fouled rudder. I briefed Two-tooth hurriedly on my interview with Schuyler. He listened expressionlessly with an eye cocked on the saloon doorway. As I went aboard I said, 'Where's Lucky?'

'Nicked off without a word soon after you did.' He followed me across the gangplank. 'And I wish now I'd had the sense to do the same. I said all along that that bloke'd get us into the . . .'

'So! The captain, he comes aboard, eh?' Zaghrali appeared in the doorway, grinning from ear to ear and making a tweeting noise that was probably intended to resemble a bosun's pipe. He seemed in the best of spirits, an attitude that was the last thing I'd have expected after the cargo we'd unloaded on him the night before. He was sporting a navy-blue double-breasted linen jacket with a crest that looked suspiciously like that of the Royal Sydney Yacht Squadron, a pair of knife-edged fawn gaberdine slacks and tan-and-white co-respondent's shoes with toes like bradawls. A mustard-yellow silk handkerchief cascaded out of his breast pocket and a matching cravat was knotted round his scrawny neck. With his pendulous nose and glossy waved hair, he looked like a dirty-postcard dealer who'd just done a brisk trade at Henley. He saluted exaggeratedly as I pushed past him into the cool dimness of the saloon. 'Looks

73

like you're all ready to cast away the anchor, yes? In a hurry, maybe?'

The radio extension speaker over the settle said rapidly, '. . . listening to the top sound on the charts all round Australia, brought to you by the makers of the toilet tissue that's used by your favourite movie stars . . .' I switched it off. 'I thought we'd agreed that you weren't to come anywhere near *Lorelei* while she's in dock?' I said curtly.

He wagged a grubby finger at me playfully. 'Aha! Thass what you reckoned on, eh? You think I don't find out what goes on, maybe?' To my annoyance, he plumped himself down on the settle, carefully adjusting the crease in his pants. The scent he was slathered with would take weeks to get out of the upholstery. On the other hand, I reflected, trying to be fair, would garlicky BO take less? 'Well, don't worry, my friend. I find out plenty. An' I just come for a little talk about las' night.'

I watched him, frowning. I'd expected him to be hopping mad with rage, and here he was, grinning all over his cheese-coloured face and as relaxed as a jelly-fish. I said coldly, 'There's nothing to talk about. I delivered the consignment as planned. If you were fool enough to let somebody take it off you, that's your affair.'

He didn't take offence. As if I hadn't spoken, he looked round the saloon appreciatively and said, 'You got yourself fixed up real nice now, haven't you, Tallon? Nice boat you got. 'Course, it must cost plenty to run, but you can afford it, can't you? Apart from what I give you, there's these little side-lines you've been running. Things you haven't had to cut me in on. Not,' he grinned at me unpleasantly, 'up to now.'

'Look,' I said abruptly. 'If you've got anything to say, say it. Then you can get the hell out of here. I've got things to do.' They included an ice-cold shower with a beer to match, followed by the *plat du jour* in triplicate.

'I bet you 'ave.' He winked at me knowingly. 'Orright, I tell you what I want. I want to know how much you been getting for all these rackets you been running be'ind my back. Like these guys you been bringing ashore, for instance.'

'So that's it,' growled Two-tooth from where he was leaning against the door. 'You think there might be a dirty dollar going into the wrong pocket. Well, you're wasting your time, mate. The only joker we've brought ashore was the one last night. And we didn't get paid for doing it, neither. We found him in the sea off Tasman Island.'

'You find 'im in the sea! Ha!' He laughed, a short bark that sounded like a dingo with its foot in a trap. He watched me speculatively while he scratched his chest under his jacket, revealing the lilac silk shirt he was wearing. When he spoke again, there was a note of grudging respect in his voice. 'You know, Tallon, I been underestimating you. Alla time I been thinking you one damn fool for refusing to bring in that little bit of heroin I want, an' for turning down that five hundred dollars las' month when that guy who shot the bank clerk wanted to leave in a hurry. An' alla time you've been doing all right. This illegal immigration racket you're working up, now. Plenty money there. Plenty Asiatics'd pay big money to be brought in an' dropped on an empty beach. Nothing to dispose of, neither, like with the slush. Yeah, you done all right for yourself. But from now on,' he rubbed his finger and thumb together, 'I take my cut, my friend. Fifty per cent, yes? You gotta remember we're partners, Tallon.'

'Not any more,' I said evenly. I'd had just about as much Zaghrali as I could take on an empty stomach. And his absurd clothes and matey manner brought home to me forcibly how low I'd sunk—to the point where a smelly little gangster like this could swagger on to my ship and congratulate me on my shrewdness as a double-crossing racketeer. 'I've got news for you, Zaghrali. We're moving on.' I glanced meaningly at the door. 'You, too.'

His face changed. 'So!' he said silkily. 'Thass the way it is, eh?' He looked from me to Two-tooth and back again. 'You got the bigger fish to cook now, an' you want to keep it all for yourself, yes? Orright, Mister Two-timing Tallon. I thought that's the way it would be. But jus' answer me this, before you start giving me the big talk about setting up on your own.' He pointed at me accusingly. 'Who was it who looked after you when you firs' come crawling into 'Obart without enough fuel in your lousy tanks to get you out again? Who was it gave you the 'elping 'and when your crazy big-sea fishing had gone bust and you didn't even have nothing to eat on board?' He tapped himself on the chest. 'Me. It was me, Anton Zaghrali, an' don't you ever forget it. You owe every goddam thing you got to me.' He sneered expertly. 'But things is different now, eh? Now you get the big money, so it's, "Go to 'ell, Zaghrali. We don' need you no more." Thass the way it is, yes?'

'No, it bloody isn't,' snapped Two-tooth. 'You ain't been no Fairy flaming Godmother to us, mate. We've earned every stinking cent you've paid us. And we told you, right at the start that we'd only run your stuff until we broke into the legit. charter business. Well, now we've done it, and . . .'

'Don' give me that crap,' the Egyptian said contemptuously. 'You ain't in no legit. business. Remember, I got contacts in this city. Many good friends who tell me things.' He leaned forward. 'I know what your boat's been hired for this time, Tallon. An' it ain't to go fishing, neither.'

'Is that so?' I propped myself on a corner of the table, watching him thoughtfully. It was true that he knew a lot of people —some of them in the most unexpected quarters. That was probably why he kept in business and out of prison. 'And what,' I asked, 'has it been hired for?'

'You think I don't know, eh? You think I don't know about this rich Mackail woman, the one who writes the books?' He grinned triumphantly at the involuntary surprise on my face. 'I tell you, you gotta be up pretty damn quick to get anything past Anton Zaghrali. I know what those packing cases are for, an' where you go this trip.' He lowered his voice slightly. 'The *Cape of Good 'Ope*,' he said softly. 'What you say to that, eh?'

'The cape of what?' Two-tooth's beard sagged like a punch-drunk hedgehog as his jaw dropped. 'But that's in bloody Africa, you nong. We're not going there.' He looked across at me sharply. 'Are we?'

I wouldn't have thought so, but I was prepared to be flexible-minded about it after the events of the last twelve hours. I said nothing and let Zaghrali hold the floor.

He enjoyed doing it. 'Don' try to bluff me,' he said without rancour. He took out a thin gold cigarette case, extracted a black cigarette and unhurriedly fitted its gold cardboard filter into a short ivory holder. 'You know damn well what I'm talking about.' He lit his gasper with a lighter that was built into the case, and its aroma mingled with that of the perfume he was wearing, a combination suggestive of a Cairo flophouse with its carpets on fire. He blew out a thin stream of acrid smoke, smirking at the rapt attention he was getting. 'You know damn well that the *Cape of Good 'Ope* was a ship that lef' Melbourne for London in 1853 and then jus' vanish—poof!' He gestured with his cigarette. 'I been checking up on it in the library 'ere.'

'Then you wasted valuable time,' said Two-tooth scathingly, 'that you could have spent getting your head examined. What the hairy hell's a ship that disappeared over a hundred years ago . . .?'

'Wait a minute.' I stared at Zaghrali, frowning as I tried to recall something I'd read once in an illustrated weekly about ships that have vanished without trace in Australian waters. 'I've heard of the *Cape of Good Hope*. Frigate-built ship of twelve hundred tons, or thereabouts. Wasn't there some theory,' I said slowly, 'that, with the winds prevailing at the time, she could have ended up on the west coast of Tasmania?'

'Of course you 'eard of it,' said Zaghrali impatiently. 'An' the cargo it was carrying, you've 'eard of that, too, I bet.' His eyes locked with mine and he ran his tongue round his lips. 'A cargo,' he said, almost in a whisper, 'of seventy thousand ounces of gold.'

The word tolled like a bell in the silence that followed. 1853 was a year that was well into the Roaring Fifties of the Australian gold-rush, the wild, rags-to-riches decade in Australian history that had opened with the discovery of the first great nuggets, the Kerr Hundredweight, on the Turon River, in New South Wales. A year when ragged, bearded diggers, Midas-rich at the stroke of a pickaxe, had lit their pipes with fivers in the streets of Melbourne. And, in the same year, the *Cape of Good Hope*, laden with the yellow harvest from the fields of Ballarat and Bendigo, had sailed from Melbourne into the unknown, taking her fabulous freight with her. 'Yes,' I said, watching him. 'I've heard of that, too. And so these well-informed pals of yours have told you we're going to salvage it?'

'I don' need no pals to tell me that. To me it is evident.' The Egyptian's eyes were glittering as if he was running a temperature. He leaned forward, gesticulating excitedly while the words tumbled out of him like the jackpot from an overfed fruit machine. 'This woman, she has spent much money on this trip—that I know. T'ousands of dollars already. An' for what? To write a book about the old wrecks of ships, a book to bring in maybe two, maybe three hundred dollars?' He shook his head energetically. 'No. She isn't writing no book. This is a salvage job you are doing—the stuff you 'ave on board proves it. An' what is there to salvage on the south-west coast?' He stared at us angrily. 'Why you not admit it's the gold you're after, instead of staring at me like butter wouldn't melt in your mouth? If she's been studying these wrecks, she'll know more about it than anybody else, won't she? An' she's spending her money buying winches an' tools an' stuff, and hiring guys like you who won't ask too many questions. Anyway, she's already said . . .' He stopped suddenly. 'I mean, she mus' be . . .'

'She said?' I frowned. 'You've been talking to her?'

'No. I don' know her. How could I?' He waved his cigarette-holder. 'But now we get down to business, eh? I got no time to waste. So I'm jus' telling you I come on this trip of yours. What you say to that, eh?'

'Beat it, Zaghrali,' I said tiredly. 'There's no gold, and we've finished with the rackets. If it'll help you keep your books straight you can keep what you owe me for last night. Otherwise there's nothing for you here.'

He stared at me venomously. 'Be careful, Tallon,' he said viciously. 'I can make plenty trouble for you if you don' cut me in on this. Nobody ever runs out on Zaghrali. Nobody. An' certainly not you, a goddam gaolbird who should have swung years ago if . . .'

'Manners, Gyppo.' Two-tooth's angry rumble sounded as dangerous as a volcano coming to the boil. He moved forward, his hands swinging loosely at his sides like a pair of mechanical grabs. 'That's no way to speak to a mate of mine. Not when yer don't know how to swim.'

'Don' start anything, pig!' The Egyptian's cigarette fell to the carpet in a shower of sparks as he came to his feet, fast and crouching, and his right hand flickered like a snake's tongue to the front of his navy-blue jacket. The thin, mirror-bladed knife seemed to sprout from his fist, and he stood balanced with it held out sword-like in front of him in the professional knife-fighter's stance, thumb on top of the blade and the point weaving protectively across his body at stomach level. 'You think you give me the same treatment as you give that 'Ydraulic, eh?' His black eyes watched Two-tooth, as evil and empty as those of a toad-fish. 'Come a step nearer, or go for that gun you got,' he snarled, 'an' I rip you open. I swear it.'

I straightened up from the table. Zaghrali's threat, far from acting as a deterrent, was the very thing most calculated to trigger the big Aussie into action. Two-tooth had never chickened out of a fight in his life. The tension crackled like static between them, so that I could almost feel it when I moved in front of the Egyptian. 'That's enough,' I said quietly. 'Put that damned thing away, Zaghrali. Nobody's going to lay a finger on you. All you've got to do is choose between leaving on your feet or the back of your neck. It shouldn't be all that difficult.'

Two-tooth moved back reluctantly, and Zaghrali's weight went back on to his heels as he slid the knife back inside his coat. He sat down again, his eyes never leaving Two-tooth, and he retrieved his cigarette from where it was burning a hole in our five-hundred-dollar carpet. 'Thass better,' he said softly. 'Jus' remember I can look after myself, that's all.' He looked up at me, fitting the cigarette back into its holder. 'An' I ain't leaving, Tallon. We're still in partnership, an' I'm coming with you to see I get my cut on this job.' He settled himself comfortably again. 'Seventy thousand ounces at thirty-five US dollars an ounce should be plenty for all of us. An' in return,' he drew on his cigarette, watching me, 'I keep my mouth shut about that phone call I 'ad from 'Ydraulic this morning. That's a good offer, I reckon.'

'I've had better.' It was the second time he'd mentioned the truck-driver. But if he thought Hydraulic was a hole card he'd have to think again. We had more than a mere case of assault and battery to worry about. 'What did he tell you that's so horrifying?'

79

'That he was beaten up on your boat an' tied into a bunk. That you gave him some clothes and filled him up with grog. An' that somebody tried to kill him las' night. He woke me up to tell me, after,' he glowered at me accusingly, 'I'd been walking alla goddam night trying to find a taxi.'

I shook my head. 'That won't get you a free passage, Zaghrali. You can . . .'

'No?' He raised his eyebrows. 'Not when they pulled him outa the river a few hours after?'

Everything seemed to go very quiet. I stared at him in stunned disbelief while the sound of the dockside traffic receded into the distance. 'You're lying,' I said slowly. 'You made this up so that . . .'

'Don't look so goddam innocent, Tallon. You think I don' know what goes on?' He pointed with his cigarette-holder at the loudspeaker behind him. 'They had a news flash 'bout half an hour ago. Some guy was found in the river near the caravan park at Moonah, drowned. Fat, bald, middle-aged guy. They're trying to find out who he is.' He shrugged, grinning at me like somebody who'd been dealt a grand slam and looked like getting it redoubled. 'If you think I'm lying, listen out for it yourself. Or you could call in at Police 'Eadquarters an' ask. In return you could tell them where he was las' night, and whose clothes he was wearing. And,' he added maliciously, 'that you've already bashed one guy back in England and killed him.'

'And, if I don't take you with me, you'll go yourself?' I stared at him with loathing. 'You would, too, especially if there was a reward. But it won't be this time. I didn't murder Hydraulic, but even if I had, there isn't a thing you could do about it. Because you can't lay information against me without implicating yourself up to the tonsils. It was you he was working for, remember, not me. And how will you explain to the police what you were doing out so late last night?'

'Me?' He looked up at me, surprised. 'Why, I'll tell them the trut', of course. That I was playing cards all evening with some very good friends, an' that I stay the night wit' them. One of them is a very ol' friend. I 'elp 'im once when his wife— a very rich, very ugly woman, you understand—fall from a

80

window. It was very sad. The police, they think he push her, but I was there to say no, it was an unfortunate accident.' He grinned wickedly. 'It is nice to 'ave such friends. As for this 'Ydraulic, I never heard of him until he ring me up at six in the morning to warn me about you, an' what goes on be'ind my back. He tell me that you promise to kill him if he breathes a word about all the currency smuggling and such that you're doing, using my fishing trips as a cover.'

'Fishing trips?' Two-tooth said incredulously. 'You've never hooked a fish in your life. You wouldn't . . .'

'Oh, yes I have,' Zaghrali pointed at me. 'I got this one.'

'Very smart,' I said evenly. 'And the truck? What happens when they find that, full of cases of slush? I suppose you don't know anything about that, either?'

'Truck?' He frowned, trying to remember. 'Oh, yes, 'Ydraulic drove a truck for you, didn't he? A truck,' he said, sniggering at the expression on my face, 'that's registered in your name, Tallon. Not mine.'

'In my name?' I said, appalled. 'Why, you filthy little squirt, I'll break your neck if you try to . . .'

'You won't.' He shook his head confidently. 'I tell you, I can look after myself. An', after all, you gotta remember you can't have it both ways. You were the one who said we ain't partners. So you can have 'Ydraulic, and the truck, and the slush, if that's the way you want it. But if I was you I'd think twice about dissolving the partnership. An', instead of telling me to go to hell, you ought to be asking me to go on this salvage trip with you. After all, while I'm here, I can't say nothing to nobody, can I?' He stood up, grinding his cigarette into the carpet while we watched him in silence. 'You know,' he said reflectively, 'I t'ink you need a good cook on this boat, Tallon. An' I ran a café once, on El Goumhouria Street in Port Said. Let's 'ave a look at what sort of kitchen you got, eh? An' then you can show me the cabin I'm going to 'ave.'

Eight

WE SAILED at sundown in the golden glow of a spectacular lighting effect that silhouetted the shadowy, brooding bulk of Mount Wellington against a backdrop of towering, snow-clad Himalayas of creamy cumulus that glowed garnet-pink where they were highlighted by the invisible sun. The light had a soft, blue, Mediterranean quality that toned down the gaily-painted houses in the suburbs to pastel shades of pink and powder blue, and the shoreline was jewelled with strings of streetlights that reflected palely in a river of molten gold—an expanse of topaz-coloured, seemingly viscous liquid that parted in two long, smooth bow-waves and turned blood-red as *Lorelei*'s stem knifed into it. Swiftly the masts and funnels of Sullivan's Cove fell away astern and the picture-windowed suburbs of Sandy Bay and Taroona thinned out into clusters of weekend retreats, each with its neatly kept landing-stage and dinghy, until the throaty rumble of the yacht's engines was being thrown back from the bush-clad hills that marched south-wards beside us. *Lorelei* slid placidly onwards to the d'Entre-casteaux Channel and the open sea while I sat at the wheel and watched the warm colours of the ever-widening river change to the blues and greys of the dusk that crept across the water. Two-tooth sat behind me at the chart-table, smoking his pipe in a companionable silence. It was as peaceful a scene as you could wish.

I only hoped it would stay like that.

Schuyler had come aboard soon after four, wearing a faded green T-shirt with crumpled khaki drill slacks and humping a bulging kit-bag. He'd taken the enlistment of our new cook without comment, apart from flatly refusing to share the fo'c'sle with him on the grounds that he wasn't shacking up with no goddam fairies. This speech had done nothing to endear him to Zaghrali, and I could see that the CIA man was going to have to watch his diet very carefully during the next few days. Two-tooth had greeted Schuyler with the mixture of suspicion and contempt he reserved for all Governmental authority, and a blunt question on how the American thought he was going to look after the *Fort Knox* by joy-riding up the west coast had been answered, equally bluntly, by his being told to mind his own business. All in all, I had the feeling that this was not going to be what the Navy would call a happy ship.

This feeling hadn't been diminished by Barbara Mackail's high-handed attitude when she'd come aboard. The rest of us had been in the galley, recovering from Zaghrali's first gastronomic masterpiece of baked beans on charcoal and listening to a fascinating account from Schuyler of smuggling methods on the western seaboard of the United States. Normally I'd have been very interested, but just then it was rather like hearing a hangman giving a drop-by-drop account of his last busy season since Zaghrali was the only one out of the four of us who didn't know from which side of the fence Schuyler was talking. I kept trying to break away to get on deck for a quiet cigarette, but it wasn't until the Post Office clock was finished striking six that the American broke off abruptly and said, 'Wasn't that somebody coming aboard, skip?'

I found the girl on the bridge, examining the mascot with her back to me. I didn't say anything about the bridge being out of bounds to passengers—especially female ones. That could be promulgated later when it was too late to get out and walk. Instead, I said politely from the foot of the ladder, 'I didn't realise you'd come aboard, Miss Mackail.'

Her reaction surprised me until I remembered the rope-soled sandals I was wearing. She spun round with a startled gasp and stared at me wide-eyed. 'Oh, it's you!' She looked as if she'd never seen me before. Then she collected herself. 'I could hear voices and I thought you were having a meal. I didn't want to disturb you.' She was wearing a sea-green linen shirt under a white Acrilan blazer cardigan, with charcoal-grey slacks. Her face, with its rather high cheekbones and vividly green eyes, was as beautiful as ever, but—probably because she was standing above me with her back to the declining sun—I got the impression that she was paler and more tensed up than she'd been that morning. 'Are we ready to sail?' she asked.

'As soon as I've shown you to your cabin.' I stood back from the ladder to let her come down to the saloon. 'Is your luggage . . .?'

'I've already dealt with that.'

She made no attempt to descend the ladder, so I climbed up beside her. As I did, I saw that she was gripping the back of the helmsman's chair so tightly that the knuckles of her right hand were as white as the sun-bleached linen seat-cover. Hell, I thought. Surely she isn't going to be seasick before we've even cast off?

She said, 'I've put my things in the cabin opposite the bathroom. It was unoccupied, so I suppose that's all right?'

'If that's what you want.' It was all right with me, but Twotooth was in for a shock. He'd have to move in with Schuyler. 'But I'd thought of giving you my cabin. There's a single bed instead of a bunk and there'd be more room for . . .'

She wasn't paying me any attention at all. She was listening, I realised, to the sound of a gravelly Australian voice that floated up from the galley. I said, a little stiffly, 'But please yourself, of course.' For two thousand dollars she could move in with Zaghrali for all I cared. 'Now, if you want to start right away, perhaps we could . . .'

'Just a minute.' She stared up at me, frowning. 'If you're up here, who's your friend talking to? I thought there were just the two of you?'

I was ready for that one. 'There's a cook and a deck-hand as well. They were ashore,' I said truthfully, 'when you were here this morning.'

'And the girl? What does she do?'

'Girl?' I was taken aback. Then it dawned on me that she must have caught a glimpse of Lucky that morning and thought she came with the boat. 'If you mean the visitor we had earlier, she's . . .'

'I think you know which girl I mean,' she said levelly. 'The one who was here on the bridge a moment ago. I saw her quite clearly from the dockside.' She eyed me coldly. 'I'm afraid there's no room for camp-followers on this trip, Mr. Tallon.'

For one horrible moment I thought Lucky had turned up again in her bottomless ensemble, ready for more free board and lodgings. Then I breathed a sigh of relief. 'We don't go in for camp-followers. I thought you'd have seen the answer to that for yourself.' I indicated the shop-window dummy that sat in the full flood of amber, late-evening sunlight. 'It was Lorelei you saw. Our ship's mascot.'

'I thought of that.' She looked at the dummy, then back at me. 'But it seemed to move. As if somebody saw me, and dodged out of sight.'

I said confidently, 'It was the reflection on the window that seemed to move as you came down the steps.' On the other hand, I remembered Lucky's attempt to hitch a ride, and her fury when she'd been thwarted. It would be typical of her to try to stow away after that. 'But,' I said thoughtfully, 'it won't take me long to make sure nobody's sneaked aboard. There aren't many hiding places on a ship as compact as this.'

'No,' she said sharply. 'There's no time for that. I want to leave as soon as possible. I'd like to look round the boat myself instead. And I'm afraid I must insist on having this—this mascot of yours removed.'

'Removed?' I raised an eyebrow. 'Why? What difference does . . .?'

'I don't intend to argue about it. I think it's odd, and I'd like it put below out of sight, that's all. You can keep it in the saloon, if you must have it on board. And now I'm going to have a look round, if you don't mind.' She dropped neatly down the ladder before I could say whether I minded or not, and a second later the sound of voices from the galley ceased abruptly.

I was left standing in the wheelhouse with the yellow sunlight glinting on the metal fittings, wondering whether that poor devil of a truck-driver had been right when he'd called the yacht a floating madhouse. Not only were we carrying a

Secret Service agent who seemed to think it was a clubhouse for Russian saboteurs, but now I'd been landed with a client who saw *Lorelei* as a sea-going bordello, complete with sex-symbols, and who searched me for concealed girls. Then there was Zaghrali, with his treasure-hunting syndrome . . . I shrugged and picked up the intercom handset to call Two-tooth to the bridge. After all, this was just another job, and better paid than most.

But later, when the yacht was lifting to the dark swell of the Southern Ocean and we were ten miles off the South-east Cape with fifty fathoms under our keel, I didn't feel quite so detached. Out on the deep water under the stars, things have a habit of taking on an aspect very different from the one they bear in the safety of a port. For the sea at night is a mysterious thing, with a primeval quality that dwarfs man and his problems into short-lived insignificance. It is a dark, timelessly rolling jungle where the artificial rules of civilisation have no meaning, an alien element where the life of a man, like that of the fish beneath his feet, depends on unsleeping watchfulness and precaution. In spite of myself, my eyes kept flicking to the revolving green trace of the radar that was bracketed to the bulkhead next to the echo-sounder. This time, if we were intercepted, we'd see the blip appear suddenly, within a single sweep of the scanner. I knew how big it would look, and how . . . Two-tooth said, from just behind my shoulder, 'What're you expecting to see on that thing? The late-night movie?'

'For Pete's sake!' I snapped. 'Must you creep up behind me like that? I thought you were asleep.'

I saw his reflection watching me in the windscreen. 'Jeez, you're on edge tonight, aren't you? What's up, Tallon? Schuyler said anything else to you?' He spoke quietly, right into my left ear.

'No. And what are you whispering for? The others have all turned in, haven't they?'

He straightened up self-consciously and said in his normal voice, 'Yeah. Sociable lot, aren't they? But I wouldn't put it past that copper to have the whole ship wired for sound. If,' he said thoughtfully, 'he is what he says he is.'

86

'He's not a copper, he's from the CIA. I saw his papers—I told you. And he went into Police HQ as if he owned the place. What else would he be?'

'I dunno. But I just can't work out what he's after, that's all. What's he hoping to get out of this trip?' I didn't answer him, and there was a silence until he said off-handedly, 'You don't reckon there's anything in this gold idea of Zaghrali's, do you?'

I looked over my shoulder at him. 'Are you serious? D'you think a ship full of gold's going to lie around for over a hundred years without somebody falling over it—even on a coast as lonely as the south-west? And, if it was there, and if the girl happened to know about it, d'you think she'd go looking for it with four men she'd never set eyes on before? Good Lord, you're as bad as . . .'

'All right, all right,' he said hastily. 'It was just that—well, you get some funny ideas at night when you're at sea. And there's something funny about that girl, too. She's either sick or scared. That dead-pan look of hers—it's not natural. She's hiding something, Tallon, I'd swear to that.'

'Aren't we all?' I said grimly. I became aware that he was watching the 'scope every bit as hard as I was. 'Look,' I said reasonably. 'We could be letting our imaginations run away with us, couldn't we? The girl could be scared stiff, but only at the idea of being shut up with four men for a few days. Schuyler might think the Russians are going to have another go at contacting us. It could be as simple as that.'

'Could it?' he said gloomily. 'You don't really know, though, do you? And neither do I.' He clamped his teeth on his cold pipe. 'All we know is that, whatever happens, we'll be right in the middle of it. Prawns. That's what we are, mate. Just bloody prawns.'

'Pawns,' I said. 'If it's chess we're in the middle of, and not a salad.'

'O.K., pawns, then. Though I always thought that was something you did with gold watches you'd nicked. But, prawns or not, it stands to sense Sweeney Todd Schuyler wouldn't be wasting his time out here if he didn't think something was going to blow up.'

And if anything did, I thought bleakly, we were in the right place for it. Out in the darkness to port lay the Sidmouth Rock, with the two-hundred-foot tower-shaped Eddystone beyond it, flanked by the Pedra Blanca and the Flying Scud Rocks—grim reminders that we were off a coast that had claimed more ships per mile than any in Australia. Ships with the quaint, euphonious names of the nineteenth century: *Dolphin*, *Active* and *Aphilo*, *Enchantress*, *Hercules* and *Karamu*. Ships like the convict transport *George III*, that had ground her life out on the rocks not five miles from our present position with a loss of a hundred and thirty-four lives. And ships of our own age like the *Brier Holme*, out of London with a cargo of dynamite, that had struck off the South-west Cape and been blown to fragments in the darkness of a November night.

The bridge intercom buzzed with an abruptness that made me clutch the wheel convulsively.

I put out a hand with deliberate slowness, annoyed at my involuntary reaction, and picked up the receiver. Barbara Mackail's voice, flat and controlled, said in my ear, 'Mr. Tallon?' When I'd acknowledged she said, 'Would you come to my cabin? At once, please.'

Two-tooth's grey eyes met mine as I hung up. The girl's voice had been clearly audible above the pulsing of the diesels and the hiss of the sea against our hull. It was significant that, instead of the barrage of ribbing I might have expected on receiving such a request at such an hour, he merely put a big hand on the back of my chair and said, 'O.K., mate. I got her.'

I slid down the ladder to the darkened saloon where Lorelei sat, aloof on the settle in the shadows, then I went down the shorter ladder that led to the for'ard accommodation. There was no sign of either Zaghrali or the American. I stood in the softly lit passageway, staring at the blank, impassive face of the panelled door of the guest cabin for a moment before I knocked. There wasn't a sound from inside.

She half opened the door. Her face was in shadow and she was still dressed in her green shirt and dark-grey trousers, but she'd discarded the white cardigan. She didn't say anything. She just looked past me to make sure I was alone, then she opened the door wide and I went in. There was only one light on, a reading lamp on the bulkhead near the bunk. It threw a pool of light on to the carpet that was dazzling after the subdued lighting of the bridge and passageway and it was a moment before I was able to see behind it and make out the figure of the man who was sitting on the lower berth. A man who stood up politely as I looked at him, so that his shadow, thrown by the low, brilliant lamp, sprawled over me like an evil genie.

It was the Russian who had called himself Nicolai.

Nine

I STARED at him—shaken, but not unduly so. I think I'd known all along, deep down inside, that a simple straightforward charter job just wasn't for me. I seemed fated to collect deadlegs the way bad meat collects flies. If I as much as tried to help an old lady across the street, I thought bitterly, it was even money she'd turn out to be an internationally sought-after axe murderess, and I'd find myself lagged as an accomplice before I'd gone a yard.

'Come in, Captain.' Nicolai's face was in shadow, but I was able to see that he'd been fitted out with an anonymously washed-out-blue shirt and grey flannels with worn leather sandals. 'It is time we had a little talk. One,' he said meaningly, 'that will be to our mutual advantage. You understand?'

I understood only too well. He thought he'd picked up God's gift to the Russian Secret Service—a boat that could be hired to do anything and that had an owner to match. And why shouldn't he think that? If you go around with a price tag on your chest you can't really complain when somebody makes you an offer. The girl said softly from behind me, 'The two thousand was only a retainer, remember? Would ten thousand be enough for the whole job, do you think?'

I swung round to face her. She was leaning elegantly against the door, her hands behind her back. 'No,' I said evenly. 'It wouldn't be enough, Miss Mackail. Not if you offered me Lenin's Tomb stuffed with roubles. We're putting back into Hobart.'

'Not enough?' She frowned. 'I don't understand. I thought . . .'

'You thought,' I said deliberately, 'that you'd got hold of a couple of crooks who could be taken for the biggest ride since Lady Godiva as long as the money was right. Well, I hate to tell you this, but you're on the wrong boat. We may not be very choosy about what we do for a living, but there are one or two things even we crooks draw the line at. And one of them is providing a ferry service for Red agents and their girls.'

'He's not a Red agent,' she snapped. 'And I'm not his girl, either. My name is Mikhailev, the same as his, but I changed it to Mackail when I was naturalised. I'm his sister.'

I looked into her sea-green eyes—eyes that mirrored the lamp over the lower berth and that were, now I came to think of it, of exactly the same green as those of the man standing behind me. I wondered why I hadn't been able to work out a little thing like that for myself. Not that it really made any difference. 'I don't care,' I said coldly, 'if you're his grandmother. Just get away from the door, will you? I'm going through it.'

'Wait!' The Russian sounded nonplussed for the first time since I'd met him. As I turned, he said quickly, 'Be reasonable, Captain. You stand to gain nothing by giving me up—just the reverse, in fact. There is the truck, remember. I know what it contains. If I am questioned by your police I shall certainly have to say where I have hidden it. I might even be persuaded to tell them you were paid to bring me ashore as well.' He paused to let the threat sink in. 'On the other hand, if you co-operate with us you will have all the money you want in your pocket and, with your ship fully provisioned, you can sail where you like afterwards.'

'I'd disappear, in fact?' I grinned unpleasantly at him. 'Oh, no. I've heard of these deals before, Mikhailev, where little men like me were going to be set up for life by doing jobs for your people. And they all seem to end in the same way, with the little man being rolled out for identification in a re-frigerated drawer. Like that truck-driver last night.'

'Truck-driver?'

'The one you coshed and left in your bunk. He was mur-dered last night. Probably in mistake for you.'

I heard the girl's indrawn hiss of breath from behind me. 'Here on this boat? They killed . . .?'

91

'Of course not. D'you think I'd be here now if he'd been killed on board? No, they tried to knife him in the middle of the night but they made a mess of it. They must have had better luck after he'd left us, because his body was pulled out of the river during the day.' I stared at the Russian. 'You can tell the police what you like. I'd rather take my chance with them than with whatever bunch of initials it is you're working for.' I turned to the door again.

Barbara Mackail had her back to it still. And the small, silver-plated revolver in her right fist was lined up, rock-steady, with my navel. She said, in a voice full of ice-cubes, 'But we're not taking chances with anybody, Tallon. Get over by the washbasin and keep your hands where I can see them. And don't try anything stupid.'

I looked down at the gun. 'When it comes to stupidity,' I said sourly, 'you're dealing with an expert.' It was a .22 Sedgley Baby Hammerless, the four-inch-long revolver they used to advertise as a garter pistol. 'But if you think you can take over the ship with a grease-gun like that you're right out of my class.' I moved forward so that the muzzle was pressing into my stomach.

'Barbara!' Mikhailev's deep voice was abrasive with anger. 'Are you out of your mind? You know you cannot use that. Captain, listen to me. I . . .'

I wasn't going to do anything of the sort. I was too busy watching the girl's eyes to see whether she'd worked herself up to the point where she'd squeeze the trigger, and I'd decided she hadn't. She looked as coldly efficient as an ice-pick—too efficient to fire a shot that would get her nowhere. And only an amateur lets you get within arm's length of his gun, anyway. I pushed it aside gently with one hand and reached for the door-handle with the other.

Something as thick and muscular as a squid's tentacle came snaking round my chest from behind me, pinning my left arm to my side and gripping my right like a vice. Another one clamped itself across my mouth and nose, shutting off my air. I felt myself being ground against what felt like the trunk of a tree, but when I lashed out backwards with my foot there was nothing to connect with. I let myself go slack, watching the girl as she snapped back the folding trigger and slipped the tiny pistol into the pocket of her grey slacks. Then I tried jack-knifing suddenly, to throw the Russian over my head at her, but I had to abandon that project just this side of a hernia. It was like trying to throw Cleopatra's Needle. A deep voice growled into my right ear, 'I regret this, but you give me no choice. Will you give me your word that you will, at least, hear what I have to say? Or do I have to render you unconscious and tie you up?'

I didn't have a lot of time in which to consider his offer. Already I could hear the sea roaring in my ears, and a cerise-coloured mist had begun to flicker in front of my bulging eyes. I couldn't speak, or even nod, but I made a belching noise that, thank the Lord, he interpreted correctly. The killing pressure round my face and chest relaxed and I sagged against him like a deflated inner tube. Then I teetered across to the washbasin and leaned on it, waiting for *Lorelei* to recover from the ninety-degree roll she seemed to have developed.

Mikhailev went to the door and snapped on the overhead light. Then he sat down on the berth again, watching me. 'So!' he said thoughtfully. 'We seem to have made a mistake, Tallon, in assuming you to be a man who could be easily bought. For that I apologise.' He looked at the girl who was leaning against the door with her arms folded. 'My sister, also,' he said, with a touch of frost in his voice. She inclined her head, but she didn't look very regretful. 'But we must have your help, whether you take our money or not. I think that, when I have explained what I am doing here, you will give it.'

I opened my mouth and told him to think again, but nothing came out except a sound like a leaking gas main, which he ignored. He leaned forward. 'In the first place, I am not, as you seem to think, an agent of the *Komitet Sovietskoi Byezhopas-nosti*—the Committee for Soviet Security. They are the very people I am most anxious to avoid. It was they who killed that unfortunate man whose clothes I took. I am sure of it.'

'You would be,' I croaked. 'Look, the only people who knew we'd picked you up last night were Two-tooth, me, a girl who came on board later, and you. And I know which . . .'

'You know!' he snapped. 'What can you know of these things? You are like a child sailing a toy boat on a pond, with no knowledge of the life-and-death struggle that goes on among the creatures beneath the surface. Do you think that because they searched you once they would let it go at that? Your ship would be under surveillance the moment it docked, I knew that. But I did not anticipate that they would make the incredible blunder of murdering the wrong man.' He glanced at the girl. 'But that is why,' he said to her, 'they have not tried again. They think I am dead.' He turned to me again. 'No, Tallon, as I told you last night, I am no spy. I am—or perhaps I should say, I was—an officer in the Soviet Navy. Engineering officer, with a rank equivalent to your commander, of a Z-class underwater-missile submarine. And I have deserted,' he said quietly. 'Deserted, not defected. There is a difference. I have come ashore here for reasons of my own, not because I wish to become a part of your effete capitalist society.'

'That,' I said, wishing my voice didn't sound quite so much like the death-rattle of a steam-rollered whoopie-cushion, 'clears the air a lot. Now all you've got to tell me is what a Russian three-ringer hopes to achieve by jumping off the conning-tower twenty miles from land. And why he didn't get shot while he was doing it.'

'I did not jump off the conning-tower,' he said impatiently. 'We never surface on patrol, except in extreme emergency. I did not plan my escape. It was a decision I made on the spur of the moment when Narumov, our first officer, reported the sighting of what he said were two Tasmanian fishing vessels, hove-to and about five hundred metres to the north of our track. We were running at periscope depth, there was no moon, and the sea was reasonably calm. It was a chance in a thousand.' He shrugged. 'I took it. In my position I could go where I liked on board. All I had to do was to change out of my uniform, pick up a life-jacket, and leave the ship through the water-spider.'

'The what?'

'The underwater escape apparatus. By the time I surfaced, I hoped . . .'

'You left while the ship was under way? And you operated the thing by yourself?'

'*Konietchno*—of course. Our equipment works on the principle of . . .' He checked himself. 'It is, naturally, more advanced than yours.'

My knowledge of submarines was limited to the World-War-Two vintage films I'd seen, so I couldn't contradict him there. He said, 'I am a good swimmer and I had a life-jacket. I saw no reason why I should not reach the ships we had sighted. As I have said, I had no time to think. It did not occur to me that the ships might not be there when I reached the surface.' He was silent for a moment, his mouth tightening as he re-lived those moments of horror in the black, choking water when he realised what he'd done. Our rendezvous with the *Haraguro Maru* hadn't lasted more than five minutes. 'I found nothing except the flash of a lighthouse that seemed to be diffused over the entire northern horizon. I had escaped only too well. And now I was going to die, without even a star to see me drown.' He shrugged. 'I struggled, of course. I remember swimming aimlessly, endlessly, and the water seeming to thicken like syrup after a time so that I could hardly move myself through it. Then there was nothing until I found myself here on your ship, with your friend leaning over me.'

The sea hissed against *Lorelei*'s hull and her engines rumbled like distant thunder as I took out my cigarettes, frowning. In spite of myself, I was convinced he was telling the truth. The quiet, matter-of-fact sentences in his precise, rather pedantic English, together with the openness of his plug-ugly face, told me that. Unless, of course, the Russians went in for such a degree of realism in their cover-stories that he'd half drowned himself just to impress me. I hammered a cigarette on my thumbnail and lit it. 'But what did you do it for?' I asked, waving the match out. 'Even if you'd wanted to change sides it was a hell of a risk to take. What's so important here that you'd go through all that, knowing you'd have both sides chasing you when you got ashore?'

'A wreck,' he said quietly. 'Barbara told you this morning what we are looking for. We have tried to tell you as few lies as possible.' He raised a hand as the girl made a movement to interrupt. 'He must know sooner or later,' he said to her. 'And he is a reasonable man, if,' he smiled faintly at me as I absent-mindedly massaged my aching ribs, 'he is approached in the proper way.' The smile vanished as he said, 'What Barbara did not tell you is that the wreck is that of a Soviet space-craft. A manned space vehicle with a crew of three.'

I'd been congratulating myself on having reached saturation point as far as shocks were concerned. I thought I'd got to the stage where even a stranded Russian nuclear submarine—stuffed, no doubt, with radioactive corpses—wouldn't have been worth a raised eyebrow. But I might have known this bizarre character wouldn't be satisfied with anything as hum-drum as that. 'A space vehicle?' I said numbly.

He nodded. 'We call it Solnishko Odno. And those three men are trapped inside it, Tallon. We are going to get them out.'

Dimly, I recognised the phrase he'd repeated over and over after he'd collapsed the night before. As I gaped at him he went on, 'Solnishko Odno—Solnishko 1, you would call it—is part of the Troika programme in which the USSR intends to put three men on the moon this year, three years before the Ameri-can target date. It was lost three days ago, after its commander had reported extensive damage caused by a collision with satel-lite debris during an orbital manœuvre. He said he was carry-ing out an emergency re-entry, and he began to give an esti-mated splash-down position to the east of Kerguelen Island in the Indian Ocean. It was then that we lost contact. His message broke off before it was completed.'

'So how do you know it crashed here?' It would be a chance in a million if it had. The Indian Ocean covers twenty-eight million square miles—one seventh of the entire surface area of this planet, a waste of water as big as the whole of Africa and Asia put together. Tasmania is roughly the same size as Scot-land.

'We do not have,' he said bleakly, 'the ground-station facili-ties that you people make available to the Americans. Much of our tracking has to be done by our navy. My ship was being used for this purpose near the Amsterdam-St. Paul group, and we were able to follow Solnishko 1 by radar until it passed over the horizon to the east. Programmed with this information, our computers told us that the space-craft would crash either in the sea or on the west coast of Tasmania.' He looked at me oddly. 'But nobody knows its exact position except you.'

'Except me?' I wondered for a moment whether the pressure he'd applied to my neck had affected my hearing, or whether his English had let him down at last.

He nodded. 'When I sent Barbara to hire your boat,' he said in his matter-of-fact, slightly guttural voice, 'I thought I had found the ideal men for the search I planned to make. Men with a powerful yacht that was equipped with radar and an echo-sounder, men who would be willing to take a risk and who would not ask too many questions. I did not dream that, by a fantastic stroke of fate, my life had been saved by the only two people in the world who knew where the missing space-craft is located.' He leaned forward. 'But after Barbara had visited you I knew. Because Solnishko 1's last transmission was at five-thirty in the evening. Shortly before your friend saw what he told my sister was a—how do you say it?—a flying saucer, landing on the south-west coast.'

'You mean,' I said incredulously, 'you're basing all this on what Two-tooth thought he saw in a bad light? Hell, it could have been . . .'

'A cloud, a mirage, an aircraft,' he said impatiently. 'I know. It could even have been a Venusian space-ship. But, backed by the findings of our computers, I prefer to believe it was Solnishko 1.' He stood up. 'It is what we are looking for. There can be no doubt of it.'

I tapped ash off my cigarette into the washbasin and ran a little water to flush it away. 'But look,' I said, well out of my depth. 'If your people have lost a sputnik on Australian territory, how are they going to . . .?'

He came and stood in front of me, his face grim. 'You begin to see the position? My government can hardly ask politely for it to be returned, as if it was a ball they had lost in a neighbour's garden. Think how the Americans would crow if they were presented, not only with the opportunity of examining one of our greatest scientific achievements, but with evidence of what they would call our technological inefficiency as well.

And, even in the unlikely event of our being granted permission to get it back, its recovery on a coast as difficult as the south-west would be a major operation. Solnishko 1 weighs twenty tons and is as big as one of your London buses.' He gripped my arm as *Lorelei* rolled slightly more than usual. 'We must get those three men out, Tallon,' he said urgently. 'This is a matter of humanity, not politics.'

I watched him disbelievingly. 'And that's why you've deserted? You're asking me to believe that you, a senior naval officer, have thrown away your career, risked your life and branded yourself, whatever you may say, as a traitor for the sake of a hunch? This thing could have come down in the sea—it probably has. And you did it, moreover, for three men you don't know? Men who've probably been dead for three days, at that?' I snorted. 'I couldn't believe a yarn like that even if I took lessons.'

He released my arm. 'I had to do it,' he said harshly. He looked at the girl, and pain stared out of his eyes for an instant like a hostage signalling from a beleaguered fortress. 'You see, Tallon, the name of the cosmonaut in command of Solnishko 1 is also Mikhailev. Igor Aleksandr Mikhailev, my younger brother.'

I opened my mouth, then shut it again when I saw the girl's stony face. She said, her voice carefully disciplined, 'When our parents died together in 1956 Igor was already in the Air Force and Nicolai had his career in the Navy. They could not look after a schoolgirl, and there was no one else I could turn to. So I went to live with my mother's sister in Prague. When she and her husband emigrated to Australia I came with them. I have not seen either of my brothers for ten years until Nicolai came to me last night.' She paused, her hands tightly clasped in front of her. 'We have all the equipment we need,' she said quietly, 'and Nicolai knows how to use it. They are trapped inside that awful thing—badly injured, perhaps. They might, as you say, even be dead. But anything would be better than never knowing what had happened to Igor. Won't you at least let us go and find out?'

I said awkwardly, 'If it's a rescue job, of course we'll go.' I studied the tip of my cigarette so as not to meet her eyes. With

Schuyler on my back, I didn't have much choice about whether I was going to be magnanimous or not. And his interest in the trip was now fairly obvious. I said, 'But how do you know they're still inside the thing? Surely, if they were . . .' I broke off.

'If they were alive they would have got out already. That is what you were about to say, yes?' He shook his head. 'But they cannot get out. The hatch of Solnishko 1 is in the form of an air-lock between two sliding doors. The air-pressure inside the cabin is always slightly higher than atmospheric to prevent the entry of contaminated air. For that reason, and also to obviate human error in space, only one door can be opened at a time. And our telemetry reported that immediately after the collision the outer door had opened and then jammed halfway. That means they cannot operate the inner one.'

'But they'll have plenty of oxygen and food?' When he nodded I said, 'So all we've got to do is either to get the outer door to shut, or else cut through the inner one with the oxy-acetylene kit you've probably got in one of those packing cases. We should be able to do that.'

The girl's breath went out in a sigh and she gave me a strained, grateful smile, the first I'd had from her. I hadn't expected Mikhailev to smile or do anything as recklessly abandoned as that, but I thought he might have relaxed a little now he'd got his own way. Instead, he stared broodingly at me, grunted, and went and sat down on his bunk again looking more worried than ever. I said slowly, 'But, of course, I'll want the whole story first. Not just the expurgated edition.'

He looked up at me sharply, then down at the carpet. A tablet of soap slithered into the washbasin behind me as the yacht rolled again, more heavily this time, and there was a creak from the built-in wardrobe. 'I don't know what you mean,' he said.

'Oh, yes, you do.' I crushed my half-smoked cigarette out and went and stood over him, looking down at the top of his cropped head. 'You said you thought Two-tooth and I wouldn't mind taking a risk. All right, what sort of risk did you have in mind?'

The girl put a sunburnt hand on my arm and said, far too quickly, 'That you might go to prison for helping us, that's all.'

'It wouldn't be for the first time, as you probably know quite well.' I shook her hand off and turned back to her brother. 'Look, Mikhailev. You know as well as I do that there's more to this than you've told me. For a start, your people aren't going to write off one of their technological top secrets as casually as if it was an empty vodka bottle. What are we going to run into when we get to the other end?' When he didn't answer I snapped, 'Start talking. Or this is as far as we go. I want the full story, or else we go back to Hobart and I'll turn the lot of us in.'

I thought he was going to call my bluff. But he wasn't to know it was Schuyler who was calling the tune, not me. He looked up. 'Very well,' he said tiredly. 'You want the truth, you shall have it. But there can be no question of turning back now. Not with something as vital as this at stake.'

He stood up, fatigue sitting heavily on his shoulders as he turned to face me. 'You see, Tallon, it is not just a space-capsule we are looking for, a mere projectile fitted with rockets. Solnishko 1 is the first of the true space-ships, a fully manœuvrable craft capable of flying not only to the moon but to the limits of the Solar System and back under its own power. Atomic power, Tallon.' He lifted a hand as the girl made to speak, and let it fall again. 'It is no secret that both we and the Americans have been working since the late nineteen-forties on the development of a self-sustaining fusion reaction using plasmas—the fourth state of matter, as they have been called. Plasmas are ionised gases, and it is common knowledge that ninety per cent of the universe exists in plasma form, including our own sun which is, to all intents and purposes, an inexhaustible source of energy. Energy released by plasma-induced fusion of hydrogen. So the theory is simple. Duplicate the fusion chain reaction that has been going on in the sun for countless billions of years, and you have an equally limitless supply of energy. And this energy is released in the fusion of deuterium, an isotope of hydrogen. It is produced from the cheapest fuel in the world. Ordinary water.'

I watched him, remembering the type of ship he'd come from and the job he'd been doing aboard her. 'And your people can do this?'

He grunted contemptuously. 'I am an engineer, not a scientist. But I know enough of it to appreciate the problems involved. For one thing, no known material could contain such a source of energy without vapourising. It would be like trying to put the sun in a cardboard box. And so, up to now, the only fusion reaction we have achieved has been instantaneous, as in the fission-fusion bomb, where all the energy is liberated and wasted in a micro-second. But until three days ago our Soviet scientists thought they had solved the problem. They have made another sun and harnessed it to a space-ship whose range is limited only by man's life-span. That is why they called it Solnishko 1. Its name means Little Sun.'

'They thought they'd solved it?' Premonitions stirred like questing maggots in the dark recesses of my mind. I grabbed his arm. 'What the hell are you trying to tell me?'

'That our instruments reported the reactor to be acting abnormally when we lost contact. The rate of fusion was slowly increasing to a point where . . .'

I shook his arm savagely. 'For God's sake, stop talking like something from Planet X. What is it you're afraid of?'

'A nuclear explosion,' he said harshly. 'That is what I am afraid of, Tallon. If those three men are unable to get the rate of fusion under control, or if they are dead, then all the energy locked in the reactor will be released simultaneously. Solnishko 1 will become an atomic bomb with a destructive force such as the world has never seen.'

'My God!' I stared at him, appalled. While the south-west itself is uninhabited, there are towns farther to the north—the small port of Strahan, outlet for the Mount Lyell copper mines, and Queenstown, the mining centre itself. Five thousand people, or thereabouts. They would go first, but they would be the lucky ones. For, on the prevailing westerlies, the radio-active debris would sweep across the entire island like a mephitic, malignant cloud laden with the seeds of radiation sickness and death. A twentieth-century plague that would burn and poison the soil, the water, the very air itself and strike down a quarter of a million people. I said urgently, gripping his arm, 'We've got to warn them. They can get somebody down from Woomera, organise the evacuation of . . .'

'Don't be a fool!' He shook my hand off violently, his voice snapping with the tension he'd kept locked up until now. 'If your people attempted to interfere with Solnishko 1, my brother would be forced to destroy it immediately. In any case, it would take your scientists months to understand it. There is no time, I tell you, no time . . .' He stopped and went over to the two-tiered bunk, gripping the chromed tubular support while he got himself under control.

'It is the whole world, not just this island, that is involved in this,' he said more quietly. 'You don't even begin to see the danger. Have you thought of the American reaction to an un-explained nuclear explosion of such magnitude on Australian territory? You know they will retaliate without question.' He stared at me with eyes like chips of malachite. 'And my government can do nothing. Even if they have already located Sol-nishko 1 with an infra-red-sensitive satellite they are power-less. As a last resort they might be prepared to put a demoli-tion squad ashore from a submarine, to dismantle the reactor and then destroy it. But with the American aircraft-carrier in the vicinity it is a risk they dare not take. All they can do is hope that the worst will not happen and that they can make such an attempt later when the danger is over. In the mean-time nobody must know of the existence of Solnishko 1. Which is why,' he said bleakly, 'they are trying to silence me. And at the same time they are preparing for the holocaust we all dread. My ship was on its way to its war station in the Pacific when I left it.'

I swallowed, my throat dry. 'In that case what do you think you can do?'

'I am an atomic engineer. I have done some research on plas-mas, and I know a good deal about Solnishko 1, since we were responsible for tracking it. I am going to bring its reactor under control, with the assistance of the crew.' He made a small ges-ture. 'And if I fail what is there to lose?'

The crash as something heavy slammed into the cabin door nearly made my heart stop. The three of us stood frozen for an instant, listening to the patter of receding footsteps in the passageway outside. Then I leapt to the door and wrenched it open.

Zaghrali, dressed in a pale blue undervest and flowered mauve pyjamas, lay sprawled on his face at my feet on the green fitted carpet.

Ten

I BECAME conscious of the increased liveliness in *Lorelei*'s
movement as soon as I stepped out into the passageway and
heard the note of the diesels deepen. We were running into
rough weather, and Two-tooth was bringing the revs down to
ease his beloved engines. The girl lost her balance as she shut
the door behind her and she grabbed at my arm to steady herself. 'Is he dead?' she asked, looking down at the Egyptian.
She didn't sound as if she'd care much if he was.

But he wasn't. He came up on his hands and knees, groaning
and shaking his head so that his mop of greasy hair fell over
his face. He stared down muzzily at the carpet, then he saw my
ankle and grabbed it. 'Tallon!' he said thickly. 'We gotta turn
back, Tallon, before it's too late. I don't . . .'

I said sharply, 'That's enough. Just tell me what happened,
Zaghrali. And how you came to have your ear stuck to that
door.'

He looked up at me, his face green with terror under the
light. 'I wasn't listening at no door,' he whimpered. 'I swear it.
I jus' wanted to go to the john, thass all, an' I heard this guy
talking, the one she's got in there. Then somebody jump outa
the bathroom an' bash me.' He started to climb up my leg, his
voice rising to a nerve-twanging wail. 'I don't want to die,
Tallon. I didn't come on this trip to get blown up. She told me
it was gold we were after, not a goddam atomic bomb. She
didn't say nothing about . . .'

'She said?' I snarled edgily. His keening voice and clawing
hands were playing havoc with my nerves after what I'd just
heard. I swung round to Barbara Mackail. 'You'd met him before you came aboard?'

She met my stare coolly. 'Of course. How else do you think I got all the things I needed at such short notice? I was told on the docks that he'd arrange anything for a price. I fixed it all up with him before I came to see you this morning.' She looked down at Zaghrali contemptuously. 'I had to tell him something. And as soon as I hinted at a wreck full of gold he practically foamed at the mouth.'

'She lie to me,' Zaghrali screamed. 'An' thass not all, Tallon. That Yank you got on board, he's no goddam sailor. I know all about him, too. He's the one who jus' try to kill me.' He knelt in front of me, hanging on to my shirt as the yacht rolled like a barrel.

I put my hand on the back of his head to push him down again. He let out a shriek like a cat with its tail in a door and collapsed, putting his hands to the back of his skull. I said brutally, 'You were coshed from behind, you liar. So how do you know who it was?'

There was a clatter from the ladder and Schuyler appeared at the foot of it. He gazed at the *tableau vivant* in astonishment and said, 'O.K., so he's a lousy cook. But—this? From where we are it sounds like Bonus Week in the Chicago Stockyards.'

The girl braced herself against the bulkhead. 'Somebody knocked him out,' she said clinically. 'He says it was you.'

'Me?' He shook his head. 'I've been up on the bridge for the last quarter hour with the Beard. Maybe the poor little guy tripped and knocked himself out. We're rolling enough.' He stirred the groaning Egyptian with his foot. 'Hey, gorgeous, what happened? Your feet get mixed up with your hair?'

'Somebody hit him,' Barbara said again. 'We heard whoever it was running away.'

Zaghrali glared up at the American, his teeth bared like those of a cornered rat. 'An' it was you,' he hissed. He flung out an accusing hand as he said to me, 'It had to be him, Tallon. Who else could it have been? He try to kill me because I know who he is. He isn't a sailor any more than I am. He's . . .'

'Give me a hand with him, skip.' Schuyler looked at me warningly as he bent to take him under the armpits. 'That crack on the head must have really knocked him off kilter. Let's get the poor little guy into his sack.'

He wasn't much of a weight, but he kicked and fought us like a wildcat, and the corkscrewing roll that *Lorelei* had developed didn't make the job any easier, either. He kept screaming that we were all going to be blown to hell if Schuyler didn't get us first, in a way that made my flesh crawl. Then suddenly, as we were manœuvring him down from the saloon to the galley, he gave a sigh and went limp. We got him into his bunk in the fo'c'sle and Schuyler leaned over him, panting. 'Out like a light,' he said, rolling back Zaghrali's right eyelid to reveal the sclerotic coat, yellow and bloodshot. 'Just as well, too. We'd have had to give him a shot if he hadn't.' He stood up. 'Can we lock him in? I don't want him running around spreading the word when he surfaces.' He tucked a blanket round the stertorously breathing Egyptian while I checked that the fo'c'sle hatch was secured and that there was nobody in the crew's shower, right up in the heaving bows.

The fo'c'sle had two doors, one of them flush-panelled and painted white to fit in with the colour scheme of the adjoining galley, the other the heavy watertight door that was always clipped back. I followed Schuyler out, locking the wooden door behind me, and he leaned against the refrigerator, breathing hard. 'Now, Tallon,' he said coldly. 'You've got some fast talking to do. What the hell did you go busting into that cabin for? And don't try telling me it was the blonde you were after, because . . .'

'Don't be bloody silly.' I pocketed the key. 'She sent for me, and I found . . .' I broke off. Pieces of the puzzle were clicking into place. Not only why Schuyler had come with us, but why he'd kept us yarning in the galley here after tea. 'You knew he was in that cabin. You arranged it so that there was nobody on deck when she came aboard, didn't you? So she could smuggle her brother aboard.'

His eyes crinkled. 'You're learning fast, pal. I've got those two right where I want them. Unless,' his eyes hardened, 'you've been shooting your mouth off to them about me?'

'I haven't told them anything.' I thought how ironical it was that it had been Mikhailev himself who had stopped me from turning the ship round and thus blowing Schuyler's plans, whatever they were, up in his face. 'It was the Russian who did all the talking.'

'Very wise. Because if you louse this up after all the trouble I've taken I'll fix you so it'll take them a couple of days just to read out your indictment when we get back. Bear that in mind, friend.'

'If we get back.' I watched him sombrely. 'Does the name Solnishko 1 mean anything to you?'

'Are you kidding? What d'you think I'm doing here?' He paused, and then said, raising an eyebrow. 'He told you about it, did he? Well, I'm darned.'

Everybody on board this ship, I thought caustically, seemed to know exactly what he or she was doing except the two who were supposed to be running it. 'He told me, all right. He said it's come down in the south-west, and that its reactor's unstable. If they don't get it under control it'll cause a nuclear explosion that could . . .'

'. . . precipitate a major crisis. Maybe an atomic war.' The air of brash confidence seemed to fall off him like a cloak. He said soberly, 'I know about that, too.'

'You know?' I stared at him incredulously. 'You mean—our people know there's a potential thermo-nuclear bomb lying out there in the bush, and they're doing nothing about it?'

'We're doing plenty,' he snapped edgily. 'I told you, that's what I'm here for. This plasma engine's a completely unknown quantity. It's a security assignment, not a job for the military. That's why we've given Mikhailev so much rope. We knew the Russians'd put somebody ashore to fix Solnishko 1, so what we're . . .'

'But they haven't. Mikhailev's deserted from their navy to do this. His brother's one of the cosmonauts inside it.'

'His what?' His yellow eyebrows shot up. Then he said pityingly, 'He was put ashore, for Pete's sake. I don't know what he's told you, but he's been landed from a submarine to do two jobs—make sure their space-shot doesn't explode nuclear-wise, and then blow it to iron filings. After that,' he said grimly, 'he'll be taken off again. When he's shot all the witnesses and sunk the yacht.' There was no schoolboy grin now, just a pair of ice-blue eyes watching me out of the lean face. 'My job's to let him carry out the first part of his mission, then move in before he can do the second.'

'But,' I said slowly, 'if they wanted to put him ashore, why do it a hundred and fifty miles from his objective when the south-west's wide open? They could have dropped him there without any trouble at all. Instead, they unload him in the approaches to Hobart, twenty miles from land. Then they leave him to arrange his own transport and put the whole thing at the mercy of the first two people he happens to meet. It just doesn't add up.'

'How do I know why they do these things?' he said wearily. 'Maybe they don't know where Solnishko 1 is. Maybe something went wrong with their programme . . .'

'And I thought,' I said stubbornly, 'that you didn't know what he was up to? You said it was the aircraft carrier that he . . .'

'Be your age, Tallon. You think I was going to tell a small-time crook like you what was going on? You just go on driving your boat and leave the command decisions to people who know what they're talking about. And if you find yourself believing whatever bedtime story it is that Mikhailev's been telling you, just keep it under your hat, that's all. Or else you might start me wondering whether you're trying to play two sides at once.' He paused, and his eyes narrowed speculatively. 'Maybe you are, at that,' he said softly. 'Maybe that's why Zaghrali got slugged—because he heard you making a deal with the other side. How else would he have found out who I am?'

'Perhaps he reads the comic strips,' I said angrily. 'And he said it was you who hit him, remember, not me. Are you sure you weren't competing with him for the keyhole at the time?'

'Don't get smart with me, Tallon,' he said coldly. 'You can ask your pal where I was just before that fink started yelling.' He straightened up. 'O.K. So neither of us did it. But who does that leave?' He reached inside his shirt and hauled out what looked like one of the Guns of Navarone, a big blued-steel Government Model Colt .45. 'Let's go take a look, shall we?'

We went over the heaving, swaying yacht from the galley aft to the rudder-post. Together we searched the cabin Schuyler and Two-tooth were sharing, and the saloon where Lorelei in her yellow dress sat aloofly in the shadows. I locked the saloon doors on the inside so that, with the fo'c'sle hatch secured, nobody hiding on deck could get below. Then we went in to the engine-room and the bathroom, with me reminding myself all the way that this was the second time somebody had suggested we might be carrying an extra passenger, and that on the first occasion it had turned out to be true. The American stayed discreetly outside Barbara's door while I knocked and went inside to search her cabin as well. I was taking no more chances. Then the two of us went through my quarters and out on to the cockpit, where a blast of ice-cold air struck savagely at us out of the darkness, howling like a police siren in the aerials as it tried to tear the door out of my hand. The temperature had gone down with a run and we were butting into a Force 7 gale—a gentle zephyr for the Roaring Forties, but enough to flail the black immensity of the Southern Ocean into battalions of white-capped, spiky waves that marched westwards, hung with flares of moonlight under the ragged, racing clouds.

Lorelei ploughed into the seas like a destroyer, meeting them with a noise like a thunderclap and flinging them disdainfully aside in sheets of spray that hung over her momentarily like a luminous veil before they were blasted astern. In the roaring black-and-silver darkness the warm, friendly rectangles of light from the bridge windows seemed infinitely remote as I struggled with a torch among the packing cases, checking that their lashings were indisturbed and cheering myself with the thought that if somebody hiding in one of them gave me a shove I'd probably end up in New Zealand. It seemed pretty silly in that sort of weather to check, as Schuyler insisted, that there was nobody trailing alongside on a line, but we even did that. Finally, we went for'ard, one on each side, to make sure there was nobody on deck. If there'd been a cockroach on board we'd have flushed it out. But we found nothing.

Which was just as well, I thought, as we fought our way aft again, soaking wet and chilled to the bone. Any more stowaways and I'd have to go in for a bigger boat.

Two-tooth was hunched over the wheel when we got back to the cosy warmth of the chartroom, an empty pipe jutting out of his beard. He said, above the screech of the wind that tried to force its way in after us, 'Well, it's nice to know there's somebody else on the bloody boat besides me. While you've been out enjoying yourselves in the fresh air I've been stuck here with no tobacco and nothing to do but lay odds with meself on who was getting himself murdered. What was all that screaming and yelling about? What with a young hurricane to cope with . . .'

'How long was Schuyler up here?' I asked, my teeth chattering.

'Schuyler? Came up soon after you went below. Then he nipped off to see who was getting the bamboo stuck up his fingernails.' He screwed round in his seat to look briefly over his shoulder. 'Anyway, he's here, isn't he? Why can't you ask him? And what d'you want to know for? Jeez, is everybody nuts except me?' He turned back to his kicking wheel. 'And listen, mate. Before the screen got cluttered up I got a bloody big contact about twelve miles to the south. A ship that's keeping station with us as far as I could tell . . .'

'I know about that.' Schuyler was watching me, frowning. 'D'you think Zaghrali might have knocked himself out, after all?'

'Too right he could,' said Two-tooth, his back to us. 'Capable of anything, that bloke. But never mind him. What is it out there? And how do you know about it?'

'No, he couldn't,' I said. 'Because both the girl and I heard somebody running away. She said so. Mikhailev heard it, too . . .'

'Mikhailev?' Two-tooth shook his head uncomprehendingly, peering out through the spinning clear-view screen. 'Who the hell's he? And how do you run away on a boat this size? If you ask me . . .'

'So there's nobody else on board.' Schuyler was leaning on the radio table, staring at the set. 'I don't get it.'

'That,' said Two-tooth loudly, 'makes two of us. Now, I'd be the last one to pry into anybody else's affairs, but if I could just ask . . .?'

'Shut up,' snapped Schuyler. 'Just take a look at this, Tallon. We seem to have another little mystery on our hands.' He swung round abruptly to Two-tooth. 'When did you touch this radio last?'

'Michaelmas Day,' snarled Two-tooth to our reflections in the windscreen. 'I remember it well, because that's the day I change me singlet. Why the hell should I be the only one who isn't peculiar around here? And if you'll come and take this bloody wheel for a minute, Tallon, we'll see who's going to shut up . . .'

'Look, Two-tooth,' I said hurriedly, 'I'll tell you all about it later.' I'd just seen what the CIA man had noticed—the small black hole that marked where the crystal-selector switch had been. He watched me in silence as I unscrewed the transmitter panel. Then I looked up at him. 'So that's what the Mackail girl was doing when I found her up here,' I said flatly. 'Making sure we wouldn't talk.' The whole of the unit that controlled our radio frequencies had been wrenched out, and for good measure she'd smashed the valves as well.

'Aw, fair go, mate!' Two-tooth's pipe fell out of his mouth with a clatter. 'How d'you know she did it?'

'Because one of us has been here ever since.' I screwed the panel on again. 'We can still receive, but otherwise we're down to a signal lamp. And we're passing the last point before we round South-west Cape where even that could be of any use to us. There's a manned light on Maatsuyker Island, about ten miles to the north.' But with *Lorelei* trying to impersonate a bathyscape, I reflected, it would be well-nigh impossible to get off a coherent message without going in close. And I wasn't at all anxious to have to dodge rocks like the Needles and the Sisters at night and in this sort of weather—not with a radar so cluttered with wave echoes that it looked like a map of Antarctica. My dripping clothes suddenly felt icier than ever as it came to me that we were completely cut off from the outside world.

The worried look cleared from Schuyler's face as he saw me watching him. He leaned back against the transmitter as the yacht ran head-on into a punch that made her shudder. Seawater, livid green in the light, swamped the windscreen and was instantly whipped away in suds of white foam. 'We couldn't use the radio anyway,' he shouted above the uproar. 'Too public. We might need the lamp, but it won't be to talk to lighthouses with.' He grinned confidently at me. 'I'm not so dumb that I'd try to hit a homer like this without bringing the rest of the team along to back me up. That ship you got on your radar's flying the Stars and Stripes, Tallon. We'll have an anti-submarine frigate shadowing us all the way, and I happen to know her captain's just living for the moment when our friend's sub comes into the picture.' He straightened up. 'And now I'm getting out of these wet clothes.'

As I made to follow him with the same idea in mind, Two-tooth threw me a hard, bitter look over his shoulder. 'That's right. Push off below. I only work here, and I don't expect to be told what the big brass is up to. But you might bring my tobacco up if you happen to be round this way again. And I wouldn't mind a cup of coffee. Unless,' he added cuttingly, 'it turns out that our Barbie's sabotaged the bloody stove as well.'

Eleven

THE wind eased before daybreak, and a cold grey dawn crept out of the Indian Ocean in a steady downpour of rain that flattened the sea into a slate-grey wilderness streaked with whitecaps, a desolate waste of water hardly distinguishable through the streaming windscreen from the gunmetal clouds that gloomed overhead. Spray still burst like gunsmoke from *Lorelei*'s bows as she forged north-west, but her motion had lessened and the monotonous, metronomic clicking of a rolling pencil that had fallen off the chart-table during the night had become irritatingly audible. Neither Two-tooth nor I had felt like sleep after I'd finished telling him what we'd let ourselves in for, and we'd spent the night dozing alternately at the chart-table. Now, he was preparing breakfast while I sat alone at the wheel. The click of the rolling pencil was as regular as that of a time-bomb, and I found myself listening to it and waiting for it to stop as I stared towards the invisible coastline that was five miles to starboard, morbidly picturing the uniform greyness of sea and sky riven by the searing, white-hot flash of a second sunrise as a change in temperature or a shift in Solnishko 1's weight caused the seed of destruction inside her to blossom into flame and atomic devastation. I wondered whether the men on the ship I could now see clearly outlined on the radar were thinking the same thing.

Schuyler came springily up on to the bridge after he'd had his breakfast. He was freshly shaved and wearing a navy-blue roll-neck sweater and blue denim trousers and he looked as if he hadn't a care in the world. But I saw the quick glance he shot at the radar as if to reassure himself as he said, 'How far to go,

Tallon?' He peered out of the side window. 'Jeez, we could be off Cape Cod for all I can tell.'

'I wish we were.' I rubbed my unshaven chin. 'I don't know how far we'll have to go. As far as the bearing on the chart's concerned, we've already passed it. But we can't get ashore there. So we're going a couple of miles up the coast to an anchorage that some fisherman told Two-tooth about once. If we can't find it we'll have to think again. This is a hell of a place for getting ashore.' I looked across at him. 'Have you had a look at Zaghrali?'

'How could I? You've got the key. I haven't heard anything from in there.' He shrugged. 'To tell the truth, I'd forgotten about him.'

'Hey, Tallon!' Two-tooth's bearded head emerged from the saloon. He had a slice of thickly buttered toast in one hand and a mug of coffee in the other. 'What the hell d'you keep shifting my mascot around for?' he asked irritably. 'No wonder we're not getting much luck out of her, if you keep . . .'

'Lorelei?' I frowned. 'You know where I put her—on the settle. Come and take over, will you, and stop waving that coffee under my nose.' I had more important things on my mind than shop-window dummies.

'Well, she's bloody well gone walkabout, then. She not there now.'

'She'll be under the table,' I said impatiently. 'I didn't tie her in place. Are you going to take over or not?'

'And that's not all,' he said indistinctly, the toast between his teeth pirate fashion as he hoisted himself up the ladder. Finding his breakfast interfering with his diction, he took the toast out and pointed it at me dramatically. 'Me gun's gone, as well.'

'Gun?' Schuyler looked at him sharply. 'You had a gun?'

'.32 Scott & Webley, with a full clip.' Two-tooth sipped his steaming coffee, watching the American over the rim. 'It was under my pillow when I went to cook breakfast, and you were asleep in your bunk. When I got back it was gone. And so were you.'

Schuyler's eyes narrowed. 'I didn't take it. I didn't even know you . . .'

'I didn't say you took it,' said Two-tooth cleverly. 'But if you didn't, then this bloody ship's haunted, that's all I can say. And by a ghost that's carrying a gun now, at that.'

'I'm going to have a look at Zaghrali,' I said abruptly. It was a thing I should have done earlier. There seemed to be so many things to think of, all at the same time. 'You can start looking for this anchorage of yours, Two-tooth. The farther we go, the farther we'll have to walk back.'

He switched on the echo-sounder and we changed places. With rain blurring the big windows, the saloon looked cheerless and cold in the grey light as I crossed it with Schuyler behind me. Most of the books had slid off their shelves and the ashtrays had spilled a mess of cigarette-ends, used matches and ash on to the carpet. But, apart from one or two other small articles, they were the only things out of place. Lorelei hadn't just toppled off the settle. She'd vanished completely.

Schuyler said, testing the door that led out on deck, 'Could it have fallen through here when the ship rolled? The door could have slammed shut afterwards.'

'Having slammed open first? I locked those doors, remember. Anyway, what does it matter?' I made for the galley. Zaghrali could be seriously ill, and I'd done nothing for him at all.

'It could matter a hell of a lot,' he snapped. When I turned, I saw the strain showing through the cracked façade of disciplined austerity in his face. 'Why did you bring it down here anyway? It was up on the bridge when I came on board.'

'That blasted girl wanted it moved,' I said liverishly. I felt on edge, too, but I was hungry and tired as well. And it seemed a long time since I'd had simple, uncomplicated things like life sentences to worry about. 'She seemed to think it had some sort of Freudian significance. I suppose she could have gone a stage further and slung it over the side.' I looked out at the grey, heaving sea. 'Or perhaps it was because she mistook it for somebody hiding on the bridge when she came aboard. I don't know. There's something funny about her that . . .'

He grabbed my arm. 'Somebody on the bridge? Why didn't you tell me?'

'There wasn't anybody,' I said wearily. 'For Pete's sake,

you're not going to search the ship again, are you?' I stared at him. 'What's so important about Lorelei, Schuyler?'

'Nothing, I guess.' He let go my arm. 'I just had a hunch, that's all. Maybe the girl thought you had the doll bugged. Microphones in the ears, cine camera behind the eyes . . .'

'To be brutally frank with you,' I said sarcastically, 'we never even fitted her out with a pair of panties. Two-tooth was always too shy to go into a shop and ask.'

He gave me a long, level stare. 'O.K., wise guy,' he said bleakly. 'Let's look in on Zaghrali. I'm beginning to realise how the Secretary-General of the UN feels, dealing with you lot.'

The galley was fragrant with the aroma of bacon and coffee as we went through it, and I thought wryly how illogical it was to feel ravenous when we were less than ten miles from the ground zero of a possible nuclear explosion. But I couldn't eat until I quieted my conscience about the Egyptian. I fitted the key into the white-painted door of the fo'c'sle and opened it.

Zaghrali was out of his bunk. He was sitting on the deck, wedged comfortably in the far corner by the door that led off to the crew's toilet. He watched me with his head cocked quizzically to one side and his mouth open, grinning at my surprised reaction to his eccentric attitude. The fo'c'sle was lit by a queer, underwater twilight that darkened as *Lorelei*'s bows bit into the sea with a roar and the portholes were obscured with spray. I switched on the light and saw that the Egyptian was still wearing his pale-blue singlet and gaudy pyjama pants. It was icy cold, but that didn't seem to worry him.

Nothing else was going to worry him any more.

Schuyler pushed past me with an oath and went down on one knee beside the body. He put his hand on the stiff, outflung arm and the impression his fingers made on the dead, waxy flesh remained there after he'd taken his hand away. 'Stone cold,' he said quietly. The sea beat on the hull like a drum and he raised his voice. 'He's been dead for hours.'

'It's like a refrigerator in here.' I remembered self-accusingly how Zaghrali had always hated the cold. I looked down at him, at the neck that looked, with the black hairs bristling out of the yellow skin, like that of a plucked chicken. What I'd thought was a grin was a mouth drawn back in a rictus under the gigolo moustache, and the eyes that had seemed to be watching me were blind and bloodshot and already filmed with death. He hadn't wanted to die, he'd said. He'd fought and struggled and pleaded with me, but he'd died just the same, terrified and alone, here in this noisy, pitching ice-box. And I'd left him to it. I picked up a blanket from the bunk. 'What happened to him?' I asked harshly. 'Was he got at?'

Schuyler looked up at me, an odd expression on his face. 'Why? Should he have been?'

'He was hit over the head. Somebody might have come back to finish the job off.'

He raised an eyebrow. 'That,' he said deliberately, 'would be kinda awkward for you, wouldn't it? Unless there's another key to this door.' He watched me for a moment, then he turned back to the body again, examining it swiftly and professionally.

'There's no other key,' I said steadily, 'but locks have been known to be picked before now.'

'Oh, sure. You go to murder a guy and stand fooling around with a hat-pin while the victim yells his head off. And, having got away with that, you waste more time locking the door behind you.' He stood up. 'But my guess is that he just died, unless he was poisoned. Stroke of some kind, heart attack or just plain fright—they'll find out when they cut him open. There isn't a mark on him, you can see that.' He dropped the blanket over the pathetic puppet that had been Zaghrali and turned to me. 'And it would be soon after we left him. There wasn't a thing we could have done for him.' He gripped my arm. 'Not a thing. I know what you're thinking, pal, but you've got nothing to reproach yourself with. Now, come on, snap out of it. We've got to concern ourselves with the living, not the dead. We've got to get Mikhailev ashore, and that comes before anything else.'

When we got back to the bridge the coastline lay spread out under the lowering sky to starboard, a sweeping stretch of rocky beach thunderous with surf, and behind it the bruise-coloured line of the bush backed by rolling, mist-shrouded hills. Low cloud trailed ectoplasmic fingers over the bleached, gesturing branches of dead eucalypts as I studied the shoreline through the binoculars, and the surf boomed like muffled drums, audible above the steady beat of our diesels as Two-tooth felt his way in, guided by the echo-sounder. Inland, I knew, there were mountains, the Junction, de Witt and Wilmot Ranges, that would, on a sunny day, have given a wild, remote beauty to this featureless, forbidding landscape. But now, under the grey sky and with the black, streaming rocks rearing out of the sea like guardian monsters, it looked coldly, implacably hostile and as lonely as Mars.

I picked up the bridge telephone and told the girl to bring her brother to the bridge. There was no point in trying to hide him any longer. Then I switched off the radar, noting that the other ship was now less than five miles out, and closing fast. To Two-tooth I said, 'I hope you know what you're doing. Was that pal of yours relying on his memory or his imagination when he told you there was an anchorage here?' The shoreline stretched away to the north without a sign of a break, and I knew that for every rock I could see there were ten I couldn't. Even a Bondi surf-boat couldn't have got ashore here in one piece.

'She'll be right,' he said cheerfully. 'See those hills?' He jerked his head to where, a couple of points to starboard, the bush had bulged out to obliterate the beach and form a promontory, rising at the same time in two small hillocks, crowned with wind-torn tea-trees, that looked like the twin humps of a Bactrian camel. 'It's in there. We go between them into five fathoms. Or,' he added thoughtfully, 'so he said.'

But the entrance to the tiny concealed inlet was there. It was twenty yards across and at right angles to the line of the coast, buttressed on either side with algae-covered rocks that appeared and disappeared rhythmically in and out of the boiling water as the sea beat at them. I didn't like the look of it at all. To put a boat with a fifteen-foot beam through a sixty-foot gap sounds easy, but with an on-shore wind and pounding surf and the sea sluicing in and out of the channel like a mill-race it was going to take split-second timing to make the ninety-degree turn that would get us into the entrance. We nosed in cautiously, the echo-sounder useless at this depth and Two-tooth using his engines shrewdly to fight the forces that were trying to drag us on to the beach.

Then, with appalling suddenness, he lost the fight. The sea took us, and to my horror I found myself studying the algae at a range of a couple of feet as the wind and surf grabbed at the yacht as if she were a paper boat and pushed her crabwise into the mouth of the channel and almost up the hill as well. Two-tooth cursed luridly as he spun the wheel and shoved the throttles wide open simultaneously, and for a moment I closed my eyes, waiting for the propeller blades, with six hundred horse-power behind them, to mash into the solid rock. But the sea tore at us again, this time to our advantage, so that we were sucked into the channel like a matchstick going down a plug-hole and on into the choppy waters of the small natural harbour.

It was shaped like the half-open claw of a crab, about a hundred yards across at its widest point and a cable or so in length. The seaward pincer was a rocky peninsula that rose fifty feet, dotted with thin scrub and terminating in one of the hillocks we'd seen. Above it, the sky to the west was clearing rapidly to a clear, rain-washed blue. The landward side was a low-lying tangle of dense undergrowth that merged into rain-forest farther inland, and the anchorage shoaled rapidly towards the northern end where there was a narrow strip of exposed mud and rock. We anchored in six fathoms and switched off the engines. The sea boomed outside in the silence as I said to Mikhailev, 'Well, we've brought you here. What happens now?'

Twelve

THAT was the first thing you noticed—the silence. The brooding, vaguely menacing silence of an old, empty house. In the jungles of Perak and Johore where I'd served during the Emergency there had never been any absence of noise. Even in the heat of the day there had been the endless shrilling of the cicadas, the chatter of a yellow-hammer, the occasional heart-stopping scream of a hornbill. Twenty-four hours a day there had been abundant evidence of teeming animal life. But here there was nothing. Only the eternal roar and suck of the surf and the dry susurration of the wind in the undergrowth, as if the only life in this desolate place came from the sea. The land was silent and empty, and the ghosts of long-dead aborigines watched us from the barricade of vegetation that lined the inlet. If Solnishko 1 blew up, I thought sombrely, this would be as good a place as any for the end of the world to begin.

Mikhailev's voice seemed unnaturally loud when he said, answering my question, 'First we locate the wreck. We take the . . .'

'Like hell we do,' Two-tooth grunted. He looked up at me from his seat. 'Have you had any breakfast?'

'No.' The thought of Zaghrali lying silent under our feet had taken away my appetite. 'You know I never eat until . . .'

'Yeah. But today's going to be different. There's plenty of stuff on the hotplate, so before we go looking for this Solnishko 1 you're going to get some of it inside you.' He looked at the Russian and his sister. 'All three of you. And while you're doing that, Schuyler and me'll get some of your equipment ashore.'

Mikhailev had shot a suspicious look at me at the mention of the space-vehicle. I said, watching his hard, closed face, 'Let's clear the air a little. We all know about Solnishko 1, Mikhailev, and you're in no danger from any of us. We're all as anxious as you are to get started. But Two-tooth's right. We know it's somewhere to the south of us and about a mile inland, and that's all. We've got to eat some time, and it'll be quicker to do it now than to stop later on. Then I suggest we work our way south along the beach to the bearing Two-tooth plotted and see what sort of country we end up in.'

'What about Gyppo?' Two-tooth cocked an eye at me. 'Is he still crook? I was thinking that maybe Miss Mackail could stay and look after him. That would save her . . .'

'He won't need any looking after.' I turned to go below, leaving them shocked into silence as I said heavily, 'He died in the night. Schuyler, will you give Two-tooth a hand with the dinghy?'

We ran into difficulties straight away. My plan of travelling along the beach had to be abandoned before it had even begun, since it was impossible to reach it from the top end of the inlet. The undergrowth that came down to the water concealed the clinging, jet-black mud of a swamp that came up to our knees. The sun had come out and in the steamy warmth we found ourselves soaked in sweat before we'd covered ten yards. I said, after we'd struggled on for a few minutes, trying to follow the curve of the inlet, 'We'll never get anywhere like this. We'll have to strike inland after all and try to get to higher ground.' I'd been abysmally wrong about the absence of life here, too. Bush-flies the size of wasps droned and buzzed round my head, crawling nauseatingly over my eyes and mouth the minute I stopped flapping them away. A leech, plum-coloured and an inch and a half long, looped its way up Two-tooth's mud-spattered trouser leg out of the ooze, and when I struck at a sudden sting on my right cheek, the remains of a mosquito lay on my palm in a smear of blood. 'If we can get high enough we might even be able to see Solnishko 1.'

Two-tooth, immediately behind me, flicked the exploring *Philaemon pungens* off his leg into the mud and tilted back the Australian bush-hat he was wearing. 'Yeah, I reckon you're right.' He tapped the breast pocket of his khaki shirt. 'Matter of fact, I made a rough estimate of its position while you were eating. That'll give us something to go on. Of course,' he added accusingly, 'if you hadn't spent so long with your nose in the trough we'd have got a lot farther by now.'

'And if you hadn't eaten every blasted thing in sight we wouldn't have had to waste time cooking our own. But never mind that. Get the compass out and see if you can lay off a course.'

'Just wait a bloody minute,' he said indignantly. 'I left four fried eggs, a pot of coffee and about half a pound of the ham I got from that bloke on the Danish ship last . . .'

I wiped sweat off my forehead with the back of the hand that wasn't gripping the canvas bag of tools. 'There was one egg,' I said, staring at him, 'and a rasher or two of ham. So somebody . . .'

'Aw, for crying out loud,' said Schuyler violently from the other side of Two-tooth. 'Who the hell cares if you had sukiyaki with raspberry jam?' He peeled off his navy-blue sweater and threw it over his shoulder. 'We've got to fix this goddam bomb, and fix it fast. It's going to be rough going, and we got no time to fool around with this who's-been-eating-my-porridge routine.'

'You're right,' I said quietly. 'Otherwise I'd go back to the yacht. To find out who ate the rest of that food.'

The swamp fell away as the ground rose. We pushed and hacked our way uphill through a tough, unyielding mass of interlacing undergrowth and tea-trees that seemed to grow thicker and taller as we advanced in single file with Two-tooth taking the lead, followed by Mikhailev, then the girl, Schuyler and me. The branches pushed aside by the American lashed back at me as he ploughed through them, his sweat-soaked blue shirt the only visible sign of the rest of the party, while the sun rose in the invisible sky above us and the whip-like twigs clutched greedily at our clothes and at every projection of the equipment we carried. It must have taken us an hour to cover the first hundred yards. Then, without any warning or thinning-out, the bush ended. There was a blasphemous shout from Two-tooth somewhere in front, then I burst out behind

Schuyler into hot sunlight, blue sky and what looked, at first sight, like a slice of Africa.

We were up to the shoulders in tufted, dark-green clumps of rapier-bladed sedge that grew in clusters with barely room to squeeze between them, a maze of huge plants like giant pine-apples that thrust drumstick-like inflorescences skywards and seemed to stretch to where the blue-hazed mountains shimmered in the distance. The size of the plants, and the way they stood separately out of the ground, gave the nightmarish impression that we had blundered into a conclave of some mobile, science-fiction vegetables that had gathered together in thousands, only to freeze into watchful stillness at our approach.

Mikhailev said, watching Two-tooth take the folding prismatic compass out of his shirt, 'We will not need that.' A two-inch slash dripped blood down his right cheek and he dabbed at it with the handkerchief in his left hand. In his right he was holding what looked like a transistorised radio receiver, a small metal case the size of a cigarette packet. Above the hum of the insects around us I became aware of an intermittent, metallic clicking, like that of a deathwatch beetle. 'This is a Geiger-Mueller counter,' he said. What you can hear is the radiation emitted by Solnishko 1.'

'Radiation?' I looked at him sharply. That was a detail I hadn't even thought about.

'But quite harmless,' the girl said placidly. She was wearing a jungle-green Aertex shirt with slacks tucked into knee-high boots. Her blonde hair was tied in a knot at the nape of her neck and she looked the least fatigued of the lot of us. 'A little more than we normally receive from the sun, perhaps, but much less than a uranium prospector would have to contend with.'

'No wonder this thing's going round like a roulette wheel, though.' Two-tooth snapped the compass shut and put it away. 'So we use that counter instead, do we? The closer we get, the faster it clicks.'

'Yes.' Mikhailev looked round at us as he hung the small box round his neck on a lanyard. 'But if the count becomes dangerous I go on alone. There is no need for us all . . .'

123

'O.K.,' said Schuyler impatiently. 'So what are we waiting for?' He hefted the gas cylinder for the portable oxy-acetylene outfit on to his shoulder, and at that moment Barbara Mackail whipped out her tiny pistol, levelled it at him, and fired.

There was no time for me to do anything about it, even if I'd been able to. I stood frozen as the shot cracked out, taken completely by surprise at the suddenness of the girl's action. And the thin, whip-like explosion was still hanging in the air when she said calmly to the American, 'I'm sorry if I startled you. But it would have struck in another moment. They get very bad-tempered at this time of the year.'

Schuyler turned, his face expressionless with shock. Still writhing in contorted coils between two of the clumps of button-grass lay a six-foot tiger snake, an evil, blackish-brown fathom of death. One of the eyes was missing from the squat, diamond-shaped head. I heard Schuyler draw a deep breath as he said, 'Thanks. That was quite a shot.'

It was, too. Anybody who could blow the eye out of a snake with a snap-shot from a gun that size certainly wasn't suffering from the tension that was affecting the rest of us. I wondered again at the girl's almost bored air of detachment as she said, 'At six feet? I could hardly miss.' She shrugged. 'It's rather warm standing here. Shall we get on?'

We wound our way laboriously among the clumps of shoulder-high plants, our ears tuned to the faint clicking of Mikhailev's Geiger counter which seemed, to my overwrought imagination, to be getting louder and more rapid with every step we took. It was impossible to follow a straight course through that maze of vegetation, and our winding, sinuous track just about doubled the distance we had to cover. The morning wore on and the sun climbed the sky, making me feel more and more like an ant that had got lost among the Brussels sprouts under an electric grill. But at last the ground began to tilt uphill, the button-grass giving way to scrubby growths of wattle and high, tangled masses of wire-grass. I paused to shift the knobbly bag of tools from one aching shoulder to the other and, as I moved my head, something metallic flashed briefly in the sun away to my left on the opposite slope of the valley into which we were climbing.

We had found Solnishko 1. When I unslung my binoculars I could see the metal panel, stripped of its paint as if by a blowtorch, wedged among the branches a quarter of a mile away. And between us and the space-craft, on the other side of the valley, was a grey-green wall of twisted, interlocking tree-trunks that not even a cat could have got through. We had come up against the horizontal—the top-heavy trees, peculiar to Tasmania, that I'd told Schuyler about. They covered the opposite slope, forming a living mat of tightly intertwined and utterly impenetrable forest, forty feet high. And Solnishko 1 was somewhere inside it, invisible, with only two or three jagged fragments of gleaming metal jammed in the tree-tops to mark her position. 'She isn't very far inside that lot,' I said. 'But we're going to have to climb over the top to get to her.' I lowered the glasses. 'They could have picked a better spot to set her down.'

Two-tooth lumbered downhill to where a creek, swollen with the rains of the previous night, gurgled at the bottom of the valley. 'If they'd put her down anywhere else,' he said grimly, 'she might have blown up on impact.' He splashed through the knee-deep water, sending up sheets of spray that soaked me to the waist. 'As it is, the horizontal's cushioned her landing, see? Like dropping her on to a trampoline, except that she didn't bounce back. No wonder they don't know where she is. Even an organised air search would never pick her out if the branches have closed over the top of her.' He zig-zagged in front of me up the slope to where the wall of slim tree-trunks, lashed together with wire-grass and bauera, stretched across our front like a natural boma. A pair of white cockatoos flapped, shrieking, out of the wattle under which he dropped his loaded kitbag. He looked up at the tangled mass of twigs and branches as we stacked the oxy-acetylene unit, the tools, the first-aid kit and the rest of the equipment in the shade. 'Who's going first? The sooner we get this over, the better.'

'I am going first. Alone.' The Geiger counter clucked gently as Mikhailev added it to the pile. 'Alone,' he repeated curtly, as Schuyler moved forward. 'It is vital that we act with the utmost caution. Solnishko 1 is equipped with a self-demolition system. Enough conventional high explosive to destroy her completely. Normally, with the reactor under control, that would not result in a nuclear explosion. But in her present state it would mean just that. If the heat-containing element is destroyed, the contents of the reactor will all fuse simultaneously, with an instantaneous release of energy on an unparalleled scale.' He looked at me, his face grey with strain and fatigue. 'My brother must see me first. Otherwise, if they think their ship is about to fall into the hands of the West . . .'

'They'll blow half of Tasmania off the map.' And, even if the atomic explosion didn't take place, we were now close enough to the space-craft to be blasted out of existence by the demolition charge. I sincerely hoped Mikhailev's brother had a good memory for faces. 'Right,' I said, suppressing an inclination to speak in a whisper. 'But take it slowly. Some of those branches will be dry and brittle, and you'll have a forty-foot drop underneath you even if you can't see it.'

'And if you do happen to fall,' said Two-tooth, 'try to break your neck. Because we'd never be able to get you out again if you dropped into that lot.'

We watched him begin his climb up the slippery, sagging trunks of the horizontal, the mud-caked sneakers he was wearing sliding as he struggled for a foothold on the smooth, dun-coloured bark. The sweat on my palms as I clenched my fists, unconsciously helping him grip the branches as he went, wasn't due to the heat. When I glanced across at Schuyler I could see that the All-American Boy look had rubbed off his face, leaving it as lined and set with anxiety as mine probably was. Two-tooth's face I couldn't see. He was sitting in the shade of the wattle with his digger hat over his eyes. Proximity to high explosive was no novelty to him, but I was sure he wasn't as sleepy as he looked. And, for the first time, I detected a tremor in the girl's voice when she said to me, 'Give me a cigarette, will you?' Her face was pale beneath the tan, and it was the first time I'd known she smoked.

I nodded, glad of something to do to break the tension. Nicolai had now disappeared over the top. Branches rustled and cracked from above in the silence as I fumbled for my lighter. The girl put the cigarette between her lips. Her eyes went to Schuyler as he swore softly under his breath, and I wondered again what it was that made them so vividly green. Greener, even, than her brother's. Then, suddenly, it hit me.

As she leaned forward into the flame, the short sleeve of her jungle-green shirt fell back to expose the small red puncture on the inside of her left forearm. She was drugged. Drugged, literally, to the eyeballs, since they had almost no pupil at all. As close as this, I could see the tiny lines that ran round her eyes and mouth, lines that had been concealed before by make-up, carefully applied. But here, in the hot glare of the midday sun, with the make-up smudged with sweat, it was as if I was seeing her face for the first time. It was like looking at a beautiful ceramic mask whose glazing had developed the myriad, tiny cracks of age. This explained her unnatural calm, her absence of emotion in the face of the danger that threatened us, her rock-steady hand when she'd shot the snake. But now the effect of whatever drug she took was beginning to wear off. I kept my face carefully blank as I put my lighter away. What she did was her own business, but I hoped she wasn't going to start going to pieces now. The minutes ticked away on my watch and we stood in the hot silence without a word and almost without moving. I was wondering how we were going to get the equipment we'd brought up to Solnishko 1, whether the crew were alive, whether Mikhailev would be able to deal with the reactor. And whether all these problems would disappear in a white-hot flash that would be the last thing I would ever see. So when Mikhailev's voice floated down to us I nearly jumped out of my skin. 'Tallon!' he shouted. 'Bring me a hammer and a cold chisel!'

Why not a pneumatic drill and a charge of gelignite? I thought wildly as I got the tools out of the bag. If he was going to smash his way in he might as well do it in style. Schuyler said grittily, 'What the hell's he playing at up there?' He watched me stuff the hammer into one trouser pocket and the chisel into the other. Then, as I took a grip of the branches, he came and stood beside me. 'I'm coming up with you,' he said quietly. 'This could be a trick to get you up there on your own. And don't get between me and him while we're up there, Tallon. If he manages to fix this thing he won't let us get back to the yacht alive.'

I looked at him sharply as he began climbing, his face wary and set. I couldn't believe Mikhailev would kill us. On the other hand, as Schuyler had said, he could hardly allow us to broadcast this story to the world. I glanced back at the girl. She had made no attempt to follow us. She stood smoking her cigarette jerkily, as a girl does when she's not used to it, but it didn't seem to be doing her much good. I could see her hands trembling from where I stood—and I could also see Two-tooth watching her carefully from under the brim of his hat.

Going up was like scrambling up rubber tubing that had been coated with butter. The slim, smooth trunks gave under my weight, swaying wildly as I clambered up, my feet kicking and sliding as I fought for a purchase. My hands were slippery with sweat and protruding branches dug painfully into my head as I bored up into them. But at last we were on top of the stuff. Holding on to twigs that threatened to snap off as I gripped them, I stepped cautiously from one resilient, inch-thick stem to the next, testing each one before I put my weight on it. Something metallic gleamed through the forest of twigs in front of me. Sweating, I paused, my right knee wedged in a fork, holding on with my left hand as I parted a tangle of saw-edged, dark-green leaves with my right and got my first glimpse of Solnishko 1.

Thirteen

I WAS level with the top of what looked, at first sight, rather like the conning-tower of a submarine, a tall cylinder of dull grey metal ten feet in diameter, pierced with observation ports, and with the initials CCCP painted round it in scorched white lettering three feet high. Below that were the Cyrillic symbols that, I supposed, stood for Solnishko 1. But instead of protruding from the boat-shaped hull of a submarine the conning-tower rose up from a smoothly curved circular base twenty feet across that rested in the depression it had made in the horizontal like a huge grey elephant on a badly sprung bed. Four tubes, a foot or so in diameter, ran in opposing pairs from half-way up the central tower to the circumference of the base, one of them supporting the wreckage of a solar panel. The whole ship was scarred and chipped—mute evidence of the beating it had taken out in the depths of space—and one of the strut-like tubes was twisted out of alignment. A snarled skein of ropes ran from the top of the ship to a mass of ripped yellow silk— the torn remains of the huge parachutes that had brought her down. Lying there in its nest of leafy branches under the corn-flower-blue sky and placidly drifting clouds that I could glimpse overhead through the leaves, its dark-grey bulk was as incongruously sinister as a tank in ambush behind a hawthorn hedge. It looked out of its element and as full of menace as an alien from another world.

Mikhailev was crouched down by the rim of the base twenty feet below us in the angle formed by the sharply inclined platform of branches and the curved hull of the ship. Schuyler said, his voice slightly off-key, 'What's he doing, Tallon?' The Russian was perfectly immobile, staring fixedly at the side of the space-craft. 'Jeez, I can almost hear this thing ticking.' He stared down at the crouching, motionless Russian. 'What the hell's the matter with him?' He raised his voice. 'Hey, Mikhailev! You O.K.?' As I eased myself down I could see that the hand with which Schuyler was holding on to a branch was trembling enough to make the leaves shiver gently. I stopped just above the Russian, feeling like a spider on a web as I hung on the tightly meshed trellis, conscious of a vaguely familiar smell that eluded me for the moment. Then I saw what the Russian was staring at, and why he hadn't looked up at our approach.

There was a narrow slit in the smooth curvature of the hull. It ran down the left-hand side of a slightly recessed, door-sized panel that had a cracked, discoloured porthole set in it. What I was looking at was a sliding hatchway, partly open. And protruding from the gap was a blackened twig with five stumpy, charred branches. It seemed to be gesturing silently and imploringly to us out of the blackness of the partly open air-lock. It was a second or so before I realised that what I was looking at was the calcined, shrivelled remains of a human hand. I recognised what the smell was, too. It was the smell you get at a barbecue when a lump of steak falls into the fire.

I felt my mouth go bitter and acid with revulsion. But from the tone of Mikhailev's voice nobody would have guessed that this disgusting, twisted thing might once have belonged to his brother. He turned to look at us. 'One of them tried to get out after they were struck,' he said neutrally. 'To carry out emergency repairs, perhaps.' He touched the flat, oxydised sliver of metal that was lodged like a wedge in the recessed slot into which the door slid. 'This jammed the hatch after it had begun to open. So it was impossible for him to operate the inner door, or for anybody else to do so. He was irretrievably trapped —cut off for ever from the rest of the crew, knowing what was going to happen to him when they re-entered the earth's atmosphere.' I wondered if Mikhailev was remembering how he, too, had been isolated from his fellow men in the air-lock of the submarine. It would be a strange freak of fate if his brother had done the same thing. He said, 'They had to re-enter sooner or later, of course. And when they did he had nothing to protect him from the heat while the door was ajar. He was roasted alive, still trying to free that deadly fragment of metal even while it was burning his fingers off.' He paused. 'There is no sign of life from inside.' He held out a hand without looking at me. 'The chisel, if you please, Tallon.'

I watched him insert the blade under the jagged slab that had once been part of a Russian or American rocket-casing, and that had been circling the earth, as potentially dangerous as a Teller mine, until Solnishko 1 had struck it. He exerted leverage against the rim of the hatchway to prise the obstruction loose. Nothing happened. He stepped up the pressure, throwing all his weight on the chisel until the veins stood out on his thick wrists. Then, suddenly, the chisel slipped. Mikhailev lurched forward as the blade scraped jarringly across the hull, and his right shoulder hit the space-craft with a force that made it shudder.

'For God's sake!' Schuyler's voice was rough with fear. 'This thing's only held off the ground by a few twigs, d'you realise that? Another push like that'll send it clean through. And if that doesn't set it off . . .' He broke off with a gasp of sheer horror. As Mikhailev leaned back, the burnt remains of the hand hooked on to the waistband of his trousers, as if trying to pull him into the air-lock. Then, as the Russian recoiled, it broke off at the wrist with a tiny, dry snapping noise. It hung at his waist for a moment, then it disappeared into the foliage below.

'Give me the hammer.' The Russian's face was as grey as the metal hull that faced us as he wrapped a handkerchief round the head of the chisel to act as a shock-absorber. Then, holding the blade in place with his left hand, he tapped gently and steadily at the top and bottom edges of the metal wedge until it started to move a fraction of an inch at each blow. I hung on to the horizontal without noticing how my arms were aching. My eyes were glued to the bulbous shell of the space-ship, wondering if it was my imagination that made me think it was beginning to radiate a gentle warmth. My heart leapt into my gullet when the chisel skidded again. But this time Mikhailev recovered before he slipped, while the dulled sliver of metal dropped free, to clink against the hull before it fell out of sight among the leaves. And, as it dropped, the outer door of the air-lock slid open, ponderously, and with a faint whirr from an electric motor somewhere within the hull.

The stench that came out was like nothing I'd ever experienced before. Gagging, I turned my head away to avoid the awful smell of incinerated meat, burnt paint, and charred insulating material that gushed out in an acrid, sickening wave of hot air. The corpse of the astronaut, reduced to the size of a large monkey, lay contorted on the floor of a compartment as big as an average-sized lift, a dark, smoky cell whose metal walls were blistered with heat and studded with valves and switch-gear. The inner door showed as a hatchway the same size as the outer one, with a similar soot-encrusted observation port, but it was set in a vertical bulkhead instead of in the curve of the hull. The Russian stepped over the coaming of the outer hatchway, placing his feet carefully to avoid what lay on the floor. As he did so, the space-ship swayed alarmingly and there was a sharp crack from somewhere below as a branch yielded to its twenty-ton weight.

'It's going!' Schuyler said in a cracked whisper. He put out a hand, as if to ward off a blow. When the space-craft settled he swallowed to relieve the dryness in his throat. 'What the hell are you trying to do?' he snapped. 'Kill the lot of us?'

'I'm going inside.' Mikhailev was examining the array of handles, burnt-out switches and electrical harness on the wall of the air-lock. He turned and looked at us. 'I shall have to close the outer door first,' he said quietly.

I knew that. And I knew what he was thinking, too. In its present state nothing on board Solnishko 1 could be expected to function with any predictability. The outer door might close and refuse to open again. Or the opening of the inner door might release a blast of radioactivity into the air-lock. He looked up at the blue summer sky, barely visible through the canopy of leaves above us, his face showing nothing. Then he pulled down on a handle that looked as if it had once been painted red.

Again the electric motor whirred in the stillness and the outer door slid to, closing slowly like the eye of a dying lizard. The noise it made sounded laboured, and it closed more slowly than it had opened. I peered in through the cracked porthole. It was pitch-dark in there, and the only air was the stinking fume-laden miasma that had belched out to greet us. I listened to Schuyler's quick breathing, and to the seconds ticking away on my watch. What was Mikhailev thinking about in there? About the escape hatch of his submarine, perhaps, where, for him, all this had begun? By this time, surely, the inner door should have opened. The American said jerkily, 'God, I can't take much more of this.' He stared at the grey, curved hull. 'Come on, you bastard,' he whispered. 'Let's get it over one way or the other.'

I said, 'If he fixes it, what happens then?'

'If he doesn't shoot us first, I take him in. The girl too.'

'After he's outlived his usefulness,' I said flatly. To a normal, well-adjusted citizen it would seem to be the only thing to do with a Russian who had carried out a one-man invasion of Western territory. But after what he had gone through to do it, and what he was going through at this very moment, I just didn't want any part of it.

'Don't start needling me at a time like this, Tallon.' Schuyler tried to stare me down, failed, and looked back at the observation port. 'He'll be handed back to his own people, won't he? It's not as if we were going to have him shot.'

'Isn't it? What else d'you think the Russians'll do to him when they find out he's responsible for your lot getting hold of the plasma engine?'

'And do you think he's going to let us just walk away from here so we can tell the world about it? Aw, for Chrissake,' he burst out, 'I don't have to justify myself to a two-bit crook like you. Where the hell is the bastard, anyway?'

'Somebody call?' Two-tooth's voice came from above and behind us. He looked at Schuyler expressionlessly and spoke to me without taking his eyes off him. 'That girl's real crook, Tallon. She's going to pieces fast. How much longer's this going on?'

As if it had been waiting for him to give the word, the hatchway slid open again with a whine from the activating mechanism that had the reluctant, overworked note of a starter motor on a frosty morning. And, with an effect like that of a stage magician's cabinet, the air-lock now held three men instead of one. Two of them were crumpled on the floor, unmindful of what they were lying on. They were dressed in shining, silver-grey space-suits, laced up and fitting tightly at the neck and wrists. This, together with their shaven heads and the ghastly blue-green pallor of their faces, gave them an eerily other-world look. They put me in mind of a couple of Martians who'd been dead for some time. Nicolai Mikhailev stood between them, a small red-painted cylinder cradled in his arms —a cylinder that seemed very heavy for its size. He stared at us without speaking.

Schuyler said, his voice harsh in the silence, 'Well? You fixed it or not?'

'Yes.' When Mikhailev nodded, I felt a sudden wave of relief wash over me. I suddenly realised how tired my arm muscles were. But the danger from Solnishko 1 was over. There would be no nuclear explosion, no international incident, no . . . Then Mikhailev's green eyes met mine as they ranged over us. There was no relief in them. Only suspicion, watchfulness, and a grim determination. He said, 'I have stabilised the reactor. Or, rather, I have completed what they were doing when they were overcome by the fumes in there. And that must have been quite recently, since they are both alive.' He looked down, briefly, at the men at his feet. One of them, in spite of his space-suit and hairless head, bore a striking resemblance to Nicolai. He was a younger version of the craggy-faced, heavily built Russian. The other man had the thick body and square Chinese face of a Buryat Mongol. Mikhailev said, 'Will you help me with them? There is still something I have to do . . .'

'Forget it,' said Schuyler briskly. He leaned back against the branches and the big Colt came snaking out of his shirt. There was a click as the thumb safety came off and he said, 'You've done all I want. From now on I'm taking over.'

The Russian stared thoughtfully at him. 'So,' he said quietly, without surprise. He looked at me. 'I expected something of the sort, Tallon. I thought it was odd that anybody as short of money as you could afford to pay a crew-member you did not need.' His voice held no reproach—only a great weariness. 'He is an American agent, I suppose?'

134

'No less,' agreed Schuyler, grinning. Triumph lent his voice an unpleasant jeering quality. 'And this is your floor, bud. So come on out, and don't try shutting the elevator door in my face. I could blast you before you could blink.'

'Perhaps you could.' It didn't seem to worry the Russian. 'But it wouldn't do you any good, my friend.' He hefted the cylinder up and down in his arms. 'Do you know what this is?'

'A transistorised latrine-bucket, maybe. But who cares?' Schuyler flicked the gun-muzzle impatiently. 'Out, out. Don't waste my time. I got a ship waiting for me back there.'

Mikhailev ignored him. He stood with his feet apart, holding the cylinder to his barrel chest. 'It is very heavy,' he said gently, 'because it has a thick lead casing. And that is just as well, since it contains enough radioactive deuterium to fry the marrow in our bones. I am holding it so that, if I fall, the shield will detach itself from the flask inside. And then nothing on earth can save us all from the most terrible death man has devised.' He looked at us in turn, his broad Slav face like a mask. 'I myself have very little left to live for,' he said softly. 'My sister is, I know, a hopeless drug addict. That is one of the benefits she has received from your Western way of life. My brother is alive, but both he and I know what will happen to us if we return to the USSR and leave you with Solnishko 1. Unless we destroy it, we are men without a home, without a country, without a future. And rather than see the plasma engine fall into your hands I would die a thousand times over.' Suddenly his voice cracked like a pistol shot. 'Throw the gun at my feet or I remove the casing. Now!'

'You lousy commie bastard!' Schuyler was almost choking with rage, frustration and indecision. 'You're bluffing. If you think I'm . . .'

'Then all you have to do is shoot me.' The Russian stared at him implacably. 'But I warn you, your death will not be as quick as mine if you do. Your body cells will begin to disintegrate the instant you press that trigger. You will suffer a living death that will last for several . . .'

'All right!' Schuyler spat the words at him as he thumbed home the safety and tossed the Colt with a clang at Mikhailev's feet. I saw his fists clench as the Russian put the cylinder down carefully without taking his eyes off us for a second. He picked up the automatic. Schuyler said savagely, 'You'll never make it, Mikhailev. You can't watch the three of us all the time. You'll slip up somewhere along the line and then I'll . . .'

'If you interfere in any way,' said Mikhailev dispassionately, 'I will shoot all three of you without a moment's hesitation.' He screwed the top of the cylinder on to its base, the gun-muzzle watching us all the time like a third eye. 'Please believe that, all of you. It is my duty as a Soviet officer to destroy Solnishko 1, and nothing can be allowed to stand in my way.' He straightened up. 'You are going to carry these two men to the beach, and I will go with you. If your ship is really there, then you will arrange for my sister and these men to have medical attention. In the meantime I will have returned here, but that does not concern you.' He moved to the back of the air-lock, out of arm's length. 'We start now.'

The hideous colour of the astronauts' faces was already beginning to fade as we dragged them, one at a time, up the sloping platform of the horizontal with Mikhailev covering us every inch of the way. Then he crawled slowly after us, keeping well out of kicking distance. But I, for one, wasn't going to start anything. I knew he'd meant every word he'd said. Without anger and without pity, he would kill anybody who tried to stop him doing what he had to do. And in his place, I thought, I'd do exactly the same. I knew, too, that he wouldn't shoot us out of hand, as Schuyler had said he would. But his problems were going to start when it came to lowering the two heavy, feebly stirring men down the last forty feet from the tree-tops.

His sister was lying under the wattle where Two-tooth had been sitting. Her knees were doubled up under her as if she had stomach cramps, and she seemed in no condition to help. But when Mikhailev spoke to her crisply in Russian she came slowly to her feet, got out the nylon rope we'd brought, and came and stood below us. I was shocked by the change in her appearance. She looked ten years older, haggard and ill, and she moved as if she was walking in her sleep. And it was Schuyler her eyes were fixed on, not her brothers. She hardly gave the astronauts a second glance. I don't know what Mikhailev said to her, but it seemed to have the effect of concentrating all her attention on the American. She stared up at him with a horribly anticipatory look in her sick green eyes that made me think of a cat waiting for a particularly succulent mouse. Her hands were shaking so much that it took her five casts to get the rope up to us. That, together with the wild swaying of the slim, top-heavy trees, made the job of lowering the two men take a long time. It was back-breaking work, but Schuyler didn't seem to mind. I heard him humming to himself, and when I glanced at him I saw a sly grin on his hatchet face. It was when the two men were safely down that I saw what he was waiting for.

Mikhailev could hardly push past us and go down first. If he did, he ran the risk of being grabbed. Or else we could vanish among the branches like a trio of Cheshire cats while he was on his way down. If he descended last, he would have to turn his back on us while he did it. And to climb forty feet down a tangle of slippery, resilient branches and cover three men at the same time is possible only if you happen to be equipped with three arms and eyes in the back of your head. But the Russian had the situation well under control. He ordered me down first. I scrambled to the ground, glad to get my feet on something solid again, and Schuyler and Two-tooth followed me while Mikhailev kept the gun on us, his free arm hooked in the trees. Then he spoke to his sister again in Russian, a series of brief sentences in which the word 'Amerikanski' figured prominently. She nodded slowly, her eyes still fixed on Schuyler, and took out her tiny pistol. The snap of its folding trigger sounded very loud in the midday hush.

The way her hand shook frightened the wits out of me. The Sedgley wobbled so much that she was able to cover all three of us at the same time. And at a range of ten feet a .22 can be just as lethal as an elephant gun if the tiny pellet strikes in the right spot. She watched Schuyler with a hungry look in her eyes that told me she'd let him have it if he as much as breathed heavily. Mikhailev surveyed the scene from above. Then he tucked the Colt into his trousers and began swarming down swiftly, his back to us.

Schuyler said conversationally, 'I'll have the gun now, sweetheart.' He took a step towards the girl, his hand held out.

Fourteen

IT WAS like watching somebody jump over a cliff. I couldn't grab him, or shout to him to stand still because, with the girl's nerves already stretched like piano wires, any move on my part would only make the outcome more certain. You fool, I said silently to Schuyler, surely you can see she's just itching for the chance to put a bullet into you? Sweat broke out between my shoulder-blades, to drip clammily down my back as I watched her drug-deprived, strangely inhuman eyes narrow while the Sedgley steadied in her hand. In her present condition the girl might not be able to shoot the eye out of a snake, but she could hardly miss Schuyler now. He was standing within reach of the gun.

Mikhailev had stopped and turned his head at the sound of Schuyler's voice, but he was caught with his weight on his arms, with no chance of getting his gun out. He shouted urgently at his sister, and it didn't need any translation to know what it was he was telling her to do. 'Kill him!' sounds much the same in any language.

But without the slightest change of expression on her face she lowered the pistol, reversed it, and gave it to Schuyler. And the American turned, raised it to the full length of his arm, aimed carefully, and shot Mikhailev just below the right ear.

As if in a dream, I saw the jet of blood jump out of his neck, glittering scarlet in the sunlight as the gun cracked like a small firework. I saw the look of utter surprise on his face. Then his hands opened slackly and he fell twenty feet on to his back with a thump that I felt through the soles of my feet. He lay very still, and quite close to his brother. The branch he had

138

been holding swung backwards and forwards until that was still, too.

Then, with an effect that was entirely macabre in the perfection of its timing, the raucous snigger of a kookaburra broke out from behind the wall of horizontal in front of us. It rang out weirdly, a burst of evil, malicious cackling with overtones of insanity that went up the scale, increasing in volume as other birds joined in until it was a mad cacophony of laughter like that of a coven of demented witches, dying away sobbingly in the sunlit silence as Two-tooth and I went across to the sprawled body of the man who would never need our help, or that of anybody else, again. 'My God!' said Two-tooth in a whisper. It was as if he was trying to convince himself that it had really happened. 'He's dead, Tallon!' He looked at me, then across at the American, his eyes like stones. 'And you killed him. You bastard. You lousy, murdering . . .'

'That'll do,' snapped Schuyler. He came over and pulled his Colt from the dead man's waistband, watching us warily. 'You saw the way it was. It was him or us, you know that. He was only using us to carry these two for him. Then he'd have had to get rid of us . . .'

'I knew him better than that. He was doing his job, that's all. He wasn't a murderer. And if he had been,' I said savagely, 'that doesn't give you the right to kill him.' I looked at the Russian's still, craggy face. When you save a man's life you've got a stake in his future, no matter who he is or what he's like. He owes his existence to you. And there weren't many people in the world who owed me anything. 'By God, Schuyler,' I said coming to my feet so quickly that he recoiled a step, 'you'll answer to somebody for this, no matter how many medals they hang on you.' And he'd done it in front of the girl, too. He'd used her gun to shoot down her brother. It had all happened so quickly that I hadn't had time to think about that. I swung round.

Then I stiffened. She hadn't reacted in the slightest. She didn't even seem to be aware of her brother's corpse lying in front of her. With a chill shock, I realised that she just didn't care. She was in the half-world of the hardened addict, where the only thing in life that matters is the next fix. She was trembling violently and, when she saw me looking at her, she said, with a begging note in her voice that made me feel sick, 'Can we go now? I've got to have . . .'

'We're going back to the boat.' Schuyler didn't even look at her as he put her gun in the pocket of his trousers. He kept his eyes on us and said, 'You two bring the space-men. And don't get in my hair, see? I got my job to do, the same as your late friend. And, like he said, nothing else matters.' He flicked the Colt at us warningly. 'Nothing and nobody. Get me?'

'What about Mikhailev?' Two-tooth's voice was like coke going through a mincer. 'You can't leave him here.' Already the fat brown bush-flies were gathering in a hungry, droning cloud overhead, waiting impatiently for us to leave.

'He'll be attended to later.' Schuyler gestured impatiently with the automatic again. 'Right now I got folks waiting for me. So let's get going.'

We got the two men to their feet. With a little help at first, they were able to walk, but I don't think they had much idea of what was happening to them—not then. They trudged, robot-like in their silver-grey space-suits, after Two-tooth and me, with Schuyler following them, the gun still in his fist, and the girl trailing behind, muttering complainingly to herself. We went down the valley in single file and out into the bright-green button-grass under a sky as blue as deep water, with the lavender-coloured hills shimmering in the hot, hazy distance behind us, and the only sound the dynamo hum of the insects and the swish of our feet in the grass. It was a good day for what should have been a victory march. We, and several thousand other people, had narrowly escaped a horrible death. We would live, and the plasma engine would no longer give the USSR superiority in the space-race. Two of the three astronauts had been rescued, and Schuyler would get whatever it is they give Secret Service men who bring off a coup of this sort. We, no doubt, would qualify for a handout for our part in the operation, if only to make us keep our mouths shut, and Barbara would get her charter fee back to buy LSD, or whatever it was she got switched-on with. In fact, everybody would come out on the credit side. Except Mikhailev, of course, and nobody was likely to worry much about him.

When we reached the belt of bush that masked the coast, Schuyler came up from the back of the column and took the lead. I followed him downhill and into the trees, so preoccupied with my bitter thoughts as I squelched through the black mud that I failed to notice where we were heading. It was only when I crashed out of a stand of tea-trees into the brilliant afternoon sunlight of the open beach that I realised we had missed the inlet altogether. The Indian Ocean stretched sparkling blue and limitless in front of me, foaming into dazzling white surf on the yellow sand, and half a mile out a scruffy-looking tramp steamer of about two thousand tons was riding at anchor. But Schuyler, after one brief glance, didn't take much notice of the ship. Nor did he seem very concerned that it wasn't the American anti-submarine frigate he'd been expecting. He was studying the helicopter that was parked not fifty yards away, its tandem four-bladed rotors swinging idly in the cool westerly breeze that came off the sea.

It was a big job, painted matt black all over, with no identification letters or markings whatever. Judging from the two men who were standing beside it watching us, it was twenty feet high and eighty or so in length, with a big, square-section fuselage and a high pylon at the tail that carried the rear rotor and the dihedral tailplane with a square, vertical fin at each tip. It stood massively on four pontoons, a pair just aft of the cockpit and the other pair at the tail. These were mounted on angled tubular-steel struts that protruded ten feet out from the fuselage like the legs of some enormous grasshopper that was ready to leap into the air at any moment. It reminded me of a photograph I'd seen in a magazine recently—a picture of a helicopter being used as a flying crane on a dam the Egyptians were building. This one was of the same type. It was a Yakovlev 24-A. Schuyler, I thought wryly, hadn't been so smart after all.

The chunky Russian astronaut who broke out of the bush behind Two-tooth recognised the helicopter, too. I heard a shout and I swung round to see him break into a clumsy run towards it, a grin of relief on his sweat-glistening Mongol face. He shouted again in Russian, gesticulating to the two waiting, motionless men as he ran. Schuyler didn't attempt to stop him. He said sharply to me as the girl stumbled out of the trees, 'Where's the other one?'

'The other . . .?' It dawned on me that Igor Mikhailev should have been in front of the girl.

'He'll be back,' said Two-tooth grimly, 'as soon as he knows his pals have arrived. What the hell did you want to bring us out here for? If we'd gone back to the yacht . . .'

'They're not his pals, you moron,' said Schuyler contemptuously.

'You mean—they're your people?' I tried to work it out as I watched the silver-grey figure scuttle through the soft, powdery sand. Neither of the two men by the helicopter had moved. One of them was a Negro in a gaudy Hawaiian shirt and khaki slacks. The other, a white, was wearing a baseball cap, blue denim overalls and about twenty-four stone of fat. They didn't look like Russians. But why should the Americans use a Soviet chopper when they'd plenty of their own?

The squat Mongol astronaut had stopped just short of them, realising something had gone wrong with the programme. He said something and gestured angrily at the Yakovlev. The two men moved forward silently and grabbed his arms. He evidently didn't like that. He lashed out sideways with his laced, calf-length boot and got the white man squarely in the crutch. Fatty didn't seem to like that, either. I heard his grunt of agony from where I was standing. Then the Mongol ducked, smashed his bullet head into the Negro's face, turned, and made off at a fast shuffle for the shelter of the trees, leaving the Negro reeling with his hands to his face and the fat man down on his knees in an attitude of prayer. Two-tooth grunted appreciatively. 'Jeez, he put the boot in there all right. He's . . .'

His voice was lost in the heart-stopping crash of a .45 from immediately behind us, an explosion so close that I felt the hot breath of the discharge on the back of my neck. Instinctively, I ducked. As I recovered, I saw that the Russian had stopped running. He was standing as if in deep thought with his right hand raised. Then, abruptly, his knees folded and he collapsed like a grey rubber doll in a puff of loose sand. Schuyler said from behind me, 'Too bad. But I can't spend the afternoon chasing these guys round the countryside, can I?'

142

I turned slowly, but I didn't speak. It was Two-tooth who said, in a voice I hardly recognised, 'Why, you bloody murderer! Give me that gun!' He lurched forward. 'CIA or not, that's the last . . .'

I grabbed his arm. I was watching Schuyler's eyes, and they told me everything I wanted to know—everything I should have known right from the beginning. They were as inhumanly expressionless as a killer shark's, as empty as if he was looking at us through two pieces of blue glass. 'He isn't a CIA agent,' I said heavily, 'any more than you are. We've been hooked again, Two-tooth.'

Fifteen

THE cold, killer's eyes watched me remotely as Schuyler grinned—a sneering caricature of the friendly, schoolboy grin that had so annoyed me when I'd first met him. 'So you finally got around to it,' he said jeeringly. 'Shrewd thinking, for a Limey.' The Colt was settled dead in line with my breastbone. 'You know something? It took you so long, I was beginning to wonder whether you were playing me for a sucker, instead of it being the other way round. Hell, I never thought I'd meet up with a guy so dumb that he'd stand around while I got rid of somebody who was trying to tip him off about me, like you did last night.'

'You mean—you killed Zaghrali?' I felt dull-witted and stupid, and he knew it. The grin broadened as he watched me ask myself how you can kill a man behind a locked door without leaving a mark on him.

'Sure. The little rat was trying to fill you in about me when we picked him off the deck, remember? He was yelling like crazy, and I had to shut his big mouth, but fast, before he got through to you. I'd taken his head and shoulders, and I know enough karate to find the nerve in the neck that can paralyse a guy if you lean on it hard enough. So I leaned, just enough to put him out so he'd still be breathing when we got him into his bunk. It was dark in the saloon, and you didn't see a thing.' He chuckled. 'He got the rest of the treatment while you were checking there was nobody hiding in the shower. One chop with the side of the hand, and I'd bust his dirty little neck. He must have fallen to the deck during the night. And,' he said conversationally, as Two-tooth moved forward convulsively, 'one move out of your Piltdown pal and you die just a fraction

144

of a second before he does. So keep him on the lead, will
you?'

Two-tooth moved back reluctantly, his big hands opening
and shutting longingly. He looked at me, swallowed, and said,
'But you told me he had a letter, signed by the . . .'

'You think you got a monopoly of the forgery business? It
wasn't even a good one. But you were so goddam grateful I
wasn't a cop you'd have believed anything.' He sniggered. 'You
should have seen the way you ran when you saw me go into
Police Headquarters—to ask the way to the Tourist Bureau,
incidentally. It was your guilty conscience that got you into
this, Tallon.'

He was right. Conscience, I thought dully, not only makes
cowards. It makes for vulnerability as well. Anybody else
could have checked up on Schuyler in five minutes, but I'd
been too busy keeping away from the police to do that. A gull
screamed derisively from down the beach as I said, 'Who are
you working for?'

'Me. Just me.' Without taking his eyes off us he bawled at the
two men over by the helicopter, 'Hey, you guys! What is this,
a beach party? Ziegler! On your feet, you fat slob, and get that
egg-beater turning. And you, Eight-ball, put that stiff on board,
outa the way. Then get over here, but fast.' To me, he said,
'You might say I'm in the same line of business as yourself,
Tallon. The supply-and-demand racket. But while you deal
with dockside scum like Zaghrali, I trade in a big way. With
governments. Like, I'm the supermarket, see? You're the
barrow-boy. While you play around with a few lousy crates of
slush, I got Solnishko 1 to sell. To a very eager buyer.'

'You're selling Solnishko 1?' I said disbelievingly. 'To the
United States? You're mad. They'd never . . .'

'The United States!' he said contemptuously. 'Hell, no. My
clients want the plasma engine a whole lot more than the good
old USA. And they don't want it for no goddam space-race,
either. No, the guys I'm dealing with are in the market for Solnishko 1 because they've managed to develop an atom bomb
but they've got no missile to deliver it with. They figure that
the power unit out of this sputnik'll provide them with the
means of sending a rocket to hell and back. And if the first

145

one,' he said viciously, 'wipes out New York, that's O.K. by me. I spent too long in their lousy pens to worry about a little thing like that.'

'You and me both, boss!' The Negro had come up in a loping run after dumping the body of the astronaut in the Yakovlev's cargo compartment. He had a build like a sumo wrestler and a face like an Easter Island wood-carving. Blood had streamed from his flat nose and been wiped across his thick blubber lips, making him look as if he'd been drinking the stuff. He looked at Schuyler obsequiously, the whites of his eyes showing yellow as he rolled them at us and said, 'You want me to liquidate these guys?'

'Who asked you to speak, you black bastard?' asked Schuyler coldly. He turned his expressionless blue stare on to the Negro. 'I'm not sure we've got any more use for you, Eight-ball, after the way you let that little guy beat you up. I'm not sure you've earned your fix, after the dumb way you acted.'

The hideous face went grey as the Negro stared, horrified, at Schuyler. 'Aw, no, boss, you wouldn't do that,' he said huskily. 'Not to good old Eight-ball, you wouldn't. I sure am sorry, boss, truly I am. I was jus' caught off balance, that's all. I'll do any mortal thing you say, boss, honest to God I will. I'll . . .'

'Sure you will,' Schuyler said softly, his eyes flicking back to us. 'You won't make any more dumb mistakes, will you, Eight-ball? Not with these two guys. I want them to disappear, get me? And their boat, the way we planned it. You know that if there's one matchstick left floating on the water afterwards you'll be cold turkey, don't you?'

'Oh, my Gawd, boss, sure I do. I know what to do, boss, and I'll do it real good.' The mention of cold turkey—junkie talk for the goose pimples that are symptomatic of complete withdrawl from heroin—made him roll his chocolate-brown eyes in terror, and he watched Two-tooth and me as if his life depended on it.

Schuyler grinned again mirthlessly at us. 'No staff problems, you see, Tallon. He'll look after you, all right. Get them on heroin and they're yours for keeps.'

'My God,' said Two-tooth with revulsion. 'Is anything too

low for you? Jeez, I hope he turns on you one of these days and pulls your head off.'

'Don't be stupid.' Schuyler raised an eyebrow. 'You ever see an addict deprived of his fix? A living death, pal, that's what it is. And that's what they'd get if they killed the goose that lays the golden eggs, and they know it. It'd cost them a fortune to buy the quantity I give them for free. Hell, they're the best bodyguard you can get. If anything happens to me, they lose their next fix. And to a junkie nothing else matters. Nothing at all.'

'Not even a brother.' I looked past him at Barbara Mackail who was crouched on the sand just clear of the trees, her dull eyes fixed on Schuyler like those of a sick dog. 'She gets the stuff from you, too, doesn't she? That's how you found out about Solnishko 1. And when she put the radio out of action it was for you, not for Mikhailev.' I watched him with loathing. 'You used her, and you used him. And when you'd finished with him you shot him.'

'You're catching on fast.' Again I got the weird impression that he was empty inside, that there was nothing at all behind those pitiless ice-blue eyes. 'But she didn't get her stuff from me direct. She got it from the guy who handled the distributing end, a pusher called Zaghrali, no less. Yours isn't the only boat he had working for him, you know.' He shrugged. 'So, when he rang me up early yesterday and told me the Mackail girl wanted an extra supply to take on a trip, and that he'd told her your boat was available for some treasure-hunt or other she wanted to go on, I became interested enough to pay her a visit. I got the full story out of her in no time, after I'd threatened to get Zaghrali to cut off her dope. About how her long-lost brother had turned up in the dead of night full of secret information. From then on it was one mad scramble to get my own ship over from Melbourne, get in touch with my prospective clients, and move in on you with the CIA cover. Then you and Mikhailev did the rest for me. Zaghrali had to come, too, in case he talked after we'd gone. With a ship full of gold for him to play with it wasn't all that difficult.' He cocked an ear as the engine of the Yakovlev started up with a shattering roar. 'And I don't reckon it'll be all that difficult to lift Solnishko 1 with

147

that chopper, either. All we want is a head start. Which is why,' he shook his head regretfully, 'all the evidence has to be removed. Sorry, fellers, but that's the way it is.'

'You've forgotten one thing,' I said levelly. 'Who was it who coshed Zaghrali?'

'Who cares?' He transferred the Colt to the Negro's outstretched hand. 'I got to go now. Been nice knowing you, but I don't think we'll meet up again. You know what to do, Eightball. If I were you I'd make them walk to their boat before you shoot them. Otherwise you'll have two heavy corpses to carry, because I don't want a trace of anybody or anything left. Get it? The other Russian I'll deal with myself. We'll soon pick him up from the air.' He turned to go. Then he said offhandedly, 'Oh, and the girl goes with you, too.'

'With him?' She came to her feet quickly. 'No. I can't do that. I've got to go with you. Now that Zaghrali's gone, you're the only one I can get a fix from. You said we were going back to the boat . . .'

'Sure, sure.' Schuyler was already walking away. Over his shoulder he said, above the twittering roar of the twin rotors, 'I left some for you in your cabin. You'll be all right. Just go with Eight-ball, will you?'

'But what will I do afterwards?' She gave a small gasp of horror as she stared at the American's retreating back. 'You're going to have me killed,' she said, her voice rising. 'You can't do that. I've got to go with you.' She trotted alongside him as he strode towards the helicopter. 'I've done everything you wanted. And you know I've got to get my fix soon. You've got to give it to me. I'm coming . . .'

Schuyler hardly broke his stride as he struck her across the face with the back of his hand and sent her staggering. 'Get outa my hair, will you?' he snarled. 'Eight-ball, get this nut under control, will you?'

She jumped, clawing desperately, at him. The Negro watched us, a hunted look in his eyes as he shouted, 'Aw, gee, boss, how the hell can I? These guys won't stick around if I do.' Then he stiffened at the look on our faces as we watched Schuyler half turn and give the girl a vicious short-arm jab to the chin that toppled her over backwards. The American broke into a run, swung up into the glasshouse of the Yakovlev and slammed the cabin door. Simultaneously, the rotors spun faster, chewing at the air as the fifteen-ton machine hauled itself upwards in a cloud of sand. 'Don't start nothing, you guys,' said the Negro harshly. 'Or you'll get it here and now.'

The helicopter's fat pontoons were only just clear of the sand when Barbara Mackail dragged herself to her feet and ran, shouting incoherently, to jump and grip the horizontal member of the front starboard undercarriage strut. Then, before our horrified eyes, she was lifted fifty feet in a matter of seconds, hanging on by her hands and screaming soundlessly at the two men who were sitting side by side in the glasshouse, her blonde hair plastered flat against her face by the blast from the two 1700-horsepower Shvetsov engines. I felt my stomach contract as I watched, and Two-tooth whispered, 'My God! She won't be able to hold on for long. He'll have to come down, and fast, before she . . .'

But he didn't come down. The big helicopter steadied two hundred feet above the surf. Then, its rotors glittering in the sunlight, it swung and headed out towards the ship that was anchored offshore. I watched with the agonised impotence of nightmare as the tiny, swinging figure, outlined against the blue sky, kicked desperately in an effort to haul itself up on to the strut against the slipstream that was tearing its arms out of their sockets. I saw the flash of sunlight on perspex as the cabin door opened, and I drew a deep, shuddering breath, waiting for Schuyler to lean out and pull the girl in.

Instead, he threw something out. Something with a loop attached that dropped over the struggling girl's head and jerked her away from the strut as if she'd been pulled from below.

She seemed to take a long time to fall. Above the diminishing beat of the rotors there was a thin, wailing scream that was cut off abruptly when the blue water spouted a plume of white. Spray arced a small, brief rainbow that vanished on the wind, and then the sea smoothed itself again as if Barbara Mackail had never been.

The Negro said, 'No floating stuff, like the boss said. That was a fifty-pound pulley block he done slung round her neck.' He sniggered. 'Seems like it's getting her down.'

Something seemed to snap inside my head and I jumped him. It wasn't the most sensible thing I'd ever done, but, with the girl's last despairing scream still in my ears, his callous, sadistic attempt at humour was enough to send me off. And for an instant I thought I was going to get away with it. He was off guard, staring past me with his white teeth bared in a moronic grin at his own wit. But I had too much ground to cover, while he only had to crook his right forefinger. I heard Two-tooth yell, but it seemed to come from a long way off. And, as I went forward, his shout was cut off by the boom of the heavy automatic that exploded in my face like the end of the world. I felt nothing, but my forward momentum seemed to go on and on into a great, silent blackness that swallowed me up as I pitched forward into oblivion.

Sixteen

I WAS still toppling forward when I came round. But, instead of falling on to the sand, I was hanging over a star-shot void into which I was tumbling endlessly and nauseatingly, head over heels, to the accompaniment of a bass drum that somebody inside my skull was beating rhythmically. He'd cut a trapdoor in the top to get in, because I could feel it banging up and down with the pressure every time the drum boomed. The pressure on my eyeballs, too, was agonising. I thought muzzily that perhaps they'd bulge out a bit and ease the strain if only I could get my eyelids open. It wasn't going to be easy, but it was either that or having my eardrums blown out like bubble-gum.

With an effort that felt like putting the shot with a pair of Steinway Baby Grands, I opened both eyes. Before they snapped shut again with an almost audible clunk, I saw a vaguely familiar diamond-patterned steel mesh screen in front of me. I discovered, moreover, that I was wearing a handcuff on my left wrist. It passed through the mesh to some large, immovable object on the other side of it. And my left arm was completely without feeling. I tried to think, but as soon as I shut my eyes the sickening, swooping sensation started again. I levered them open wearily, wishing I could sink back into the nice comfortable unknowingness I'd just left.

I was lying on my back on the lower of the two-tier bunks in the cabin the Mikhailevs had occupied. The steel mesh was the base of the upper berth that had had its mattress removed. And the police bracelet I was wearing went up through it to a hairy wrist with an even hairier face behind it that was peering down at me concernedly. I said, in a voice that seemed to have aged a lot recently, 'For a moment I thought I was in Taronga Park Zoo. All you need now is a banana in your other fist.'

I became aware of the laboured beat of a helicopter's engines from not far away. Two-tooth said, 'You don't look so bloody glamorous yourself, mate.' He was leaning on his left elbow, grinning with relief. 'You ever see a bloke struck by lightning while he was opening a bottle of tomato sauce?'

I put up my hand, listening to the dwindling sound of the aero engines. The crust of blood that coated my face made it feel like a badly constructed Ho mask. I looked at the strands of singed hair, mud, and dried blood on my hand and said, 'What happened?'

'As a suicide bid, it started off all right. But little black Sambo didn't allow for the kick of that howitzer of Schuyler's. He spoilt your hair-style, that's all.' He added accusingly, 'It was a bloody inconsiderate thing to do. I had to carry you all the way here.'

'Where's the Negro?'

'Ashore. He made me dump you in here, then he took me with him to Schuyler's cabin to get the bracelet. He's been well briefed for this. The idea,' he said unemotionally, 'is that we get shot. The handcuff's to avoid any chance of our bodies floating to the surface after they sink the boat.' He raised himself a little to look out of the porthole. 'Schuyler's cabin's in a hell of a mess. The mattress ripped open and stuff all over the deck. What would he leave it like that for?'

I stopped myself from shaking my head just in time. It was aching blindingly, and I felt that my brain would fall out of the top of it if I wasn't careful. Two-tooth stiffened as he looked out and said, 'Looks as if they picked up the other astronaut, Pat. That bloody black's putting him into the dinghy. I reckon he's dead.'

I noted the ominous use of my Christian name. It didn't look as if Two-tooth thought we'd much longer to go, either. We listened in silence to the splash of oars as the dinghy came alongside. There was a thump, followed by the pad of footsteps up on deck and a sinister dragging noise. Then we heard the Negro come slowly down the companion and go along the passageway to my cabin. A door slammed, then a key rattled in the lock outside. Chained together as we were, I wouldn't have thought it necessary to lock our door as well, but it looked as if Eight-ball was taking no chances after Schuyler's threat.

He stood in the doorway with his hands on his hips and the front of his flashy shirt open, surveying us. His black, muscular chest shone with sweat and I could smell a sour, musky odour from him, like the acrid scent of a fox. 'Hi, fellas,' he said, flashing his teeth at us. 'I sure am sorry to keep you so long. Had some trash to dispose of.' He picked up a small crystal bottle off the dressing-table and unscrewed the top. 'But I won't keep you guys waiting much longer. No, sir.' His flat nose flared as he sniffed at the flask, and Barbara Mackail's perfume filled the cabin as he put it down. 'Well, now,' he said, grinning as he took out the Colt slowly and ostentatiously. 'You got any last messages for the folks back home?' He let us see the safety-catch go off, enjoying himself and taking his time.

'Only,' I said deliberately, 'that you must be the world's worst shot.' What we had to do was lure him across the cabin to where we could get our free hands on him. Even if he hadn't got the key to the handcuffs we'd be a lot better off with him out of the way. 'If you can miss somebody who's leaning on your gun-muzzle,' I said with a sneer, 'we haven't got much to worry about as long as you're standing there.'

'Too right,' said Two-tooth, catching on. 'And I reckon you must be the world's smelliest shot, too. Jeez, that scent's a hell of an improvement on the stink you brought in with you, Sambo.'

The Negro's grin faded as his slow brain took the insults in. For a moment I thought we'd got him when he took a lumbering step towards us, his ugly, bloodstained face twisted with fury. But then he saw Two-tooth's free hand lying like a side of ham across his body and he stopped. 'You white filth,' he snarled. 'You won't be so chipper by an' by. Not when I've done with you.'

'Maybe.' Two-tooth looked down at me. 'But it'll be a hell of a relief to get out of this, even feet first, won't it, Pat? I'll lay you ten dollars I don't smell as bad as him when I've been dead six months.'

When the muzzle of the Colt came up and steadied on Two-tooth's head, I thought, despairingly, that we'd pushed the Negro too far. If ever there was murder in anybody's face I saw it then. Death hung in the cabin, brushing us like a chilly, invisible cobweb. But Two-tooth didn't flinch. He stared back, straight into the Negro's face, and belched as loudly as only he knew how.

And the muzzle was lowered again. I relaxed weakly on the bunk, watching the Negro's chocolate-coloured eyes. They were still as murderously enraged as before, but there was a look of frustration in them that made me realise that what he wanted was to enjoy his killing. In his drug-diseased mind he craved the sadistic pleasure of seeing us beg and plead, or, at the very least, go numb with fear. 'No,' he said softly, the fury fading out of his black face to leave it set and anticipatory in a way that chilled my spine as his rage had failed to do. 'No, fellas. You want it slow, you can have it that way. I'm gonna tell you what I got in store for guys like you.' He tucked the automatic into his trousers, grinning twistedly again. 'We're gonna tow this boat out, 'bout fifteen or twenty miles. And then I'm going to scuttle her. There's four hundred fathoms, ten miles out—four thousand, if we go far enough. Places where no diver can ever reach, places where there's only the dark an' the cold an' a pressure that'll squash you flatter'n a nickel long before the fish get at you. You'll sure wish I'd given you a bullet then. Because you'll feel her going all the way, with the water rising nice an' slow, and you two pulling one another's arms off as you try to get away. You'll die by inches, you bastards. And,' he stopped, his woolly head cocked on one side, listening. 'And we start as from now,' he said malevolently. We, too, could hear the chug of a motor-launch coming into the anchorage. He stood for a moment, watching us, but when the voice from the launch hailed him he backed out, leaving the door open.

The steel mesh that Two-tooth was lying on was hooked on to the tubular-steel frame of the berth. With my free hand I tried to twist one of the hooked ends loose. I might as well have tried to snap the steel chain on my wrist. Two-tooth said, 'You're wasting your time. D'you think I haven't tried that?

154

These bunks were made to take punishment, yer know.' I gave up, my headache nearly blinding me, and lay listening to the shouts from up for'ard as the launch took *Lorelei* in tow. They'd cut or slipped the anchor cable, for I felt the jerk as the tow-line took up the strain without any sound from our electric winch. 'We're moving,' said Two-tooth unnecessarily. He swung his legs off the bunk and sat with them dangling, twisting round to look through the porthole. 'And by this time Schuyler'll have Solnishko 1 stowed away in one of the holds of that rusting bag of rivets we saw offshore. The bloody anti-submarine frigate,' he said bitterly, 'that was supposed to have been trailing us last night. They'll have used the helicopter as a crane, then used their derricks to lift it on board. They wouldn't be able to land a thing as big as that on her decks.' He looked down at me. 'But if he's got the space-craft, why's he going to all this trouble with us? Why didn't he just shoot us and the two astronauts and leave us in the bush? That's what he did with Mikhailev.'

'You heard what he said. He doesn't want a trace of anybody left. He'll have brought Mikhailev out and dumped him in deep water, with the man he shot on the beach. He's got to cover his tracks. Because,' I said grimly, 'if the Russians found out that two of their astronauts had been found dead here they'd track him down like a she-bear chasing somebody who's pinched its cub.' I looked up at a golden-tinted cloud that appeared in the porthole and then swung away as *Lorelei* turned. I said, puzzled, 'What time is it?'

'Just turned five.' He was looking at the sky too. 'You were out for an hour or so. And we're out of the inlet. Easier passage than this morning.' It seemed years ago.

I felt the swell take *Lorelei* and she rolled heavily as the launch tugged her out. Then the motion increased as the distant splutter of the engine died away, leaving the yacht wallowing helplessly. Two-tooth said, 'They'll be picking up their launch. The rust-bucket's taking over the tow.' Golden sunlight flashed into his face and his shadow swung dizzily up and down the bulkhead opposite. 'Can't see a flaming thing. If only there was a fishing boat out there. I could flash the sun back at it . . .'

155

'There won't be any fishing boats. Schuyler's bound to have radar. He'll make sure we haven't got an audience.'

The jerk came again as the tow-rope tightened, pitching Two-tooth over sideways. The cabin door slammed, and from then on we had to hang on like limpets. The towing effect of the launch had been small, and *Lorelei* had responded to it slowly but smoothly. Now, the more powerful engines of the steamer wrenched at the yacht brutally, dragging her out to sea like a reluctant puppy. We endured the battering, listening to the protesting shouts from Eight-ball up at the wheel, until after what seemed an age the vicious tugs at *Lorelei*'s bow ceased. The sky that swung down into my line of vision, then up again, was a perceptibly darker blue and dusted with the gold of the approaching sunset. We heard the Negro go forward to cast off the tow. Then there was the thump of his feet on the companion as he came below to go for'ard to the fo'c'sle. There was a series of ringing hammering noises, then the sound we'd both been waiting for—the splash and gurgle of inrushing water. It sounded louder when the cabin door opened and the Negro said gloatingly, 'O.K., you guys, this is where I get off. I sure am sorry for smashing up that neat little jakes you got up for'ard, but we got to let the sea in somewhere, and that seemed kinda appropriate. And the guy in there won't be using it, I guess.' He grinned wolfishly. 'Not got quite so much to say now? I could have done the job a whole lot faster by letting the water in at the bathroom opposite, but that'd be too quick for you bastards.' He stared at us for a long moment. Then he spat, 'I hope you rot in hell.'

After he'd gone I tried vainly to compress the bones of my hand enough to get it through the handcuff, knowing it was futile as I did it. I gave it up, wondering how many other men in the past had tried to get rid of their chains on this coast in the same way. There was a dull splash as the Negro went over the side, and Two-tooth said, 'Jeez, I wish now I'd had a go at rushing him as well. But he said he'd shoot you again if I did.'

'It didn't get me anywhere.' Already I could feel a strangeness in the way *Lorelei* sat in the water, and the bottle of perfume that the Negro had put down on the dressing-table toppled over with a tiny crash, its contents leaking out drop by

drop. As if pushed by a ghostly hand, the cabin door swung to
with a click and there was the clatter of a saucepan falling in
the galley. Then there was another sound, one that brought
my head up sharply. A sound I'd heard once before, in this
very cabin. Above the gurgling death-rattle of the dying ship
I could have sworn I heard the pad of soft footsteps in the
passageway outside. I said to Two-tooth, in a whisper, 'Can
you hear what I hear?'

He nodded. 'There's somebody outside. Somebody the
Negro hasn't got on to.'

And somebody I hadn't got on to, somebody who could hide
out on a fifty-foot yacht so well that even I, who knew every
square inch of the boat, hadn't been able to find him. I'm not
superstitious, but I swear at that moment I felt the hair rising
on the back of my neck. Queer things have happened at sea—
strange, unexplained things. And if other ships could be
haunted, why not *Lorelei*? Her very name was that of a spirit,
one that had lured seamen to shipwreck and death. As my
Lorelei had done. I wondered how I would feel if the door
opened and Zaghrali stood leering at us, his face distorted by
death as I had last seen it.

There was a loud slam from for'ard, and the gurgling
stopped. We heard the soft, hesitant footsteps come aft again,
down the companion. They stopped outside the door. There
was a long silence in which I could hear Two-tooth swallow
noisily. Then the handle turned gently and the door opened.

Seventeen

WE LAY staring speechlessly at the figure framed in the doorway. It was a figure that had drawn a good many speechless stares in its time—a small-waisted, slim-hipped figure in a black, well-ballasted roll-neck sweater and tight, dark-blue trousers. She had wide tawny eyes and a .32 Scott & Webley that had once belonged to Two-tooth in her olive-brown fist. She sniffed, wrinkling her small nose delicately, and said, 'If it's a new fly-spray, I don't like it.'

'Lucky!' I said feebly. 'How the hell did you ...?'

'Can we,' she said crisply, 'stay afloat with the fo'c'sle flooded and the watertight door shut?'

'You beaut!' I heard Two-tooth's sigh of relief and I lay back, grinning at her foolishly. 'In weather like this,' he said happily, 'we'll stay afloat all right. Is that what you've done?'

'Among other things.' She didn't smile back and my grin faded as she stared critically at me while she put the automatic away. She looked different somehow, not at all like the lush gold-digger we'd left behind in Hobart. Instead, she had a purposeful poise that reminded me unpleasantly of policewomen. I noted the competent way she handled the gun, together with the fact that both her accents—Australian as well as Italian—seemed to have disappeared. She came into the cabin and said, in her new, clipped voice, 'I always said your head needed seeing to, Patrick. I suppose we'd better fix that first.' Before, she'd given the impression of knowing as much about first-aid as a mongoose.

'My head's all right for the time being,' I said curtly. 'What are you doing here? And how did ...?'

'Who cares?' Two-tooth grinned down at her. 'Just nip

158

down to the engine-room, sweetheart, and bring me the cable cutters out of the tool-kit. We'll have Schuyler's narcotics squad back before long.'

'In that case,' she said coolly, 'we'll have to fight them off, that's all.' She took a ring with two keys on it out of her trouser pocket. 'But he won't expect us to sink instantly. We've got a few minutes in hand, which is all to the good. Because my job is to delay him as long as possible.' She tried a key in the lock on my wrist. 'I found these when I was going through Schuyler's cabin. I think this is the one.'

'Your job?' I stared up at her.

She touched my head gently. 'That wound does need attention, Patrick,' she said concernedly. 'I'll get some water and . . .'

'You'll do nothing of the sort.' After the last hour or so, water was the last thing I required. 'What job are you talking about?'

She straightened up, the handcuffs clinking in her hand, and smiled at me for the first time. 'I think it's time you knew,' she said gently, 'that I'm not the pickle-merchant's home-wrecker, after all. In fact, there never was a pickle merchant. My real name doesn't matter, but I might as well tell you now I'm working for the Department of Trade and Customs.'

For a variety of reasons the cabin swam dizzily as I swung my legs off the bunk. Two-tooth stared at her, as horrified as if he'd found a red-back spider in his underpants. 'A Customs nark! Jeez, I don't believe it.'

'Not really,' she said. 'I'm on loan from Naval Intelligence. I'm a lieutenant in the WRANS, you see.' She put the handcuffs down on the dressing-table. They seemed to make a hell of a noise. 'Smuggling's become more than a crime—it's a threat to national security, especially when it involves narcotics and illegal immigration. So the Government's decided to treat it as a counter-intelligence job—to use the smugglers' own methods and smuggle people like me into their organisations. I've been on to you two for a long time. But it was the people in the background we were after, the respectable citizens who always pay their taxes and who never get their hands dirty. People like Anton Zaghrali. You were only little fish who could be useful as bait, and I was told to let you go on swimming while you were busy with your watches and cameras and transistor radios.' She paused. 'But then,' she said quietly, 'you got in deeper, and went on to forged currency. You were following the pattern of behaviour that all professional smugglers conform to sooner or later, a career that starts off with a few cartons of duty-frees and ends up with a cargo of rifles or dope. I thought it was time to stop. I was sure of it when I found you'd been fool enough to bring a Russian in, and I was going to have you pulled in that very night. But then I decided to stay on board and see whether your boss turned up. And then the blonde came into the picture. She was, I knew, tied in with Zaghrali and also with a man called Todd Schuyler, in whom the FBI are very interested and who's done time all over the USA. So I stayed on the bridge, listening.' She turned to Twotooth. 'You remember? I could see you both heading straight for life sentences once you got into Schuyler's clutches, and I tried to warn you off, but you wouldn't listen to me. So I decided you'd have to take your chance, because it looked as if this trip was going to be a golden opportunity to get enough evidence to put both Schuyler and Zaghrali where they belonged. That's why I stowed away.'

'It was you outside this cabin last night,' I said slowly. 'It was you who knocked Zaghrali out. But where the devil did you hide afterwards? We searched the whole ship.'

'I know. I was sitting on the settle in the saloon while you did it,' she said, smiling mockingly at me. 'I was wearing a yellow dress. You walked right past me, both you and Schuyler.'

'Lorelei!' I said, thunderstruck. It was like seeing a two-year-old complete a puzzle I'd spent hours over. 'You changed clothes with the mascot!'

She nodded. 'I hid in your cabin when I first came aboard, hoping to find an empty one, but they were all occupied, and I was getting worried in case Schuyler called the whole thing off if he knew I was on board. I still thought it was dope-running, you see. We sailed, and you didn't come down to your cabin and I thought everything was going to be all right—until I heard you coming below last night. But then you went into the girl's cabin.' She paused and coloured slightly for some reason or other. 'I went and listened at the door. Then I heard Mikhailev talking, and I knew I'd stumbled on something that was dynamite. I heard him tell you about Solnishko 1, and then Zaghrali came along. I had to dodge into the bathroom. He got his ear stuck to the door when he heard Mikhailev's voice, and I knew I was in a spot. He'd nip into the bathroom, too, if anybody came along. So I had to lay him out with the lavatory brush. As soon as I'd hit him I realised what an idiotic thing I'd done, because everybody else on board was accounted for, and I knew you and Schuyler would turn the boat upside down. I raced up to the saloon, took off my slacks and pulled on the doll's dress. I'd thrown her over the side and I was sitting on my trousers in the shadows when you and Schuyler came past with Zaghrali. After you'd searched the ship, hiding out was easy. No hiding place is safer than one that's just been searched. I threw the dress away and spent most of the time in your cabin. I was even able to risk stealing a meal from the galley.'

'But if you knew Schuyler was a crook,' I said angrily, 'why the hell didn't you tell me?' When she didn't answer I said levelly, 'I see. You thought he was a pal of ours. Is that it?'

'How was I to know? I couldn't afford to trust anybody. And you seemed to get on very well together. What I wanted to do was to get at the radio.'

'He told me he was a CIA agent,' I said. 'And he had papers to prove it.' I paused, reflecting that, as well as classing me as a drug-smuggler, she would now put me down as a mental defective. 'But it's not important now.' I looked up at Two-tooth. 'What's he doing?'

'Steaming round us in circles,' he said, 'like a dingo round a dying brumby. And any minute now he'll be asking who's stuck his toe in the plughole.' He scrambled off the bunk. 'Let's get up on deck where we can see . . .'

'No!' said Lucky sharply. 'If he sees us, he won't have to ask any questions. He'll murder the lot of us and steam out into the Pacific where he'll be just another dirty, innocent old tramp. No, we've got to tie him down here for as long as we can. Until the Navy gets here.'

'The Navy?' I stared at her incredulously. 'Coming here?'

161

She nodded. 'The *Fort Knox*, with an escort of four RAN destroyers.'

I watched her bemusedly. 'They know about Solnishko 1? Then why didn't they . . .?'

'Of course they don't,' she said impatiently. 'How could they? They're on their way to Fremantle. They left Hobart this afternoon. But they can't be all that far away.'

I looked at her silently for a moment. 'Are you,' I asked bitterly, 'much of a hand at telepathy?'

Two-tooth said gloomily, 'We couldn't even outsail that garbage can of Schuyler's in our present state, if you're thinking of making a run for it. Our screws'll be out of the water, for a start. And we've got no transmitter, so we can't . . .'

'I know that,' she said, exasperated with our dullness. 'How do you think I passed the time while you were ashore? But I've had my bullfrog switched on since last night.'

'You have?' I put my hand to my splitting head. 'You know, I think I'll have that water, after all. With Scotch. I could have sworn you said . . .'

'BULFRO,' she said clearly. 'Beacon, Ultra Low Frequency, Robot Operated. The Navy calls them bullfrogs. They transmit a continuous, almost undetectable distress signal—like those things secret agents stick on cars on television. It's only the size of a pocket radio. I switched it on last night when I found out about Solnishko 1. It's in your wardrobe now.' She shrugged. 'Our destroyers will pick it up all right. They won't know what it's all about, but they'll recognise a bullfrog when they hear one. They'll be here.'

'I see.' I stood up, staggering on the unfamiliar tilted deck, trying to clear my head of the merciless, throbbing pain that, until now, had blotted out any thought of constructive action. I thought of Barbara Mackail's miserable death, the treacherous murder of Nicolai, the callous killing of the two astronauts. Any plan, however fantastic, would be better than sitting here waiting for the grinning sadist who'd done these things to come and finish us off. If only we could get in a smack at him before . . . I said thoughtfully, 'He can't hang around here much longer. He's relying on his disguise to get him through, so he'll want to get out into the shipping lanes where he can melt into the background. On the other hand, he can't leave us here. We might be picked up and blow the whistle on him before he gets to wherever it is he's going.' I stared at Two-tooth, filled with a joyous, primitive lust for revenge. 'What would you do in his place?'

'Surrender, before you came and bit me.' He eyed me warily. With my face plastered with mud and blood, my hair singed and my eyes glittering, I must have looked like Hallowe'en in the ward where they don't allow knives and forks. 'Look, my old cobber,' he said soothingly, 'why don't you just lie down and . . .?'

'And he must know he can't hope to fight it out once he's stopped. So he's not likely to be carrying anything heavier than a sub-machine gun.' With a suddenness that made them both jump I snapped, 'Lucky. Get up to the saloon, but for God's sake keep your head down. I want to know the minute Schuyler makes a move, and how he bears when he stops circling us. Two-tooth, start up the engines. Slow ahead both. We won't be doing any steering, so you can work them from the engine-room. Right?'

'No,' he growled. 'It bloody isn't. I told you, the screws'll be out of the water. And, even if they're not, we'll be rumbled the minute Schuyler sees we're moving.'

'I want him to see us moving.' I grinned at him, and he backed out of the cabin, his eyes popping as I added, 'All I want is a carton of cleaning powder from the galley, plus one or two other odds and ends. Then we're all set for the Battle of the South-west Cape.'

I saw him tugging at his beard worriedly and pretending to examine the engine-room switchboard as I went for'ard, down-hill, with Lucky behind me. Everything in the saloon that had been hurled to the deck during our tow had slid forward as the bows had gone down and ended up in a chaotic mess against the bulkhead. Lucky took up station with my binoculars behind the cocktail cabinet that dripped a variety of expensive liquids on to the carpet while I ploughed through the shambles of smashed crockery, jam and cornflakes that lay in drifts in the galley. I found what I wanted—the carton of cleaning powder, a half-pound packet of Conde's crystals that we'd bought for snake-bite and never used, and a small bottle three-quarters full of glycerine in the medicine cabinet. From behind the watertight door there came an unpleasant sucking noise as I searched among the debris, and something soft bumped heavily against the bulkhead. I thought of Zaghrali floating in there, his eyes sightless in the black water, then I put him out of my mind. I was working against the clock now, and when I heard Lucky shout excitedly I thought I was too late. But it was only to tell me that the steamer had hove to on our port beam. This was better than I'd hoped, but even so the sun was sinking fast and Schuyler would soon have to take the logical step that would send us to the bottom. I emptied the contents of the cylindrical carton into the mess that littered the galley and I was on my way to the engine-room when Two-tooth started the diesels. Even though I'd been waiting for it, their coughing, tigerish roar made me jump. Two-tooth was leaning over them lovingly. He throttled them back and shouted, staring at what I had in my hands, 'What the flaming hell are you up to, Tallon?'

I was busy filling an empty beer bottle with some of the petrol we kept for our small auxiliary-lighting generator. 'Molotov cocktail,' I said briefly. 'Slow ahead now. But give me full astern when I yell for it.' There was no time to explain, and I went up to the saloon feeling *Lorelei* begin to move sluggishly through the water.

The steamer lay a quarter of a mile to port, smoke from her filthy funnel hazing the clear blue-gold of the evening sky. Behind her, the sun was sinking into a cloudless, mother-of-pearl sunset, but it was still high enough for me to see the detail in the ship's outline when I took my Zeiss glasses from the girl. A knot of men was gathered aft on her poop-deck, but I ignored them when I found what I was looking for—the tarpaulin-covered bulk that marked where the helicopter, its rotors folded, was secured on the foredeck. It was, I had reasoned, far too big to fit anywhere else. The sea was flat calm, with the sheen of shot silk, and the reflection of the ship's superstructure wavered in the quiet water, surrounded by glinting amber shards of sunlight. Lucky said shakily, 'Have you looked at her stern?'

I swung the glasses back along the flaking, rusting hull. I stiffened. 'So that's why he's taken so long,' I said softly. 'It's the Negro. Schuyler's found out that he didn't shoot us as he'd been told to do.'

Eight-ball, his hands tied behind his back, was hanging from the rail right at the stern on the end of a warp that went under his armpits. I could see the insane terror on his ugly face and hear, now that I was listening for it, the thin animal howling that came from his gaping mouth—a display of fear that seemed absurd from a man who was only up to his waist in water.

But his madly kicking feet were only about a yard away from the ship's propeller.

'When they start moving,' Lucky said in a whisper that I could only just hear above the purring of our diesels, 'he'll be drawn into the screws. God, what a fiendish thing to do. That's why Schuyler's been so long, Patrick. Even though we're moving, he knows we can't get away. Perhaps he wants to make us watch it . . .' She stopped. Suddenly the reflection of the steamer in the sea had been shattered. White foam boiled under the stern, mercifully hiding the Negro from sight, and the outline of the ship appeared to shrink horizontally. 'He's turning towards us.' Lucky stared at me in consternation. 'Patrick, he's going to ram!'

'Of course he is,' I said shortly. I was emptying the purple, shining potassium-permanganate crystals into the cylindrical carton, taking care not to spill the petrol from the bottle I'd tied to it. 'Now get below, will you? He'll probably open fire on us as well.' She dropped down the companion, eyeing my chemistry set doubtfully, and I turned the glasses on to the steamer.

At the rate she was closing us I wouldn't be needing them for long. Her hull and superstructure might have looked as if they'd been the subject of a Victorian lithograph, but the bow-wave she was already piling up would have done credit to a corvette. The exhaust gases that jetted from her thin, old-fashioned funnel came from something a lot more recent than a steam-engine. She had a power unit that was hurling her across the flat, oily water like a runaway rhino.

'Two-tooth!' I bawled. 'Full astern both! And give it all you've got!' God, she was much faster than I'd bargained for. What if I'd left it too late? The heavy binoculars shook as I trained them on the other vessel's wheelhouse, feeling like an apprentice matador faced with an unexpectedly agile bull.

My hands steadied with the fatalistic realisation that we couldn't be any worse off if I failed. I concentrated on the swarthy, thickset helmsman whose head and shoulders were almost filling the eye-pieces so that I felt I could reach out and deflect his wheel. I could see Schuyler, grim-faced, standing behind him. And I could see, too, that the other vessel wasn't coming straight at us. Knowing that we were under way, Schuyler was aiming his ship slightly ahead of us so that we were on a collision course with him. If we maintained it, he'd cut us in half and trample the pieces underfoot. That was what I'd anticipated. So we'd go astern, like the matador side-stepping to avoid . . .

But we weren't going astern. The yacht's engines were bellowing with a high, unfamiliar note, but they weren't even slowing us down. Desperately, I looked aft out of the starboard saloon door. Sheets of spray from our stern told me what had gone wrong. With her screws partially out of the sea, *Lorelei*'s engines were only exerting a fraction of their thrust to brake the yacht's seventeen tons. We were continuing to move slowly and ponderously into the path of the two-thousand-ton vessel that now seemed to hang over me like a rust-caked, riveted cliff on to which we were rushing flat out. Without knowing what I was doing, I saw my hands methodically pouring the contents of the glycerine bottle on to the crystals in the cardboard container. But it was useless. I could hear the swift, triumphant pounding of the other ship's diesels above our own, and the crash of the sea against the high, old-fashioned bow that was going to slice through us like a cheese-cutter.

Schuyler saw what was happening before I did. Even without the glasses I saw him shoulder the helmsman aside and spin the wheel to starboard. Because *Lorelei* was going astern. Agonisingly slowly, with her engines racing their bearings out as the screws clawed at air and water alternately, but astern none the less. And too late. Far too late. I'd failed to allow for the unexpected speed of the other vessel which was now so close that her wheelhouse was cut off from my line of vision by her starboard bow. The name *Kowloon* in what had once been white paint hung over me like a curse and I could see glistening lengths of seaweed on the corroded flukes of her anchor. She couldn't miss us now. Schuyler's course correction would easily compensate for our sluggish struggles to get out of his way.

But it was Schuyler who had miscalculated. For, owing to the position of her rudder, a ship answers her helm like a car being reversed. Her mass and inertia compel her to pivot about a point forward of midships when her rudder is first put over. Then she will skid sideways for a period depending on her speed until finally her bow comes round. And the *Kowloon* was moving very fast indeed. So the only effect of Schuyler's attempt to cut the corner was that the stern of the other ship moved away from *Lorelei* slightly, but her bows didn't deviate by a centimetre. She was rumbling past like an express train only a few feet from our half-submerged bow before I woke up to the fact that she'd missed us.

It was the warmth from the container I held in my hand that galvanised me into action. I'd been given the opportunity I wanted, but I only had a second or two in which to take it. I jammed the metal foil top back on to the carton that was beginning to give off thick clouds of acrid smoke. The sprinkler holes in the top would give it all the oxygen it needed. I fitted the cork loosely into the mouth of the bottle of petrol, checking that it was tied firmly to the cardboard cylinder. Then I ducked out through the starboard saloon door, swung my parcel back as if lobbing a grenade, and heaved it in a high parabola over the bulwarks of the *Kowloon*'s foredeck.

No sooner had it left my hand than *Lorelei* was struck by the bow-wave of the other ship. Caught off balance, I fell over backwards as our bows came up out of the sea. The yacht rolled wildly to starboard, white water cascading off her foredeck. Then she recovered, swinging in towards the *Kowloon*'s hull like a toy boat caught in a millrace. I lay sprawled on my back on the deck, looking straight up at the head and shoulders of a man who had appeared on the wing of the *Kowloon*'s bridge

167

high above me. A man with a crew-cut and a faded blue T-shirt, leaning far out to open fire with the Schmeisser sub-machine gun that was cradled in his arms.

A fraction of a second before *Lorelei* could smash herself against the side of the other ship she was boosted outwards. This time I swear her mast must have touched the sea. She'll go right over, I thought, as she rolled so far to port that I fell vertically through the saloon doorway, catching as I did so a cinematographic glimpse of blue flame fluttering from the muzzle of the Schmeisser that Schuyler was firing straight down at me. Splinters flew from the deck where I'd been lying only a second earlier, and the windows on the starboard side caved in with a noise like the end of the world. But when *Lorelei* righted herself, slowly and reluctantly like a punch-drunk heavyweight, the *Kowloon* was drawing away rapidly. A bullet whipped over my head as I crawled across the see-sawing carpet, but for the time being we could breathe again. I shouted, 'Two-tooth! Stop both!' If the *Kowloon* made another pass at us, our engines wouldn't save us again.

Two-tooth appeared beside me as I knelt propped against the settle. 'Just checking to see which way up we are.' He looked sideways at me. 'You know you won't be able to get away with that trick again?'

'I know.' I grabbed the binoculars that had ended up under the settle and searched the *Kowloon*'s foredeck as she heeled, belatedly, to starboard. Nothing. No excitement, no clouds of smoke, no . . . I held my breath. The backside of a crewman had sprung into view. He was clambering over the tarpaulin-shrouded helicopter with the air of a man who'd been sent to look for something.

Two-tooth grunted. 'Ah, well,' he said loyally, 'I reckon you did all right to last out this long. But, let's face it, you didn't have much show of stopping them with a bottle of petrol, did you? And what was the other stuff in the carton?'

The other vessel was continuing her turn to starboard, coming about for her second—and final—run. I said, 'For a Molotov cocktail you need a lighted fuse to go with the petrol. But that can go out when you throw it. Mine was a dodge I picked up from the terrorists in Malaya. I had glycerine and potassium permanganate—Conde's crystals—in that container. Both of them perfectly harmless, and you can get them at any chemist's. But mix them together, and you get a chemical reaction that burns white-hot after a couple of minutes, an intense, searing heat that'll crack a crucible. More than enough to set fire to a tarpaulin, if you throw in a little petrol to spread the fire around.'

The crewman had found what he was looking for. A sheet of bluish-yellow flame flowered silently in front of him as I watched through the glasses. I saw him stagger back, his hands to his face, before the cloud of sooty smoke billowed up and hid him. It spread out, hiding the wheelhouse that was swinging round towards us. 'Maybe so,' said Two-tooth flatly. 'But it's going to take more than that to stop Schuyler. And here he comes now.'

'Under the tarpaulin,' I said, trying to keep my voice down, 'there should be a good deal of vaporised aviation spirit.'

Two-tooth turned slowly towards me. 'Strewth,' he whispered. 'You carbolical bastard. And there was I thinking you were off your bloody nut.' He stared back at the *Kowloon*, where the men were beginning to scatter away from the foredeck. 'Why, that should . . .'

A searing orange glare flashed fifty feet up into the calm evening sky as the Yakovlev's petrol tanks ignited. Black, unidentifiable objects hurtled up with it, to be swallowed up in a soaring, blood-red fireball that became a pillar of jet-black smoke with a roaring inferno at its base. The sullen boom of the explosion echoed like that of a twelve-inch gun across the water, and the *Kowloon*'s foremast sagged tiredly and fell into the flames, throwing up gouts of flaming petrol to start fresh fires. Two-tooth said thoughtfully, completing his sentence, '. . . should take a fair bit off that tub's resale value, I reckon.'

The ship continued her turn until she presented her port side to us. Then she hove to, half a mile away. I only hope, I thought grimly, that Schuyler was still on the bridge when it was swept by the blast. The pink glow of the setting sun tinged with a lurid, hellish glare the smoke that enveloped the *Kowloon*'s foredeck, and the jets from the fire-hoses that were beginning to play uselessly on the flames looked like streams of blood. Two-tooth stood up. 'I'll see if the radar's working. If Lucky's right, we ought to be getting a contact before long.' With one foot on the bridge ladder, he said, 'Where is she?'

'I sent her below. But in those two rolls we did, she might have been . . .' I clattered down the companion. 'Lucky!' I shouted. After the tumult of the last few minutes, everywhere seemed deathly quiet.

'I'm here.' Her voice, oddly preoccupied, came from behind the closed door of my cabin at the end of the passageway. 'Don't make a noise, Patrick.'

It seemed an odd request after what had been going on. But when I opened the door I found out why. She was kneeling by the grey-clad body of Igor Mikhailev who was stretched out on the deck. 'He's dying,' she said quietly. 'I tried to stop him crashing about, but there isn't much else we can do for him.'

Blood was seeping thickly from a patch of scarlet over the astronaut's abdomen, and his face was almost the same colour as his space-suit. He was fully conscious, hanging on desperately to Lucky's hand, and when he saw me his whispered, 'Well, Englishman? Your American friend has sent you to finish me off, yes?'

He thought Schuyler and I were working together. He hadn't been with us on the beach. 'No,' I said gently. 'It's not like that at all. He's not working for the Americans, and I'm not working with him.'

'I do not believe you.' He bared his teeth in a grin of pain. 'You and that traitor who used to be my sister helped him to kill Nicolai. This is an Anglo-American plot to steal Solnishko 1.'

'No. You've got it all wrong, Mikhailev.' It seemed strange to be using that name again. 'And your sister was sick. She didn't know what she was doing.' I didn't think it would ease his last moments to know that she was dead.

'I do not believe you,' he said again, in a voice that I could only just hear. 'But it does not matter now. None of you will get Solnishko 1. You will all die, as I am going to die.' He closed his eyes, and I thought it was all over. But then they opened tiredly and he said, clearly and distinctly, 'You see, when I got away from you I went back to Solnishko 1. When your American ally shot me down from his helicopter he was too late. I had already done what I had to do. I had activated the self-destructive system in the space-craft.'

'You did what?' I stared down at him, wondering if he knew what he was saying. 'You mean—you've blown it up? Then what . . .?'

'No. That would have been too dangerous.' His voice trailed off as he whispered, '. . . delay mechanism.'

I felt a horrible cold shock of premonition. 'Mikhailev!' I dropped to my knees beside him as his eyes closed again. 'Mikhailev, listen to me! If Solnishko 1 blows up now, will it affect the reactor?'

He didn't answer me for a few seconds. Then he said, in a voice so weak that I could hardly hear it, 'It has not had time to become fully stabilised. There will be an instantaneous fusion reaction.' His eyes were still closed and his face was already relaxing into its waxy death-mask. 'But the innocent will not suffer. It will explode far out at sea. Where it can harm no one but you.'

'When?' I said urgently. I leaned over and grabbed his shoulder. Lucky seized my arm indignantly, but I shook her off. 'When will it go off? Answer me!'

He opened his eyes for the last time, staring past me at the golden light that streamed in at the port side. 'Sunset was a good time to choose. As one sun dies, so will the other. Solnishko. Little Sun.' He began to say something in Russian and he died quietly and without any fuss in mid-sentence.

Two-tooth's voice came down from the bridge into the silence as Lucky and I stared at one another across the body of the Russian. 'Hey, Tallon! Come on up and take a look at this. I got a king-sized blip that can only be the *Fort Knox*, together with four little ones. Our tin cans are coming, and bringing the Yank with them!'

And *Lorelei*, like the siren she'd been named after, was luring them with the song of a bullfrog to the ground zero of a nuclear explosion.

Eighteen

WHEN I raced up to the bridge with Lucky just behind me, Two-tooth was sprawled comfortably in the control position with a hiss of static coming from the radio receiver and his eyes glued to the five brilliant blips that formed a neat pattern at the extreme limit of the radar screen. The fire on the *Kowloon*, half a mile to starboard, had spread aft to her bridge, but I only gave her a passing glance. I was staring the other way, westwards, to where the sun was falling into a sea the colour of leatherwood honey.

'You can't expect to see them yet,' Two-tooth said, thinking I was looking for the five naval vessels. 'They're a good twenty miles away. I got the radio on the distress frequency in case they call us up.' He took out his pipe and began filling it. 'And Schuyler can't see them at all, not after you knocked his foremast down. It had the radar scanner on it.' He chuckled happily. 'My oath, is he going to get a shock in the next hour or so!'

I looked at him for a moment. 'He won't be the only one,' I said grimly. I told him why.

'My God!' He put his pipe down when I'd finished, his eyes fixed on mine. 'And those ships are sailing right into it.' He turned to the girl. 'Lucky, can't you use that frog gizmo of yours to warn them off? Or stop the bloody thing altogether?'

She shook her dark head. 'I could smash it, but they'll have a pretty good bearing on us by now. Even if it stopped, they'd still come to investigate.'

'Besides,' I said, 'we're a lot closer to land than Igor thought we'd be. With the astronomical data he had available, he'd have been able to work out the time of sunset here to a second. He must have heard Schuyler mention a ship, and so he planned the explosion to happen well out at sea. But he didn't know we were working against Schuyler, and that we'd pin him down like this. So they're bound to be affected ashore, if it's only by the fallout.' I looked across at the *Kowloon*. 'No, there's only one thing we can do. We've got to get over there and stop it going off. It's an outside chance, but it's the only one we've got.' And, I thought as I looked at the setting sun, we've got about half an hour in which to do it.

'No!' Lucky put her hand on my arm. 'It's crazy, Patrick. You haven't even an outside chance of doing that. You wouldn't even get on board alive. They'd shoot you before you'd . . .'

'If that thing blows up,' I said impatiently, 'we're all finished anyway, so what's the difference?' I put my hand on hers. 'I think we can get away with it. There's plenty of smoke to cover us, he's got his hands full getting the fire under control, and a boarding party's the last thing he'll expect.' I looked at Two-tooth. 'And you're the bomb-disposal king. Nicolai said the self-destructive charge consisted of conventional explosive. Think you can handle it?'

'What can we lose?' He stood up. ' "If at first you don't succeed, you won't be around to try again." That used to be me old squad's motto. And this can't be hairier than some of the problems the Nip engineers used to set us with their bloody open-and-closed-circuit detonators. I'll get me tools.' He pushed past me to the ladder.

'The bare minimum.' I kicked off my mud-encrusted boots and pulled out a tangle of flippers, goggles and snorkels from the locker under the chart-table. 'I'll carry half the stuff you need, but we'll be swimming underwater most of the way. We can't take much. And that rules out your gun, too.'

'That,' he observed as he disappeared, 'makes it so much easier. 'I'm quite looking forward to boarding a burning ship full of homicidal junkies with an adjustable spanner between me dentures.'

Lucky said hesitantly, 'Patrick, before you go, I want to say . . .' She stopped as I turned towards her. Then she came and stood on tiptoe to put her arms round my neck.

Somehow, it was far more effective than the last time she'd

done it. Then she'd pasted herself to me like a postage stamp, giving me full coverage from the toes upwards. And it hadn't stirred me in the least. Without knowing the real part she'd been playing, I'd seen through it as part of the act. But now, when she looked at me with her heart in her golden eyes, hardly touching me at all, I felt my pulse-rate going off the clock and my spine turning to the consistency of sweet, warm porridge. I put my arms round her firm, slim waist and kissed her—the way you'd kiss a girl, too, if you'd suddenly discovered you'd wasted your whole life until that moment and that now you'd only half an hour or so to live.

Two-tooth tapped me on the shoulder, standing on one leg to put a flipper on the other. He was still wearing his shirt and trousers and his pockets were bulging with tools. 'Sorry, mate. But there's no time for the diplomatic coughing bit. Stick this Mole wrench in your pocket and let's get started.'

Lucky disengaged herself swiftly and kissed him on the beard as he dragged his goggles over his head. 'She'll be right, mate,' she said, covering up with her lady-of-easy-virtue act. 'I know that if anybody can make a pig's ear of this, you can.'

'The last naval lieutenant,' he said coldly, 'who tried kissing me got a poke in the puss and ten years on a very serious charge. See yer later.'

It was only the acid, stinging lash of the salt water in my head wound that enabled me to keep up with Two-tooth. He barrelled along just below the surface with an incredibly fast shimmy—a weird blend of crawl, breast-stroke and dog-paddle that slammed him through the water like a whiskery torpedo, even though he was carrying most of the ironmongery in his shirt. I plugged along beside him, trying desperately to whittle down the twenty-five minutes I'd estimated for the half-mile. But that would only leave us five in which to deal with Schuyler and Solnishko 1. We'd never make it. I'd been insane even to think that we might. My arms and legs were beginning to feel like pig-iron already, and I couldn't get enough air through my mouth-piece. We'd still be swimming in this hopeless race against time when the sun dropped into the sea. And then Lucky would die, and we'd be blasted wide open like dynamited trout. Or vaporised. Two-tooth surfaced to check our position. I trod water gratefully beside him and he mouthed from behind his snorkel, 'Current. We're nearly half-way.'

When the water was suddenly darkened by the hull that stretched away into the bottle-green distance, I found him clinging to the ghostly-wavering rudder post of the *Kowloon*, stripping off his flippers. I got rid of my equipment and we surfaced cautiously, sheltered by the overhang of the ship's stern. For a panicky moment, I thought the light had gone. Then I realised we had emerged into the unnatural twilight of the pall of smoke that hung overhead. There was the acrid smell of burning paint, and a confused shouting from above. Then something brushed against me, something wet and slimy and rubbery that moved away as I turned, to swing back again ponderously with its dead, goggle eyes looking down crazily into mine and its blubber lips stretched in a silent snarl.

The truncated corpse of the Negro Eight-ball.

Two-tooth let go of the rudder-post and sank, his strangled yell coming out in a stream of bubbles. I fended the loath-some thing off, fighting down the stomach-heaving urge to vomit as it tried to nuzzle up to me—the head, arms and chest of what had once been a man, ending at the waist in a disgust-ing tangle of chewed cloth, bloody flesh and entrails. Anything that had hung in the water had already been dealt with by the fish, and now it swung just clear of the surface, revolving slowly in the rays of the setting sun. Trying not to look at what I was doing, I pulled out the sheath-knife I'd brought and severed the loop that supported the arms. It dropped into the calm water, blood drifting from it like red smoke, just as Two-tooth came up again. 'Strewth,' he spluttered. 'What the hell happened to him?'

'Schuyler found out that he didn't shoot us.' I took a grip on my shaking nerves and grabbed the rope. 'But he solved the boarding problem for us. Up you go.' I tried not to think of how, after the half-mile swim, my paralysed muscles were going to cope with a twenty-foot climb with no footholds. He went up effortlessly, hand over hand, paused at the top for a look round, then he went smoothly over the rail.

I gripped the rope and took a deep breath. Then, in the clear water, a ten-foot shape, beautifully streamlined, slid like a grey ghost from behind the rudder, heading for the torso that was bobbing just behind me. I went up the rope effortlessly, too, and hurled myself flat on the poop-deck behind the rusting, ancient winch that was sheltering Two-tooth. He said, looking sideways at me, 'Jeez, that was quick. Bit sharky down there, is it?'

Nobody saw us, and we saw no one as we dropped down to the after-deck. Smoke still hid everything forward of the funnel, but it was thinning rapidly in the light breeze that had sprung up to ruffle the sea. They were getting the fire under control. There was no guard on the after-hold, and a three-foot gap had been left in the hatch-covers at the point where the access ladder led below into the darkness. And, through the gap, we saw the bright gleam of bare metal on the dome of Solnishko 1. I didn't dare look at the sun as we slid down the ladder. We were down to a matter of minutes now.

The space-ship, secured by a scrambling net attached to ring-bolts in the deckhead, almost filled the hold. It towered above us as we stood in front of the entrance hatch, open as Igor had left it, but with a rubber-covered electric torch lying just inside. The silent shade of Nicolai Mikhailev seemed very close to me in the darkness as we climbed up into the black, yawning mouth of the air-lock which still smelt unpleasantly of roast meat. I picked up the torch and switched it on. The sooty, blistered walls of the tiny chamber showed up starkly in the white glare, and I pointed to a handle that still bore traces of red paint. 'That operates the doors.' My voice sounded hollow and metallic and my palms were sweating. 'How the hell will you know where to start looking?'

Two-tooth's bearded face looked like that of a stranger as he hauled down on the handle as I'd seen Nicolai do. 'A delay mechanism can be any one of a hundred things.' The motor whined, and the outer door began to close with agonising deliberation. 'Acid eating through a wire, a bi-metal strip, clockwork, electrical, magnetic—take your pick. I've seen booby traps that depended on water dripping from a tap. But clockwork's the most dependable. And clocks usually tick. What the hell's the matter with this bloody door?'

Each time I'd seen the doors operate, they'd moved more sluggishly. The batteries, I thought suddenly, as the outer door finally slid shut. They're running out. What if we get trapped in here? There was a faint hiss, and I felt a slight discomfort in my ears as the air-pressure in the lock built up above atmospheric. Then the inner door began to open, inch by painful inch. I could hear Two-tooth's harsh breathing in the silence. He said, his voice unnaturally quiet, 'Leave your watch out here. I'm hoping to God it's a clock. And if it is, I want to locate it quick.' The inner door stuck when it was only six inches ajar.

My stomach came up and stuck in my throat. I put out a hand to the metal rim of the door and at that moment I felt the space-ship tremble. As the door began to move again, Two-tooth said grimly, 'Schuyler's starting his engines.'

Schuyler! I clenched my fists to suppress a hysterical urge to reverse the door again and get out of this claustrophobic death-trap. The first thing Schuyler would do would be to finish off *Lorelei*. And Lucky was on board her, alone. Two-tooth said urgently, 'He's not under way yet. We've got to do this first, Pat.'

I nodded as the door slid fully open. If we didn't locate and deal with the demolition charge in the next minute or so, it wouldn't really matter what Schuyler did. I saw Two-tooth squeeze into the dark, tomb-like chamber where the chromium and glass of banks of matt-painted control panels winked at me as I passed the torch in to him. It didn't seem possible for one man to fit into that switch-studded, instrument-filled dog-kennel, let alone three. It smelt of stale sweat, rubber, and chemical WCs. But when I held my breath, it wasn't because of the smell. It was so that I could be sure I'd heard, above the gentle vibration of the *Kowloon*'s diesels, the fast, impatient ticking of a clock.

White-painted Cyrillic lettering flashed in the torch beam as Two-tooth swung it rapidly up and down, trying to locate the sound that seemed to come from all around us. The light flicked upwards, to steady on a red-painted panel directly overhead. He looked up at the clock-face that was set in it, stiffened, and I heard him gasp under his breath.

'Hold this!' he snapped. 'Quick!' I reached over his shoulder, took the torch, and shone it on the panel. A screwdriver flashed up into the light. It spun anti-clockwise four times, and at each lunge a screw fell rattling on to the metal floor. Two-tooth's big, capable hands were as steady as vices as he eased the panel down by its chromium grips. He held it up, an Atlas supporting the world, with his left hand and his right dived down into his pocket. It came up holding a pair of pliers, and there was the clip of cut wire. Then he swung the panel down and leaned on it, gripping it with both hands and turning to grin forcedly in the glare of the torch as he said, 'She's right. But, strewth, I've never cut it as fine as that. It was on to its last minute, mate. There were only forty bloody seconds left.'

The torch beam was trembling unashamedly, and I could feel my heart slamming away like a pneumatic drill. I sagged weakly against the hatch-way and at that moment the spaceship's metal hull carried up to us the deepening rumble of the *Kowloon*'s engines. I straightened up and grabbed Two-tooth's arm. 'We're under way! And Lucky's . . .'

He nodded. 'I got that worked out.' He put his hands into the recess where the panel had been, and lifted down a block of what looked like dark-brown toffee with a small battery wired to it. 'Plastic explosive. There'll be a few more of these dotted around for complete destruction, each of them detonated simultaneously by the clockwork mechanism. This one should be enough for what I want. All we've got to do is connect up the clock again, and we've got ourselves a bomb with a forty-second fuse on it.' He detached the clock from its panel and pocketed it. 'Now let's get out of here,' he said, backing out into the air-lock. 'It smells like a bloody bridewell.'

I pulled the door-operating handle up, and the inner door moved three inches and stopped. I gripped the edge of it and pulled. It slid to with a reluctant groan and there was the hiss of air pressure adjusting to atmospheric again. Then the outer door trundled slowly open. The circle of light cast by the torch flashed out into the *Kowloon*'s pitch-black hold. And dead in the centre of the beam was the grinning muzzle of a .45 Colt.

If I hadn't been so unnerved by the last few minutes I might have stopped to think before I acted. I might have decided that the only thing to do was to put my hands up and hope to get near enough to Schuyler to take the gun off him. If I had, it would have been the end of all of us, because he wasn't one to go in for a lot of Aha-I-have-you-in-my-power nonsense. It was shock as much as anything else that made me jerk the heavy rubber torch straight at the face that hung, twisted with fury, in the gloom like a bad dream. At the same time, I dived out of the air-lock and to the right. There was no force behind the throw, and the torch didn't even hit him. But it was enough to make him duck instinctively, so that his three shots came high and late. The heavy, nickel-jacketed bullets whanged into the metal roof of the air-lock, sounding like a steam-riveter in the confined space—a racket that drowned the noise I made as I hit the deck with stunning force. I struggled to get to my feet in a tangle of netting and ropes, but I was still on my back when I saw Schuyler, outlined against the patch of light from the end of the hold, lining up his automatic. But not at me. He was taking aim at the figure that was scrambling up the ladder as hard as it could go, a block of explosive tucked under its arm. I lashed out with both bare feet and kicked Schuyler's legs from under him.

The Colt thundered again and metal screamed grindingly as the slug ricocheted off the dome of Solnishko 1. Then the gun clattered away into the darkness and, before Schuyler could recover it, I dived full-length at him. He twisted like a cat and swung a chopping karate blow at the side of my head. I went down as if I'd been hit by a truck.

Then he was on top of me, his thin, bony fingers digging into my throat and his legs wrapped round my body, pinning my arms to my sides. I tried to get my knees up into his groin, but he clung to me like a Derby jockey. I threw my weight sideways, to roll him, but I couldn't move. After the fall I'd taken and the blow on the head, I could feel myself drifting off into choking unconsciousness as my lungs begged for air. I panicked and wasted what strength I had by writhing uselessly as I realised that my struggles were getting weaker.

He panted into my face, 'This is the end of the line for you, you stupid bastard. This is what happens when anybody tries

179

to get in my way. You and your buddy'll be feeding the fishes by the time I've cut that boat of yours in half.' I made one last attempt to get my arms free, but I knew it wasn't any use. I don't think I'd have been able to lift them even if his legs hadn't been clamping them to my sides. As I heaved he stepped up the iron grip that was bursting my lungs and snarled, 'Die, goddam you. You're wasting my time . . .' There was a dull, flat explosion from somewhere, and I felt the deck heave beneath my back.

Schuyler fell over sideways as the ship lurched, his hands going out to save himself. As my own hands came free, I groped desperately, with arm muscles that felt like elastic bands, trying to get to my feet before he came at me again. As I did so, my flailing hands touched something hard and rounded. The torch. As Schuyler recovered and sprang at me again, sobbing with rage, I swung it in a short, tired arc and caught him on the left temple. He collapsed in a heap, and I lay whooping for breath, listening to the roaring in my ears that almost shut out the sound of distant screaming. There should have been another noise, but I couldn't think what it was.

The engines, I thought dizzily. That's it. They've stopped. I wonder why. I dragged myself to my hands and knees, and at the same time Schuyler lashed out at me with his fist, missed, and tried to get to his feet as well. But he was having the same trouble as I'd had with the netting that secured Solnishko 1. His foot was caught in it. But when he gets up, I thought feebly, he'll come in for the last round. I wouldn't be able to fight him off for long in the state I was in. But, with the gun, it would be different. I set out like a drunk on my hands and knees to look for it.

It was lying not three feet away. In fact, if I'd been able to stretch out my hand while Schuyler was choking the life out of me, I'd have been able to pick it up. Its cold, checkered hand-grip made me feel a lot better. 'Stay where you are,' I said wheezily. I flashed the torch briefly down on to the gun to let him see I'd got it.

'Give me that!' He glared at me in the light of the torch. 'You haven't the guts to use it.' He took a step forward. 'You're finished, Tallon. My boys'll be down here, and you've only got four shells left. But I'll make you an offer. Give me the gun, and I'll put you and your pal back on your boat and leave you.' He was edging forward all the time, talking to distract my attention until he got within reach.

As he put his foot forward again I said levelly, 'Move the other leg, and I'll blow it off. I don't have to kill you, Schuyler. Just damage you a bit. And it's you who's finished. There are five Navy ships on their way here.'

He sneered at me. 'Aw, for Chrissake, grow up. You think you can bluff your way out of a spot like this? I know you've got no radio, remember. There can't be any ships, and you know it. You might as well . . .'

He stopped. Above the clamour up on deck, a voice yelled, 'Lower away, you bastards, and hurry it up. You want to be around when the Navy gets here?' Two-tooth, I thought, had been spreading a little alarm and despondency.

I said, 'Your engines have stopped, Schuyler. Or hadn't you noticed?' As he listened, I added, 'If your radar had been working, you'd have seen the ships for yourself. We had an emergency distress transmitter on the yacht.'

'You had a . . .?' I saw his fists clench and he made a move at me, so that I thought I'd have to shoot him after all. But he stepped back again as he hissed, 'My God! You lousy, interfering small-timer. I should have sent you the same way as Zaghrali while I had the . . .' Before I could drop him he had leapt out of the torch-beam and up into the air-lock. He slammed down the operating lever and, as the door started to close, he snarled, 'I'm not through with you yet, Tallon. What those commie spacemen could do, I can do. If you don't call off those lousy ships, I'll blow the lot of us to hell and back!'

'You're wasting your time.' I grabbed at the door with my free hand to stop it closing and he snapped a numbing blow with the side of his hand at my wrist that loosened my grip. 'You won't be blowing anybody up, Schuyler. Come out of there.' The door groaned protestingly on, to jam three inches from the end of its travel as Solnishko I stirred uneasily in her lashings. The *Kowloon* lurched again, listing heavily to starboard, and this time she didn't come level.

Schuyler shouted, 'What the hell goes on?' He was listening

to what I had thought was the roaring in my ears. But now I knew what it was. It was the thunder of the sea pouring into the stricken ship.

I said, 'There's no explosive you can use in there. Two-tooth's taken it out. He's used it to blow a hole in your ship.'

He looked out at me through the three-inch gap with more hatred in his cold blue eyes than I'd thought it possible for one man to possess. 'One day,' he said softly, 'we'll meet up again, Tallon. And God help you when we do.' He paused for a moment, then he said savagely, 'O.K., damn you. I'm coming out.' He jerked the operating handle up, but he couldn't move it. The door had to shut completely before it could open again. Impatiently, he tugged at the edge of the jammed door, whipping his hand away as it slid completely shut. Through the cracked observation panel I watched him wrench again, viciously, at the handle. This time, it came up. But the door didn't move a millimetre.

It was a little while before he realised what was going to happen to him. I watched, hypnotised, as he tugged again and again at the handle, and there wasn't even a murmur from the door. And in my imagination there were others who watched him from the blackness of the hold that was already awash with gurgling water that chilled my feet: Barbara Mackail, her long, golden hair now dulled and matted with mud and sea-weed; Nicolai Mikhailev, big, broad-shouldered and impassive; Igor and the Mongolian, in their shining space-suits; the Negro Eight-ball and Zaghrali. And when at last it came to him that the steel door would never open again I think he saw them, too, and he knew they were waiting for him.

It was horrible to see the way his face changed. He flung himself at the door, clawing at the steel, his eyes glaring at me through the armoured glass that had been built to withstand the impact of a meteor in deep space. I saw his mouth open, and I knew what he was screaming, although I could not hear. Curses, prayers, threats—anything that would move me to open the door for him. But I couldn't have opened that door even if the batteries had been fully charged. I'd never seen Solnishko 1 opened from the outside. Only the Russians he'd murdered knew how to do that.

I turned away and sloshed through the water that was rapidly filling the hold, pitying him in spite of what he was and what he had done. For no revenge that the human mind could devise would be worse than what he was going to go through. He wouldn't even die with his ship. Solnishko 1 would withstand the water and the pressure as the *Kowloon* slid down into the black, silent deeps. Down into the places where, as Eight-ball had said, no diver could ever reach and there is only the dark and the cold. He would last until his oxygen—or his reason—gave out. He'd wanted Solnishko 1, and now he'd got her all to himself. For eternity.

I climbed the ladder wearily and met Two-tooth at the top. He had a Schmeisser sub-machine gun slung over his shoulder and he said urgently, 'I was just coming down for you. We got to get out of here fast before she pulls us under.' He'd commandeered an inflatable life-raft and, as we lowered ourselves into it from the starboard rail that was almost flush with the sea, he said, 'What about Schuyler?' He shot a quick look at me. 'He won't be coming with us, I reckon?'

'No.' I told him what had happened to Schuyler as we paddled with clumsy haste away from the doomed ship. We had a long way to go. The *Kowloon* had been moving away from the yacht when Two-tooth had dropped his bomb down into the engine-room. She'd been swinging round in a curve to work up speed to ram. *Lorelei* lay like a ghostly white bird on the purple sea that reflected the fading glow of sunset—a sea that heaved suddenly as the *Kowloon* sank noisily behind us and flung the raft into spinning gyrations. Faint shouts and the distant splash of oars marked where the ship's crew were pulling hopefully for the land.

As the sea smoothed itself and the raft settled, Two-tooth leaned across and grabbed my arm. 'There they are!' he said, grinning. He pointed to the faint amber glow to westward that was all that separated the sea from the night sky. Breaking the smoothness of the horizon was a cluster of small silhouettes, twinkling with lights, that were climbing over the rim of the sea towards us. 'The Navy's here!' Staring at the ships, he said thoughtfully, 'And when they get here, I suppose there'll be that little matter of smuggling to sort out. Wonder what they'll do about that?' He let go of my arm and sat with his paddle poised. 'Well, let's go and find out. If we don't get a move on, we'll be swanning around in the dark when they arrive.'

Suddenly, *Lorelei*'s riding lights came on. I looked at them, and at the small figure I could see waving frantically from the lighted bridge. 'Not in the dark,' I said. 'The stars are coming out.' I dug my paddle into the water. 'Come on, Two-tooth,' I said. 'Let's go home.'

Author's Note

My collection of material for this book was augmented by some unscheduled field-work when, on the 10th of September 1965, the de Havilland Beaver in which I was a passenger ended up on its back in a swamp in Tasmania's rugged south-west. Although nobody was injured in the crash except the Beaver, my three companions and I might have taken up permanent residence there had it not been for the mirror flashed by our pilot to attract the attention of another aircraft that, by a chance in a million, also happened to be in that remote area.

And so my fervent thanks go to Jack Legarde, the passenger in the Cessna 172 who saw our distress signal and who later collected us in his launch *Arcadia II*; to William Workman of the Southern Aero Club, who was flying the Cessna in the right place at the right time; and to Austin Miller, veteran pilot and holder of the Australian national land speed record, who wielded the mirror.

I should also like to acknowledge the assistance given to me by Pat Lyne and Eric Birtles of the Tasmanian Aero Club, who were with me in the Beaver; by Frank Ellis, Director of the Queen Victoria Museum; and by all my other Tasmanian friends who were so helpful with information about the little-known part of their State that I have used as a setting for this story.